Hammerfall
Hammerforged Saga Book Three

ANDY WANG

Copyright © 2023 Andy Wang

All rights reserved.

ISBN: 9798865997696

DEDICATION

To James, thanks for being the catalyst for this crazy journey.

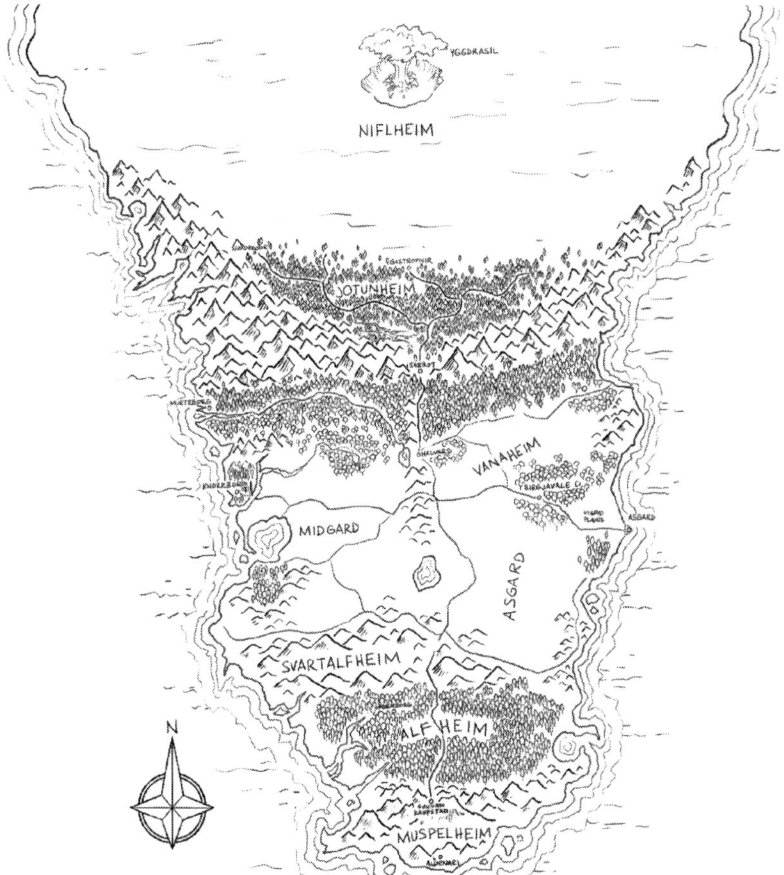
YGGDRASIL
NIFLHEIM
JOTUNHEIM
VANAHEIM
BIRGJAVALE
ASGARD
MIDGARD
ASGARD
SVARTALFHEIM
ALFHEIM
MUSPELHEIM
DAUDR HAF
N

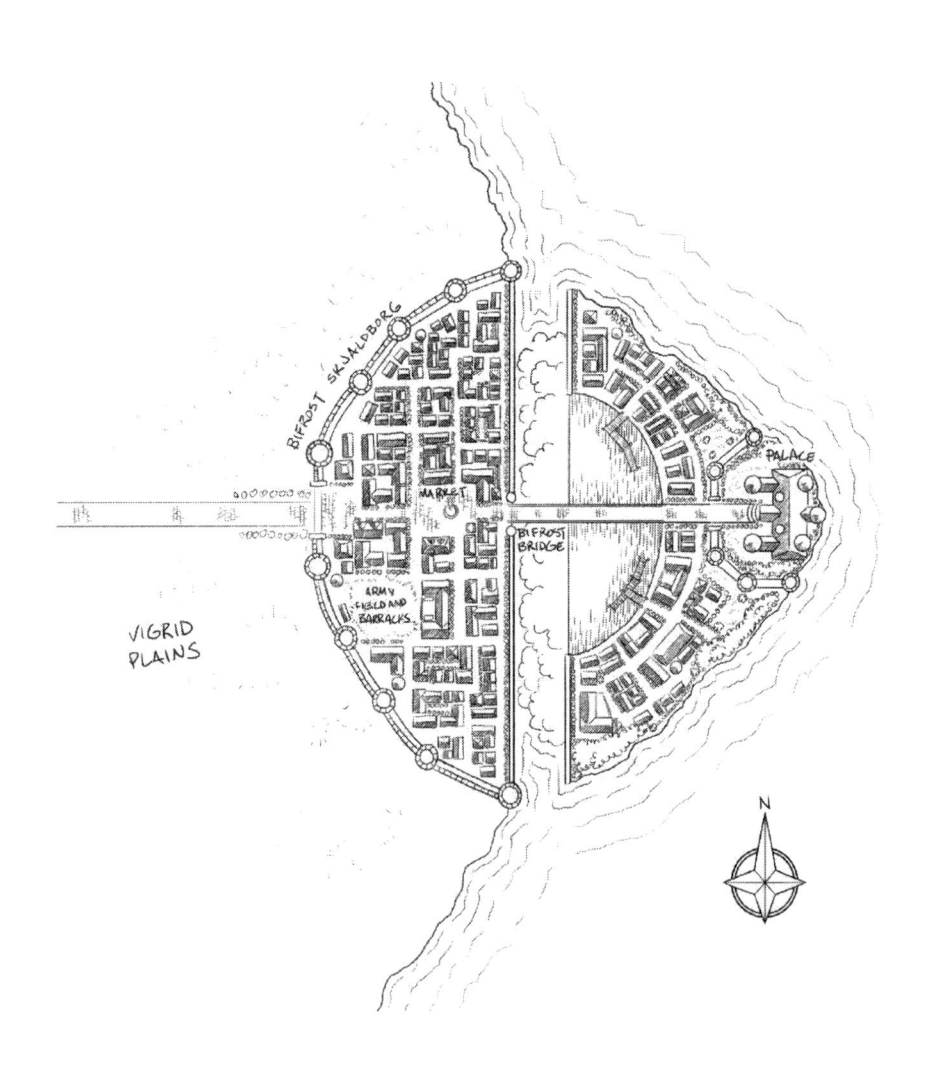

ANDY WANG

A world bursting with life
Nature's bounty for all
Peace lasts not forever
And pride leads to the fall

When summer has gone
And winter reigns
When Nidhogg flies
And daylight wanes
The Skjaldborg sunders
Will Asgard remain?

Past sins come home to roost
As Asgard weeps in sadness
War is never ending
Driving all to madness

When summer has gone
And winter reigns
When Fenrir rises
And daylight wanes
Odin's power fails
By darkness claimed

Rising up united
With shackles cast aside
Flaming sword held aloft
Surtr ushers in the tide

When summer has gone
And winter reigns
When the serpent strikes
Heroes fight in vain
Yggdrasil expires
The world ends in flames

PROLOGUE

Metal rang out as swords and axes struck shields and armor. Thousands of soldiers fought across the once pristine beauty of the Vigrid Plains. Over the last week of combat, the broad expanse of verdant low grasses, shrubs, and pastel wildflowers had been churned and trampled into a rotting brown mixture of mud, dirt, and blood. Just a mile to the east, soaring towers glinted against the azure dome of the sky in the full light of the midday sun. The white marble walls of Odin's palace stood shimmering and bright, in the heart of the capital city of Asgard, which sat upon a finger of rock jutting out into the sea. Sheer cliffs dropped off precipitously, a hundred feet down into the crashing waves.

From the west, the Vanir and Jotnar armies had marched together as a motley ensemble, rowdy and undisciplined. Jotnar soldiers, their fur in various shades of green, wore ironbark armor. Ironbark trees were difficult to work with, but the Jotnar had a way of coaxing the wood into the shapes and pieces they wanted. Even so, the armor appeared to be cut and pieced together with a blatant disregard for aesthetics or order, with branches and leaves jutting out all over at random angles and scrawled emerald markings carved into the wood. Silvery metal accents bolted onto the ironbark were covered in runes that glowed in shades of greens and whites. These same white iron reinforcements had been added to their helmets, made from the skulls of aurochs and giant Svelbjarg rams. Each suit of armor was, despite its clumsy appearance, unique to the wearer and proved robust and functional.

The full leather gambesons of the Vanir were more uniform and well crafted, with dozens of three-inch tall rectangular white iron plates sewn into neat, regular rows in a lamellar configuration. Similar to lizard scales, this pattern gave the wearer an effective balance between protection and flexibility. Like the Jotnar armor, green runes of Ethlivald radiated against the burnished white metal. The ivory skin and dark hair of the Vanir were almost entirely concealed by the enclosed helmets in addition to the full armor.

On the opposing side, the defending columns of the Aesir Army presented a solid, united front that executed their maneuvers with exacting timing and precision. The golden-hued armor of these men and women complemented their complexions. In a kindred style to the Vanir armor, it fully protected their torsos with interlocking layers of metal laced onto leather. Locks of auburn and blond were braided tight and tucked away beneath their helmets. Valkyries prowled the field of battle, distinct in their lack of head coverings, the plaits of their hair tidy and composed, never impeding their ability to fight.

"The Aesir's dominance has come to an end, Thor!" Freyr shouted from the Vanir line as he made eye contact with Odin's firstborn son. "Asgard is surrounded, and your father isn't here to save you this time." He gestured his sword to the east, where Odin stood on the far side of the vast chasm separating the city of Asgard from the continent.

"As I recall"—Thor's sword blazed with golden light and cut across three Jotnar in a single stroke—"Freya has done the wolf's share of the fighting." Green light and a flourish of vines and leaves burst out along the arc of the sword. The soldiers were thrown to the ground and writhed in pain though still alive. With the backswing, Thor's sword knocked away two charging Vanir soldiers, the Mithlivald runes of their enchanted armor absorbing the destructive power of Thor's Reginvald. "All you did was stand at the flank and watch."

"Say what you will, but we outmaneuvered you at every turn," Freyr snorted. "From the forests of Jotunheim and the golden fields of Midgard to the rocky crags of Svartalfheim and the fiery volcanoes of Muspelheim, you Aesir have been woefully outmatched." He feinted, lunged, and riposted, cutting into Thor's side.

"Woefully outnumbered, you mean." Thor gestured with his sword arm at the vast Vanir-Jotnar Army surrounding them. Streaks of golden blood glinted in the sunlight as they ran in rivulets from the cut in his side.

"Outmatched or outnumbered, the Aesir will continue to lose," Freyr said with a laugh. "If Odin hadn't used Gungnir to separate Asgard from the rest of Ymir, we would have taken it by now."

"Be thankful he did not turn Gungnir against all of you and lay waste to your pathetic mess of an army in a single blow," Thor roared above the battlefield din. His sword clashed against Freyr's, the blades deflecting amid a shower of gold and white sparks.

"And if we decided to use Mjolnir, Asgard would tumble into the sea," Freyr said with a smirk.

He then bounded forward and cut a path through the Aesir soldiers. Thor pushed his own troops out of the way with one hand, his other brandishing a sword overhead. The bright energy of Reginvald flared out from the blade as it struck Freyr's weapon. It was as much a clash of wills as it was a physical attack. With their weapons locked, the white Mithlivald light brightened until it subsumed the golden glow of Thor's sword. Freyr's snarl turned to a toothy grin. Thor roared with impotent rage as Freyr flung the Aesir off his feet. Leaping at his downed opponent, the Vanir brought his sword crashing down with his full weight behind it. It was with the narrowest of margins that Thor brought up his weapon and intercepted the strike. The white and gold energies flared out again at the point of contact.

Despite Freyr's superior position, Thor was stronger and redirected the strike to one side and rolled into it, pushing the Vanir prince off at the same time. Both fighters scrambled to their feet in moments and found their footing and rhythm in the ebb and flow of battle, circling one another. They dodged friends and dispatched foes until they had created a miniature arena, everyone giving them a wide berth. They reengaged with a flurry of blows and powerful explosions of magical energy.

All around, the soldiers in closest proximity stumbled away as arcing bolts of energy lashed out and struck with no regard for ally or enemy. And yet, just beyond that shock wave of power, Jotnar and Vanir soldiers continued to undulate in a surging, chaotic mass. A faint aura of white light surrounded them as the Mithlivald-infused armor and weapons flared. The runes engraved into the metal Vanir and Aesir plates glowed as they protected their wearers from the damaging effects of the attacks. For the Jotnar soldiers, the Ethlivald runes, carved into the living ironwood itself, regrew the bark wherever it had been damaged. They shone white and green as the rowdy and disorganized mob of Vanir and Jotnar crashed into the regimented line of the Aesir. Again and again the seething waves of troops pounded into the golden wall of shields, bristling with spears. Pale light surged against gold.

Freyr and Thor continued to trade blows, circling left and right, cutting and blocking, parrying and riposting. The maelstrom of strikes and slashes, metal striking metal, rose to a deafening crescendo.

Thor stood opposite of the Vanir; the tip of his blade grazed the ground as the Aesir panted hard, his posture hunched over. By now, the sun was half a palm's width from the western horizon. The fighting at the front had not moved in either direction since midday. Enchanted armor had kept fatalities to a minimum, and injured soldiers were pulled from combat to the rear by their comrades with haste and efficiency. As the orb of the sun at last dropped from the sky, horns blared from both sides and the battle came to an abrupt halt. With measured and deliberate movements, the two sides disengaged and withdrew to their respective encampments.

"Your mother is calling you home," Freyr taunted through ragged breaths. His body sagged, and he allowed his guard to drop. With visible relief, his arm fell limp at his side, grip light, fingers not quite curled around the hilt of his sword.

"And your mother is calling you to Hel!" Thor uncoiled and leapt up at full strength and speed.

Although Freyr's fatigue vanished, he was caught with his weight on his back foot. Thor's blade rushed towards him.

Inches from Freyr's shocked expression, the blade came to a stop. Freya's sword had intercepted the strike, though she could have easily chosen to kill the Aesir.

"Enough!" She punched Thor with her free hand and knocked him back a yard while Freyr stumbled and dropped to the ground, landing on his ass with a heavy thud. "The fighting for today is done. We will withdraw to our camps and retrieve our dead and wounded like civilized people."

Thor stood and wiped the golden blood from his split lip. Freya's skill, strength, and gauntleted fist had dealt considerable damage. Thor would need a fostra to reset his jaw. "Civilized?" he sneered. He spat as he eyed Thrym leading his Jotnar away. They were a raucous and savage lot, dragging their weapons along the ground with little care and even breaking into song. Despite their long collaboration, the Vanir had yet to gain any fluency with their allies' native language, Jotunmal. But their tone and cadence made it clear that it was irreverent and implied a certain levity and lack of respect to the serious business of war. "These fools know nothing except how to waste the bounty of everything we fought so hard for in the Great Awakening."

Meanwhile, the Vanir and Aesir troops withdrew in regimented, coordinated lines. Though on opposing sides, they had similar reactions to the Jotnar's antics. Those Aesir soldiers who acknowledged the Jotnar at all eyed them with sneers of disgust. The Vanir averted their gaze, doing just about all they could to ignore their own allies, who danced and pushed their way into their orderly formation.

"Tell Odin that the civilized alliance of Vanir and Jotnar are prepared to meet him on the field of battle tomorrow, and the next day, and every day after until Asgard is but a smoldering pile of rubble and ash," Freya said with a flourish and a bow.

She helped her brother up, and the siblings walked away as Thor stood upon shaky legs. He gave a quick glance to his father, who had not moved from his place in front of Asgard. There was a glint of light in his eye and the barest nod of his head.

—

Though the bodies had been removed, severed limbs, broken weapons, shattered armor, and other detritus littered the mud-brown Vigrid Plains. Pillars of smoke rose, angry black scars across the blood-red sky as it darkened. The Jotnar and Vanir camps in the west were dug in and the Aesir were entrenched with their backs against the chasm separating the Ymir continent from Asgard in the east.

Hedgerows of thorny briars made up the defensive perimeter of the Jotnar and Vanir camps. Most of the Jotnar milled about as they walked their patrols, while those who were off duty rested out in the open. Austere tents served as shelters for the Vanir troops. To the rear of the encampment, several large, ornate tents served as the command center for Freya, Freyr, and their senior officers. At their center stood one twice the size of the others. Two Vanir guards stood vigilant watch at its entry despite its distance from the front.

"Hey, Gudmund," hissed one of the guards. "Did you see Thor on the battlefield today?"

Gudmund responded without turning his head. "Certainly not, Thyra. I was fortunate to be far from his side of the fighting. Even without Mjolnir, I wouldn't want to be within striking distance of his sword."

"Aye, you speak the truth of it," Thyra said, maintaining her stoic posture. "Fortunately, Freyr kept him occupied for most of the day. Many of our soldiers are still in the infirmary being attended to by the fostra"—she paused and looked to the glow of the funeral pyres that blazed outside of the encampments—"or were sent to Hel by his hands."

"Do the Jotnar even believe in Hel?" Gudmund asked, shifting his eyes just enough to catch Thyra's. "They don't even burn their dead. They entomb them in the ground… trap them under the cold, hard dirt. It's…" He lowered his voice so that Thyra just barely heard his next words. "It's so savage."

"Whatever they believe in, they are our allies." Thyra gave Gudmund a reproachful look. "They died by Aesir blades just as we did, and they deserve our respect in that sacrifice at least."

Gudmund rolled his eyes in response. "They're our allies because their chieftain, Thrym, stole Mjolnir while Thor was busy chasing after Lady Sif. There's no honor in theft. And perhaps more of them wouldn't have died if they knew how to fight as an army and follow orders. If they are anything, they are a liability. Their only assets are their vast numbers"—he folded his arms across his chest—"and that their leader has Mjolnir."

"They also have some considerable power of their own." Thyra, her brows knit, gestured out towards the hedgerows. "And yes, they lack fighting skills and military discipline, but when they fight, they fight with passion."

"Misplaced passion." Gudmund patted at a dent in his pauldron and rubbed at another on his helm. "Passion without discipline is a recipe for chaos. I've been struck at least a half dozen times by our 'allies' in the heat of battle. I swear, I don't think that they can tell the difference between an Aesir and Vanir."

"Hush," Thyra snapped under her breath. Muffled shouts came from one of the officer tents nearby. "Speaking of discipline, we should maintain ours. If Freyr caught us chattering on like this, we'd have latrine duty for a month."

"Are you insane?!" Freyr bellowed as he paced around his sister's personal tent. "You can't seriously be considering this."

"Quiet." Freya threw him a sharp, reproachful look. She sat at the center table and turned back to her guest, poised and with a thoughtful expression on her face. An ornate bed sat along the wall opposite the tent flap. Four chairs were set around a table covered with maps, various scrolls, and loose sheets of paper detailing tactical information. Atop them all was an unfurled scroll; its wax seal was broken yet still sparkled with golden light. Across the table sat a peculiar sight: a figure wearing armor very similar to Freya's, with strands of auburn hair peeking out from under a conspicuous black wig.

"I can *not* believe that worked." Freya put her hand to the side of her face and gestured with her other hand at the figure seated across from her.

"And I can't believe you shaved your beard," Freyr added.

"That should tell you how serious we are," Thor replied, pulling off the wig, his long red locks flowing free. The first son of Odin rubbed at his chin as he tossed the dark tresses onto the empty fourth chair.

"This war has been costly," Freya replied, her eyes intense as she stared over her steepled fingers at him.

"We are at an impasse," Thor added. "This has been quite a war of unexpected turns. Our forces at Muspelheim, Alfheim, and Svartalfheim have held out against your incursions there. You may have taken some of the villages, but those can be easily rebuilt with the workers and resources at the regional garrisons."

Freya waved her hand with a sigh. "You must know that those were not serious efforts to take those lands. They were designed to draw your forces away, thinking that we were targeting your supply lines."

"Of course, you were quite clever." Thor coughed and nodded. "You may have been able to mask your attack upon Asgard, but you will never take it. Even with your combined numbers and power, we were ready for you."

"Odin's response was… surprising," Freya said with a smirk. "Using Gungnir to carve out a chasm between us and Asgard."

"At least he did not use it against your armies," Thor offered. "I think that we can agree that neither side wishes to unleash the full power of Mjolnir and Gungnir."

"I'm certain that Odin finds it more difficult to dictate terms from on high without having both of these weapons in his possession," Freyr added with a sneer.

"Odin finds the manner in which you acquired Mjolnir to be"—Thor paused for a moment while he sought the most appropriate word—"distasteful."

Freyr snickered. "And he surely sent you disguised as Freya as punishment for losing it while in your possession."

"Odin's terms are interesting." Freya cut off Thor before they devolved into more petty bickering. She gestured to the opened scroll. "But how can he expect us to simply betray our alliance with the Jotnar? Especially while Thrym holds Mjolnir."

"That is the key point for the truce," Thor said. "Someone must be held accountable. And Thrym was the one who stole the hammer and set off this entire war. He and the Jotnar shall bear the entirety of the blame. We will make an example of them so that none will be tempted to repeat this ever again. With the Aesir and Vanir united and in possession of both Gungnir and Mjolnir, we can ensure that no one will be in a position to threaten us in the future. It will be the birth of a second age of peace and prosperity. And you will have been responsible for it, a steward for a new legacy, like your father, Njord."

"All of this proves that we have the advantage, sister." Freyr stopped pacing and stabbed his finger towards Thor. "We don't need to bargain or meet their terms. With Mjolnir and the combined might of the Vanir and Jotnar, the Aesir will fall."

"But you do not have Mjolnir." Thor waved his hand to the tent flap. "That fool, Thrym, wields it like some toy that he won in a game of chance. The Jotnar have no sense of the state of the nine realms. And I have heard that he seems to think that he will take you as his bride." He gave Freya a knowing wink.

She put her hand to her face again and shook her head. "I still can't believe the Jotnar were so blind that they were fooled by such a shoddy disguise." Freya waved her hand at Thor. "Why did we spend so much time having them cordon off our lines with those hedgerows of briars and brambles if they're just going to let anyone walk in?"

"It's true. They have never understood the way of things," Freyr conceded. "We had to explain to them how and where to put them up. They treat everything as frivolous, as some lark with no rules."

"Everything is a joke to them." Thor's voice had an edge to it. "They have served their purpose. They stole Mjolnir and gave you enough of an advantage to threaten Asgard itself. Odin recognizes the power and value of the Vanir. That is why I am here. To negotiate terms to end this conflict."

"And what will befall the Jotnar?" Freya raised her eyebrow.

"Wars need to end with winners and losers," Thor offered with a shrug. "They will simply have to be the losers."

"They don't deserve that," Freya said, her voice just barely audible.

"And we deserve more." Freyr's voice increased in intensity. "No longer will we defer to Asgard for guidance in how we govern Vanaheim. We require autonomy from Odin's decrees."

"We demand self-governance," Freya added, her voice calm yet stern, the plight of the Jotnar quickly forgotten. "But we will not be cut off from the resources of the other realms," she added as Thor opened his mouth to respond. "Vanaheim will stand as Asgard's equal among the nine realms, or this war does not end. All resources delivered to Asgard must be divided equally between us."

Thor sighed. "Mother suspected you'd say something like that. Truly she should have come here to negotiate directly. However, I am here, lest you and your allies see that as an opportunity to take a hostage." Thor's hand came to rest on the sword on his belt. "Lady Frigg acknowledges the Vanir aptitude for logistics but argues that two governments would be confusing for the other realms. What I can offer is this: The Vanir will unite with the Aesir as one people and merge the realms of Vanaheim and Asgard in all but name. Your ruling class will live in Asgard with us"—Thor raised his hand to head off Freyr's objections—"as equals, with key positions in the pantheon."

"Why did you not simply open with that?" Freyr snapped.

"Father is always looking for the most advantageous deal," Thor admitted with a sheepish grin. "He wanted to see what you would accept."

"That conniving, petty, old—"

"Now, now," Thor interrupted Freyr's tirade. "Let's not say anything that we can't take back."

"Fine," Freya acquiesced at last. "I suppose I will need to retrieve Mjolnir from Thrym."

"Wait." Thor held up one hand and picked up the black wig with the other. Standing with a grin and donning the wig, he said, "Please, allow me."

CHAPTER 1: STOKING THE EMBERS

"What did you say?" Freyr rounded on the Eldjotnar with auburn fur. The other Eldjotnar at their forges stopped, everyone eying the commotion.

"I said *oflati*, you traitorous, back-stabbing Vanir," she spat. "It means—"

A sharp crack echoed in the otherwise silent chamber. Freyr had slapped her across the face with the back of his hand. Freya placed a hand on his arm, stopping him short as he moved to strike her again.

"How dare you sully our ears with that filth you pass off as a language? You are in the presence of Asgard's council." Freyr turned and gestured to the procession that included himself, Freya, Thor, Ydun, and Bragi. He turned to the Aesir captain accompanying them. "You allow those under your charge to utter this barbaric language, Captain Hillevi?"

"No, sir," she replied without hesitation. She snapped her fingers and pointed at the offending Eldjotnar. Two Aesir guards hurried over and grabbed her arms. They splayed her against the wall, pressing her face into the warm, soot-covered stone. Hillevi uncoiled a whip hanging from her belt.

"No!" A young Eldjotnar ran forward and threw his body between Hillevi and the prisoner. Freya mentally noted that his fur and facial features had a fair resemblance to that of the restrained female.

"Surtr, stay back!" the prisoner shouted over her shoulder.

One of the nearby Eldjotnar stepped forward and pulled the boy back, even as others tensed their muscles and gripped their tools tighter. Two other Aesir guards eyed the crowd. Their weapons remained sheathed, though their hands had moved to the hilts. Freya felt the tension manifest as heat; the air in the room shimmered.

After a quick look to Freyr for his assent, Hillevi flicked her wrist. In a blur that moved faster than her eye could follow, the whip cracked and sliced through the woman's tunic. A luminescent red-orange blood, the color of molten lava, seeped out of the gash in her back.

"Stop!" Surtr shouted again, fighting against the Eldjotnar holding him back. "Let go of me, Erland!"

"The punishment for speaking Jotunmal is ten lashes." Hillevi's voice was impassive as two more cracks sounded.

Despite the deep cuts from the whip, the female Eldjotnar gave no audible cry. Six more lashes, and she still did not so much as whimper. Yet the physical toll it was taking was clear; her muscles tensed with each crack before they went slack. She remained standing only due to the guards' unyielding grip. Surtr was bawling into Erland's powerful arms. With a flourish, Hillevi let loose the final stroke; the crack echoed in the silence of the smithing room. The guards released the woman, who collapsed to her knees, her face and arms still pressed up against the rough masonry.

"Ma!" Surtr ran to her, slid to his knees, and embraced her. His hands clasped around her back, where her tunic was in tatters and the fur and skin nearly flayed off. She winced at his touch and yet bore the pain in silence.

"Back to work." Hillevi coiled the whip and placed it back on her belt, still dripping with blood. The droplets sizzled when they hit the stone floor.

"Nanna, are you alright?" Erland ran over to Surtr and his mother. He had to speak louder as the hammering and bellows resumed their activity in earnest.

The procession of Aesir and Vanir swept out of the room. Freya's gaze lingered for a moment upon the mother and son even as Freyr and Thor resumed their idle chatter. Nanna's eyes blazed with anger and defiance as they met the Vanir's gaze.

CHAPTER 2: BANDITS IN THE BRANCHES

The powerful muscles of the four aurochs flexed and strained against the yokes as the heavy-laden wagons lumbered forward. Abundant shadows from the dense, leafy canopy overhead helped to keep the beasts cool on this warm summer day. The dappled light of the tree-lined highways cast the vast forests in a calm and serene yellow-green hue. That was one of the things Hilder loved about her tours in Alfheim. Still, she was disappointed that the vista was obscured by the burlap sheet covering her and the rest of the supplies laid out in the bed of one of the wagons.

As the light danced across her vision and the chassis of the wagon swayed gently, the valkyrie felt her eyelids grow heavy. Before they fully closed, an elbow jabbed her in the ribs.

"They're coming," Skogul whispered. She was to Hilder's right and had been so still that Hilder had thought she was a sack of apples.

"One of these days, you will need to teach me how you do that." Hilder rubbed her eyes.

"You just need to listen. Clear your mind to catch the subtle changes in the world around you. And cleaning out your ears once in a while would help too," she answered as she poked her little finger into Hilder's ear.

"Stop that," hissed Hilder as she swatted away the offending digit. "We need to be ready."

"They're just simple Ljosalfar bandits," Skogul said with a shrug. "At least the Jotnar's Ethlivald makes fighting them a challenge. Brunhilda's lucky that she got assigned to Vali's detail in Jotunheim. Perhaps I should follow her example and piss on Freya's fjathrhamr the next time we're in Asgard."

"Well, these Ljosalfar have managed to steal quite a bit from our caravans while also evading the Aesir regulars," Hilder retorted.

Skogul shook her head. "The reports that they've sent make no sense. How does an entire security detail lose track of a day?"

"At least these thefts have not involved any missing or wounded Aesir."

"Can you imagine?" asked Skogul. "Odin would burn down the whole of Alfheim if there had been any casualties."

Hilder nodded. "He certainly made an example of the Jotnar. So it's a wonder why any would even try something like this. Odin's wrath is an inferno."

"Aelweiss is more of a bureaucrat than a tactician. The bandits must have figured that she poses little threat in the field. That's why Freya sent us." Skogul patted her quiver full of arrows. "We will have this whole thing in hand shortly. These boors can't even begin to comprehend the power of—"

"Halt!" The caravan jerked to a stop amid the cacophony of falling trees ahead.

Hilder threw off the burlap cloth. She and Skogul leapt out of the wagon to join the standard complement of guards. A gentle rain of leaves began falling from the canopy with a gentle swishing sound as the echoes of the crashing trees faded away. Several trees, three feet in diameter and a dozen or more yards long, blocked the road ahead and behind, but Hilder saw no Ljosalfar or any other people. The aurochs, agitated, snorted as they pawed at the ground.

"What do you see, Skogul?" Hilder whispered, her sword drawn.

"I…" Skogul's brow knitted; she swept her nocked and drawn bow left to right, up and down. Her ears twitched and her nostrils flared, straining to catch a hint of something, anything. "There's nothing."

The rustling leaves and dancing lights produced a pleasing, calming tingle in the base of Hilder's skull. She was slow to notice as Skogul began to loose arrows seemingly at random into the canopy above.

"What is it?" Hilder squinted and found that her eyes could not focus. "I-I see nothing."

"I don't know. Something's out there." The distant thud of arrows striking wood echoed in a staccato rhythm. Skogul's breathing was shallow and erratic. "I can't—I don't see anything, but I can feel them. They're everywhere."

Hilder looked around and saw that the Aesir guards were swaying on their feet, weapons lowered, just barely still in their grasp. The aurochs sat down among the carpet of leaves with muffled thumps as their snorts eased into deep, regular breaths. She could feel the edges of her vision begin to dim and her mind dull. "Enough!" she roared. Her sword blazed gold as she leapt at the closest trees, swinging wildly and cutting them down.

Skogul closed her eyes and her body flashed with the white aura of Mithlivald. She then joined Hilder in felling all of the trees in proximity. The deluge of leaves abated at last, silence returning to the woods. Skogul attended to the guards, applying a bit of Mithlivald to each one. Slowly they regained their senses, coming out of a fugue state.

Hilder returned to the caravan and found the wagons empty. "Hel's taint!"

Skogul bent down to examine the leaves on the ground, wiping away a bit of white powder and putting a dab of the substance on her tongue. "Poppies. They laced the leaves with powdered poppy and took everything while we were in a drugged torpor." Skogul kicked the wagon wheel. "Freya won't like this."

"That was a calculated risk." Hilder placed a hand on Skogul's shoulder. "One caravan is a small price to pay to discover their tactics. And these supplies were made as bait. The thieves will discover that what they stole will be scarcely worth the trouble to transport, much less use. Now that we know, we can protect against it and follow the trafficking of poppies to hunt down these bandits and everyone else involved."

"And once we do…" Skogul drew her sword; the blade flared gold. With one swing, she cleaved the logs blocking the road in two, and the guards hopped to action and cleared the way.

—

"Those two valkyries have figured us out, Eik." Two tall, dark-skinned, female Ljosalfar looked back over their shoulders at the Aesir caravan. Ahead of them ran six other Ljosalfar, pulling along wagons laden with supplies that had, until recently, been in the wagons of the Aesir caravan. They all wore sleeveless, pale green, hemp-woven tunics, affording freedom of movement, perfect for these warm, southern latitudes. Aurochs' wool scarves were wrapped tight around their noses and mouths.

"Damnation! Now we have to cover our tracks and make sure they don't discover us." Eik groaned and rubbed her forehead.

"Let's get these supplies out of here." Oydis signaled to the others and then lifted the posts on the front end of the closest wagon and rested them on her shoulders like she was carrying a litter. Eik took up the rear, and the wheels came up off the ground. The loads were heavy, but the wagons would leave ruts that were too difficult to mask and too easy to track. The four others hoisted their bounties and fell into a quick march. The final pair of Ljosalfar brought up the rear to cover their passing.

Oydis led them through the denser underbrush, away from the more obvious trails and animal runs. Despite flitting through low scrub brush, they made little noise. Though not as closely connected to nature as the Jotnar, the Ljosalfar nevertheless were well in tune with their surroundings. Eik and her team were especially adept at navigating the woods with the utmost grace and stealth.

In the shifting light of the forest, Oydis seemed to glitter and almost shine with a warm, flaxen aura to Eik's eye. She had been enigmatic when they had first met. But her strategy to use the powdered poppy was clever and had intrigued Eik. After gathering a small group of like-minded Ljosalfar, they had pilfered dozens of Aesir supply convoys and distributed the bounty to the villages most in need. The Aesir had always demanded tribute from the Ljosalfar, but they'd been squeezing harder ever since the Aesir-Vanir War.

"I don't just mean now," Eik hissed to Oydis. "No doubt the valkyries will figure out our tactics if they haven't done so already."

"We just have to make sure that they can't trace the powder used in these attacks to any specific settlement." Oydis nodded towards the oilskin satchel slung across her shoulder.

"Even if they can't trace it, they will find one of our towns and make an example of it," Eik said with exasperation. "I told you that this caravan was too convenient a target and might be a trap."

"The Aesir have only been able to chase our shadows from the Nyrvidr Woods in the east to the Gulleik Forest in the west." Eik thought she heard a titter in Oydis's voice. "Their sense of justice won't allow them to take punitive actions without proof."

"How do you know so much about them, Oydis?" Eik eyed her with an arched brow. Although they lived in separate villages, Eik had worked with Oydis for a year and would call her a friend. Yet comments like these made her wonder what Oydis did when they were apart.

Oydis stared back. "I watch. I listen. Year after year, they take great care to maintain a certain order to the nine realms. Their order."

"Right." Eik let out a long, slow breath. "You're right. I just… sometimes I do question what we're even doing. They provide for us. It's a simple life. The labor is hard, but we survive."

"We survive while they thrive," Oydis snapped. "We eke out a living, harvesting and milling the lumber, and they take every last bit for themselves while doling out scraps to the rest of us. They don't even allow us to grow our own food or craft our own tools. From the cradle to the grave, we toil in service to the Aesir. All of us have lost someone—to the mills, to the logging. We are none of us unscathed."

Eik and Oydis stood in silence. Sounds from the Aesir caravan snapped the pair back to the present. The valkyries had begun a sweep of their surroundings, looking for any signs of the bandits.

"Let's get these supplies to those who need them."

CHAPTER 3: THE ROAD NOT TAKEN

Golden light sparkled, reflected across the calm water of the secluded fjord. Aric shaded his eyes against the glare. Turning his attention back to the fishing net in his hands, he rubbed the stiffness from his fingers and then stroked his bushy beard, which was peppered with gray, before continuing the delicate knotwork.

A sharp crack behind him drew Aric's attention. With a smile, he watched the silver-maned Dagmaer coach their young grandson as he sparred against their daughter Una, both armed with wooden weapons. A wild mat of hair covered the boy's head and flopped down across his eyes. Even through those unkempt locks Aric could see the boy's strong resemblance to Una. His lanky frame and nimble movements reminded him of someone else, too, someone from a different life—a dream half-remembered. Aric shook his head, clearing those thoughts from his mind. The boy swung wildly and lost his footing. Dagmaer rapped his knuckles and made him do it again with proper form.

With a chuckle, Aric returned to his own tasks and soon finished. He held the fishing net at arm's length and admired the interlocked threads of the mesh. None of these individual strands could catch a fish, but together they brought in a bountiful harvest that kept their small family nourished and provided for their village and for the nine realms beyond.

Moving on to other chores, Aric picked up a hoe and tended to the family's modest garden. There were not many weeds, but he liked to keep things tidy, taking care of potential problems early, before they got out of hand. At the very least, it made him feel useful, and he enjoyed the feeling of sore muscles from a day of productive labor.

"Alright, everyone," Aric called out as he gathered a full plate of fish from the smoker. "Time for supper."

He had his hand on the door before he noticed that no one had responded. The clacking from the sparring grew louder and faster. Turning, he could see that the action was no longer a simple training bout. Una's face was contorted into a fierce grimace, and the young boy cried out with each block.

"It's time to eat," Aric said, his voice sounding strange—loud and uncharacteristically stern. "Stop fighting." He stamped his foot for emphasis.

His brow furrowed as the tempo of the hits increased. Aric dropped the fish as his arthritic hands cupped his mouth. "Stop fighting!"

"They can't hear you." The voice came from behind him.

Aric spun around, coming face-to-face with Freya, unchanged and looking just as she did all those years ago when she had revealed her true visage at Yggdrasil, eternally young and beautiful.

"No—"

"I'm sorry that this couldn't be your life." Genuine sadness tinged her voice.

Aric looked at his hands, no longer spotted, wrinkled, and wizened. He turned around and found that Dagmaer, Una, and his grandson were gone. The world was now dim and gray, the golden orb of the sun nowhere to be seen, lost behind the thick shroud of clouds overhead. Murtrborg, the forest, the fjord itself had been replaced by a wide-open plain, the frozen soil trampled and lifeless.

No longer empty, his hands now held a sword and shield while a fierce battle raged all around him, full of faces that were both strange and familiar. Frode and Hege were locked in combat; Lif fought back-to-back with Loki against Hertha and Brunhilda. As the conflict intensified, Aesir and Vanir, Jotnar and Humans, Dokkalfar and Ljosalfar all turned against each other and attacked with no regard for ally or enemy.

Far to the north, the sky darkened. The ground beneath his feet shook violently; his legs wobbled and his stomach lurched as a seismic wave passed through the ground. A dark, shadowy mass barreled down towards them from the north. No one looked up from their fighting, no one saw the inky black doom coming for them. Aric tried to shout, tried to warn everyone, anyone, but no sound escaped his lips. The darkness hit the edge of the fighting, consuming fighter after fighter. Jotnar, Humans, Aesir—none were spared.

Freya's hand alighted on his shoulder. "It's too late. There's nothing left to do."

Aric turned to find her gone. In her stead, Loki stepped into the clearing around him. The surrounding fighters formed a circle around them, ten yards across. Loki's face was distorted, the scowl familiar and frightening. He brandished a wicked sword, jagged and cruel. As Aric turned to run, Thor entered the circle and blocked his path. The long, billowing red locks of the Aesir blew clear, revealing the face of the mummer from the Wodensdaeg Festival so long ago. In his hand was a sword almost identical to Brunhilda's. When their eyes met, Thor and Loki charged. They were oblivious to Aric, yet as they ran at each other he found himself caught in the middle. Frozen in place, he did not even attempt to defend himself.

The swords pierced him, skewering him from the left and right. Blood spewed forth, and still no sounds escaped his mouth. All at once, the shadowy mass eating away at the edges of the battle coalesced into an enormous serpentine silhouette. A pair of glowing red ingots shone from the head. Those eyes locked on to Aric, and then the creature struck like lightning, mouth wide, swallowing them all up in one gobble of its toothy maw.

—

Aric woke with a shout, breathing hard. Lif was there to calm him before the grumbling from their neighbors turned into angry yelling. Hundreds of bodies littered the ground of the makeshift barracks in one of the cavernous halls of Aldrnari, Muspelheim's capital city. They were all exhausted from their work smithing weapons and armor or harvesting food and preparing rations.

"Another bad dream?" Lif whispered as she mopped Aric's sweaty brow with an ash-stained rag.

"Yeah, i-it's nothing," He was sitting up now and hunched forward, taking deep breaths to slow his racing heart.

"Nothing?"

Aric knew Lif could feel him shaking, shivering to the core in spite of their proximity to the rivers of molten rock that fueled the forges of Aldrnari.

"It's not nothing." Freya stood over him. "Doom is coming for all of the nine realms. The danger is real, and we must entreat Asgard for aid. They're the only ones with the knowledge and power to do anything about it. And they won't be able to if they don't know about it and if they're fighting against this coalition in a fruitless war."

Looking at Freya for a long moment, he shook his head before turning back to Lif. With a heavy sigh, he said, "Something big, something terrible is coming. The darkness—the monsters are still spreading. If they come for us while we're distracted fighting each other, no one will be able to defend against them. Everyone throughout the nine realms will perish."

With a frown, Lif glanced in the direction Aric had stared at for so long. Freya betrayed genuine sadness as she reached an intangible hand to Lif's cheek.

Aric stood and put his shirt on. He avoided meeting both Lif's and Freya's eyes. "I've got to speak with Frode and Sigrid. It's time to make them understand what I see."

"What more can you say?" Lif grabbed his arm. "At every turn—Hoddmimis Holt, Knorrborg, Svartalfheim—they've ignored you. It's like they would rather keep fighting and don't want to actually fix anything."

"I... They..." Aric shook his head. He was not prepared to debate this with her. Maybe he still was not equipped to debate this with anyone. The words would not come to him. Looking at Lif, he was surprised that she had challenged him. She was always a bit stubborn when she wanted to be. Now, instead of keeping to herself and just doing whatever she wanted, Lif took the initiative to discuss it with him. Aric blew out a long breath and ran his hand over his head. She had grown so much more talkative over the past few months. Aric was certain Lifthrasir had more than a little to do with that.

"I have to try." He shrugged and let his shoulders slump as he turned and walked away.

CHAPTER 4: FORGING ARMIES

"What's wrong with him?" Lifthrasir whispered after Aric had left. He slid over to Lif and was now lying beside her, propped up on one arm.

The hall was dim and silent. Those who had stirred at Aric's shout had returned to their slumber. It was the middle of the night, not that anyone could see the sky from so deep within the mountains. Alternating between smithing, cultivating the tuber and mushroom harvests, and military training, all of the people who had come to Aldrnari maintained a full and unrelenting schedule. They were all exhausted.

Lif just stared at him while lying on her back; a slight frown darkened her face.

"He's still convinced that we need to ally with Asgard, isn't he?" His hand balled into a fist. "It's been three months since we came to Muspelheim, and there hasn't been a single monster sighting. It's over, we escaped..."

Lif rolled onto her side towards him and placed her hand over his fist. Lifthrasir relaxed and dropped down onto his side, facing her. She leaned her head into his chest and just listened to him breathe. Lifthrasir let out a long sigh. He wrapped his arm around her shoulders and bent his head to hers and breathed in her scent. In a few moments, they were both asleep.

—

Lif was illuminated by the blazing light of the forge. Sparks showered onto her heavy leather apron as she hammered the glowing ingot, held in place by Lifthrasir with heavy, steel tongs. When the metal began to cool, he placed it back into the roaring furnace and then moved to pump the bellows. Lif wiped away the sweat drenching her brow.

Brokkr and Sindri kept a watchful eye out as they walked among the myriad smithing stations.

"Mind that flame, don't blow it out," Brokkr snapped at Lifthrasir.

"Yes, sir." Lifthrasir slowed the bellows to a steadier and more even cadence. He gave Lif a sharp look as he noticed the vein in her head pulse and the muscles in her arm twitch. Tensions were running high for everyone, and although Lif buried her emotions, he knew that she was just as agitated. She had not been allowed to go out and hunt in months, not that there was much game in these mountains. The goats here were pygmies compared to the mighty Svelbjarg rams. And with little vegetation, the rodents were small and sparse. Their only food consisted of various mushrooms, root vegetables, and funguses cultivated in the cavernous lower halls. The food from Midgard that Asgard once regularly distributed had been absent since the Jotnar Uprising. Lifthrasir was grateful for the aurochs the Jotnar had brought with them. Their milk and cheeses served to bring some welcome variety to their diet.

Sindri had stopped walking and turned at the outburst from his normally good-humored brother.

Brokkr squeezed his eyes shut and pinched the bridge of his nose. "I'm sorry. It's just that a batch of swords from last night turned out brittle and unusable. We'll have to melt them back down and start that lot over."

"I know it's frustrating and slow," Sindri said in a reassuring tone. "In three months, we've only made enough weapons to arm half of the able-bodied adults here. But we are making progress, and we have a huge cache of raw materials."

"We have mountains of iron ore but not much else," Brokkr growled above the ringing of metal. "Ax heads would be faster, but we don't have wood for shafts. These swords are crude hunks of metal with no elegance whatsoever. And that's not even taking armor into account. Leather armor would be simpler, but even if we slaughtered all of the aurochs the Jotnar brought, we would fall far short of outfitting everyone."

"And we'd be out of a very productive food source," Frode said as he entered and went to an open station, ready for his shift. "I'm surprised that they have found enough roughage to eat."

"If Ivaldi could see us now," Sindri said, shaking his head. "They were right over there." He pointed to an arched door on the far side of the hall. Runes of power had been etched into the jambs, sealing off the door after only two weapons were crafted within. "Ivaldi and his sons, crafting Mjolnir and Gungnir for the Aesir. And now, here we are making weapons to fight a war against them."

"We are honoring their legacy, united against a common enemy and working together," Lifthrasir replied. "Aligned in a shared vision to turn a hostile land into a place where we can all prosper. This time, we're not fighting against monsters. We're fighting oppression, we're fighting the Aesir."

"That's a fine sentiment, but get back to that anvil!" Sindri shouted at Lifthrasir, who was standing there, holding his tongs. Lif also stood idle, hammer in her hands. Snapping to attention, Lifthrasir hurried back to his station and pulled the ingot from the forge. Sparks burst from the metal as Lif flew back into action.

"No running!" Brokkr scolded.

—

"Soon, we will have forged enough weapons and armor to field an army to rival the Aesir," Surtr said, standing before the leadership council.

Frode, Sigrid, Hertha, Loki, Brokkr, and Sindri were seated around a square, stone slab table. Two figures sat at the far end. Although not as tall as Loki, they had a similar build to the Jotnar, though their complexions were much darker. Unlike the soot-covered Dokkalfar, the skin of the Ljosalfar was a rich brown hue. Eik and her partner, Groenvetr, shifted in their seats, uncomfortable spending so much time underground.

"According to our scouts, they have rebuilt the Skjaldborg." Eik stood as she raised this concern. "Our numbers mean little if we can't breach it."

Groenvetr stayed seated and blew a lock of hair out of her face as she added, "We've had some success in annoying the Aesir over the years. But our hit-and-run tactics will do nothing against the fortifications of Asgard."

"Thanks to you, our new allies"—Surtr nodded to Eik and Groenvetr—"we have the lumber and resources you've stolen from the Aesir over the years to build siege engines."

"Thor will not fall for the same tactics that we used in the Battle of the Bifrost Skjaldborg," Hertha chimed in. "Also, without Suttungr, we cannot create the same sapper bombs that toppled it before."

"What we need is something to rival Mjolnir." Surtr addressed this to the Dokkalfar.

"You know that the titles of Brokkr and Sindri are just titles, right?" Sindri replied. "We're old, but we're not the same two Dokkalfar who made Gungnir and Mjolnir all of those centuries ago."

Brokkr stroked the braids in his beard and exchanged a look with Sindri. "Few records remain from the times before the Great Awakening, and even then the Dokkalfar were not privy to all of the techniques involved in the forging of those legendary weapons. Ivaldi was sworn to secrecy, though his sons were present for the smithing of them."

"From the stories, we know it took the combined powers of the Aesir, Vanir, and Jotnar to enchant them," Sindri added with a shake of his head. "But without the Aesir and Vanir, we have no one to add Mithlivald and

Reginvald into the metal."

"I can do it." Loki leapt to his feet. "I have mastered the three energies." One after another, bolts of power flared across his clenched fist, alternating in color from blue to white to gold and back again.

Everyone looked in awe at his display of power.

"It's much more than a simple enchantment," Brokkr continued after silence had dragged on. "It's been said that the enchantments of Reginvald, Mithlivald, and Ethlivald were added with each fold of the metal, with each strike of the hammer."

"From what you've told us of Aesir smithing techniques, they etch runes into the metal only after forging because these powers prevent the metal from being altered afterwards." Sindri pointed to Loki before slumping down into his seat. "You're asking for the impossible."

"We used to think that defeating the Aesir was impossible," Hertha replied. "This wouldn't be the first time we have taken on the impossible."

—

"Damn!" Sindri roared as the metal ingot exploded. Iron shards pelted everyone in the forge chamber. Fresh cuts joined recently scabbed-over wounds where his skin was not covered by his heavy leather apron and smock.

"What went wrong this time?" Loki asked from behind the heavy furnace door. It had protected him from the brunt of the shrapnel.

"The Ethlivald is fighting against the heat of the forge." Brokkr wiped at a superficial cut above his brow. "I don't have any precedent for this. We're figuring this out as we go."

"Thirteen times!" Sindri struck the anvil with his smithing hammer. The sound rang out and echoed in the vaulted chamber. "Does it have to be Iss Ethlivald? The cold is making the metal brittle and nearly extinguishing the hearth. That's no way to keep the metal malleable."

"I know I can get the cold out of it." Loki's brows knitted and the muscles of his jaws twitched with the effort. Almost imperceptibly, the blue light coming from Loki's hand took on an aquamarine tinge.

A sharp pain flashed in his arm and broke Loki's concentration. The glow snapped back to an icy blue. He lurched forward and caught himself on the anvil. "Why can't we just use Suttungr's tactic?" Loki asked through heavy breathing. "I'm pretty confident that I can replicate that enchantment. Those siege engines seemed to be effective against Mjolnir."

Hertha let out a long breath. "I doubt that Thor will fall for the same trick twice. It's far more likely that someone will have to face an angry, hammer-wielding Thor on the field of battle."

"A sword requires so much more enchanting in the smithing stage than a spear or hammer." Surtr picked up a sturdy oak axe handle.

"Both Gungnir and Mjolnir had shafts made from Yggdrasil's wood," Loki countered through raspy breaths, still leaning upon the anvil. "Through those pieces of the World Tree, the Aesir weapons are bound to the primordial energy of Ymir itself." Loki tapped his foot on the ground. "A spear or hammer with simple wood handles would not be able to channel these energies, much less stand up to being struck by Mjolnir. Without a piece of Yggdrasil, an enchanted sword made entirely of metal gives the wielder the best chance to stand against Thor."

"How do you know so much?" Brokkr and Sindri asked in unison.

"I studied many of the tomes from the Folkvangr library," Loki answered with a smile.

"Freya's personal library?" Surtr asked with a raised eyebrow.

A wistful look crossed Loki's face, and the light from the forge seemed to transport him to a brighter, happier time. "It was long ago, a time when I was happily ignorant of the inequities of the world." The smile vanished, and he shuddered as if shaking off a sudden chill. "I don't know everything, but I learned much during the brief time I was welcome among the Aesir. This is our best chance in the coming war."

"Well, whatever we're doing, we need to figure it out quickly," Hertha replied. "With each passing day, we risk the Aesir finding out about our plans or simply marching their army down here and wiping us all out."

"Well then"—Loki rubbed his chin—"we need to get into the Rikrsmidja."

They all looked to him while he stared at Surtr.

"Am I supposed to know what you're talking about?" the Eldjotnar questioned Loki.

"Mjolnir and Gungnir weren't crafted with these meager forges." He waved at the nearby smithy with affected disdain. "Not that these haven't been very useful," Loki added as Surtr gave him a hard look. "But the texts mentioned that no ordinary beings could stand in the presence of the Rikrsmidja's searing, unquenchable heat. The smiths needed the protection of Ethlivald and Mithlivald to survive while working the metal."

"Why didn't you mention this before?" Hertha shouted at him. Though shorter, she stood at her full height and grabbed and pulled Loki towards her to snarl in his face.

"I assumed it was poetic license." Loki struggled to pull away. "There actually seemed to be some missing detail regarding the construction and use of the forge."

"It might have been intentional," Brokkr spoke up. "It seems likely they wouldn't have wanted anyone with the ability to create rivals to Mjolnir and Gungnir."

"Just like the Aesir to hoard knowledge and resources," Sindri sneered.

"These are the only forges that we have," Surtr said as he waved around the room. "We have been using every available forge for months to arm and armor everyone here. If there was another one we could have been using this whole time, I would not have hidden it."

"I'd wager the Aesir destroyed the Rikrsmidja," Sindri said as he held his hand out to Brokkr.

"I'll take that bet." Brokkr clasped hands with Sindri. While still holding tight, he smirked and said, "If it could stand the smithing process, it had to be very sturdy and durable. I doubt they could have destroyed it if they wanted to."

"But Gungnir can cleave through anything." Sindri smirked right back at him. "Odin himself used it to cut through the continental shelf of Ymir to prevent the Vanir from taking Asgard."

"Enough." Hertha stepped in and separated the two Dokkalfar. "Surtr, is there some place here where a forge like Rikrsmidja could exist?"

"There is one possibility," Surtr said after a long moment of contemplation. "There is a section of Aldrnari that was kept off limits while the Aesir were here. Once they left, we immediately investigated the area only to find a door that had been locked off by several enchantments. They all converge on a central triquetra seal. We tried everything that we could to break through it, but with no success. So we've just stayed away from that area. We broke a great many tools on it before giving up. Sparks of green, white, and gold seemed to ignite at random with each attempt. Gold sparks simply destroyed pickaxes and hammers. When the sparks were white, the chips in the stone just vanished as if it hadn't been touched. And rock sprouted thicker and tougher with the green."

"Ethlivald, Mithlivald, and Reginvald," Hertha and Loki said at the same time.

She turned to him and asked, "Do you think you can open it?"

"I don't think we have any alternatives," he replied with a shrug.

CHAPTER 5: THE GREAT MIGRATION

Three vargr moved through the snow-blanketed woods on the northern fringes of Jotunheim. The fimbulvinter had only intensified since the Jotnar laid siege to Asgard only two years prior. In spite of the bitter cold, a bloom of life and activity had surged down from the north in the wake of Fenrir's resurrection. Monstrous vargr and lindworms poured down from Yggdrasil, all tainted with the same blight of dark energies. The beasts were moving in random groups and clusters, though they all tended southward. They congregated and traveled among their own kind, but the broad roles of predator and prey seemed to have been abandoned. An uneasy truce existed between the various groups as long as they kept their distance from one another. The vargr trio took advantage of these gaps as they moved north against the flow.

The ground rumbled under their feet. As the shaking grew more violent, they leapt back moments before a lindworm burst out of the ground in an explosion of frozen dirt, snow, and ice. It scurried and slithered as it charged straight for them, hissing and spitting venom, its gaping maw full of sharp teeth. With military precision, the three vargr split up into a defensive formation. As they stood on their hind legs, each one drew a gleaming sword with a golden hilt. On the pommels were emblazoned two facing swans with a spear crossed over a sword in the center. The valkyries peered out from under the maw of the vargr heads, part of the skins they wore as a disguise.

With the lindworm's attention split between the three targets, Brunhilda led the counterattack, dodging an arc of venom as she slashed at its throat. Asta was on the right flank, keeping the beast contained. On the left, Bodil charged in with barely controlled ferocity. From the corner of her eye, Brunhilda saw her intensity. She empathized with the exhilaration of returning to the battlefield after an injury, but with all of the monsters in the area, she needed Bodil to remain calm and clandestine.

Even though the drone carried the taint of the dark energies, three valkyries against a single drone was child's play after fighting a lindworm queen. As the beast lunged at Brunhilda, Asta and Bodil struck at vulnerable gaps in its exposed throat. New runes etched onto the blades flared with power as they plunged in through the shadowy tendrils that writhed over the creature's body. Asta held fast against the darkness, pushing the blade ever deeper. Bodil alternatively thrust and slashed, hacking away at the lindworm's neck. Her berserker frenzy left her exposed to the thrashing tail, and she blocked one hit and dodged another before being batted aside. Asta, meanwhile, held fast, sword deep into the nape of its neck, until Brunhilda stepped in and thrust her blade through its open mouth into the animal's brain.

Brunhilda looked around to ensure that their scuffle had not drawn unwanted attention. Bodil rose to her feet and pulled on the vargr skin that had dropped off before signaling that she was uninjured. With a nod, they all wiped the lindworm toxins from their swords and sheathed them. Resuming the posture and behaviors of simple vargr, they continued on their way. With the adrenaline still coursing through their veins, they moved fast and with less caution. In their distracted state, they almost stumbled into a snarling pack of thirteen vargr fighting over the meager corpse of an anemic elk that had not managed to escape farther south. Brunhilda breathed a sigh of relief as the preoccupied animals gave them no heed.

A short while later, the valkyries arrived at their destination, the village of Gastropnir. They approached with caution as a group of lindworms chased off some other stray vargr that had wandered too close.

"What do you see?" Brunhilda whispered to Asta as they all crouched behind a snowdrift.

"It's just like every Jotnar village and stronghold we've encountered throughout Jotunheim," Asta said. "This entire realm is devoid of people. The tracks that we found indicate that everyone who was able left here months ago. Those who couldn't were killed by all of these… things."

"Well, let's go kill some of these monsters then." Bodil's hand went to her sword. Brunhilda grabbed her wrist, keeping the weapon in its sheath.

"I appreciate your enthusiasm, sister." Her tone was stern and her grip was firm. "But we cannot lose sight of our mission. We need to report back to Asgard."

"And if there are this many lindworms here, that means there's probably a queen set up in Gastropnir," Asta added.

"It took Thor wielding Mjolnir to slay the last one," Brunhilda said in response to the look of grim determination on Bodil's face. "And that was after we'd practically eviscerated it with our trap."

The focused hatred faded from Bodil's eyes as she calmed and met Brunhilda's gaze. With visible reluctance, Bodil released her grip on her sword, and then Brunhilda let go of her wrist. Even after all this time since the Battle at Halvard, Brunhilda still found it amusing when hers was the voice of patience and reason. She smiled, knowing that Hilder and Skogul would be proud of her maturity.

"Fine," Bodil snapped. "Then what do we do now?"

"It's conclusive that the Jotnar have left the north and that the monsters of the Great Awakening have broken free of Yggdrasil," Asta said.

"Indeed," Brunhilda concurred. "We still need to make our way to the World Tree. We must determine the extent of the damage and report back to Lady Frigg."

"What can she do with that knowledge?" a frustrated Asta huffed. "Njord was the most powerful magic user of all time, and if his energies have faltered, what hope have we? Freya is long since dead, and Freyr was never as adept as either of them."

"We should send the entire Aesir Army north and slay every last monster." Bodil's hand was back on the hilt of her sword.

"This will take much more than brute force." Brunhilda smirked, once again the voice of reason. "And we cannot abandon Asgard. Loki and the Jotnar Army are still—"

A low, blood-curdling howl broke through the cold, quiet air. Peeking over the snowdrift, the trio spied a dark shape bounding across the vast, frozen tundra north of Gastropnir. Once more, a towering beast made of flowing shadow darkened the world. For a long moment, Brunhilda thought she was seeing Fenrir resurrected for a second time. But as the creature came closer, its shape resolved. It was more hound than vargr, looking like a twisted, nightmare version of the dogs that some Aesir used for hunting. And it was heading straight for them.

Its baying and snarling caught the attention of the lindworms in Gastropnir. Three of the drones emerged from the village, snapping and hissing at the bounding shadow hound. They attempted to attack the beast, but it did not break stride as it bowled straight through them. In a rage, they gave chase, and now four corrupted monsters were careening towards the valkyries.

"Well, this isn't going to end well," Brunhilda said.

Whipping her sword out, Bodil growled, "Finally, a challenge." The blade flared with the golden light of Reginvald for a brief moment before it sputtered, dimmed, and then extinguished. "What?" She stared at the weapon and concentrated on it. The runes sparked to life and the cold steel looked to regain its luminance… but the power evaporated again just as quickly.

Brunhilda and Asta both drew their weapons to similar effect.

"Hel's taint!" Brunhilda spat before turning to Asta. "Can we even pierce their dark aura without Reginvald?"

"Fenrir and his pack seemed rather unaffected by even the Reginvald-infused arrows when they attacked Asgard." Asta had her eyes closed as she took deep breaths, holding her sword in her right hand and tracing her left hand along the runes of her blade.

"Perhaps withdrawal is the prudent course." Brunhilda sighed, thinking back upon her fight at Halvard so long ago. How much had changed since then, in the nine realms and within her.

"We are valkyries," Bodil said through gritted teeth. "We will not be slain by mere animals, Reginvald or no."

"Maybe they'll kill each other," Asta chimed in.

Brunhilda's eyes flashed at the comment. She put her hand on Bodil's sword arm. "Follow me!"

With some reluctance and a grimace still on her face, Bodil allowed herself to be pulled away, and the three sprinted south, back towards the woods. Brunhilda gave a quick glance over her shoulder; it appeared that their pursuers leapt onward with a newfound burst of speed. The trees would slow them down, though the valkyries would not be able to outrun the monsters for long. They reached the tree line about twenty yards ahead of the dark tendrils of the demon dog. Seconds later, the howling and snapping of branches announced the arrival of the creatures. Leaping and dodging in and out of the trees, Brunhilda, Asta, and Bodil stayed mere steps ahead.

"Whatever you're doing, you'd better do it soon," Asta yelled out.

"Trust me," Brunhilda answered through her ragged breathing.

In the very next moment, they emerged into a small clearing and fell right into the pack of vargr that they had avoided earlier. The entirety of the elk carcass had been devoured save for a lone femur being fought over by two smaller vargr. As the pack jumped in reaction to the intruders, the shadowy mongrel and lindworms crashed onto the scene. Still wearing their vargr skins, the valkyries blended in with the startled pack.

In a flurry of snapping jaws, bared teeth, claws, and limbs, the pack attacked everything that was clearly not a vargr. The sixteen furry bodies moved to circle and attacked the four foreign invaders. Gnashing and lunging at each other in a mad scrum, none noticed the three vargr skins getting ripped to shreds.

Amid the chaotic melee, the valkyries slipped away and melded into the deep shadows of the forest. Allowing for a brief glimpse back, Brunhilda saw that despite the overwhelming numbers of vargr, the demon hound appeared undaunted. The inky tendrils protected its body while its powerful jaws snapped at beast after beast. Brunhilda noted as much detail as she could see through the carnage as she absentmindedly wiped at the black sludge clinging to her armor.

CHAPTER 6: THE ROAD AHEAD

Sigrid stood outside the immense, twenty-foot-tall iron doors at the entrance to the city of Aldrnari. She had come out for a reprieve from the heat of the furnaces only to be met by the inferno of the surrounding lava fields. A river of molten rock flowed along either side of the broad, paved King's Road. Aldrnari in Muspelheim was its terminus, the southernmost city of the nine realms. Only the dark, endless waters of the Daudr Haf lay beyond.

"All roads lead to Asgard," Aric said from behind her.

"But they all start somewhere else." Sigrid turned to address Aric. "Roads connect places."

"And people."

She looked him up and down. After months of traveling together and all of their shared experiences, she felt as if she knew him well. "When are you leaving?"

He chuckled and ran his hand through his hair, looking down at his well-worn boots. She could tell that he had been ready to explain things, to argue and debate. "As soon as I've packed up enough provisions to make the trek to Asgard."

"I know that there's no talking you out of it, but there's something remarkable happening here." She gestured back towards the towering gates of Aldrnari. "Jotnar, Eldjotnar, Dokkalfar, Ljosalfar, and Humans all united together, working with each other. We have a council of leaders representing everyone. It's not one group sitting on high dictating to the rest."

"It is quite a thing to behold," Aric answered. "For my entire life, I had only heard stories of the other races from traveling mummers. But you know as well as I do that Muspelheim isn't equipped to support and feed all of these people. We've started working the land to grow crops, but the Aesir knew what they were doing when they partitioned the realms. The rocky soil here pales in comparison to the rich and fertile farmlands of Midgard. Prohibiting the Eldjotnar from growing their own food or cultivating crops left them dependent on the bounty of Midgard, distributed by the grace of Asgard. And that was before we brought tens of thousands more mouths to feed. All of these weapons that we're crafting aren't simply for defense. We have to go back and take Midgard—by force."

Sigrid scrutinized Aric. His eyes drifted to her left even though she knew that there was no one else out here. He was rather shrewd for a simple fisherman from Murtrborg. The council had been discussing this very thing earlier. "How—"

"It doesn't matter how I know all that," he cut her off. "What matters is what else I know: blighted animals are pouring down from the north, and Yggdrasil is dying. If we're busy fighting each other, this infestation will spread and overtake us all. I know that we have to fix it and that we can't do it ourselves. I'll go to the Aesir with or without you."

"Your faith in them is misplaced." Sigrid ignored his ultimatum. "They will destroy us if we show any weakness. What they did to the Jotnar after the Aesir-Vanir War... They only understand strength."

"They understand threats, and if we threaten them—"

"Enough!" She walked past him to the gates and paused to look back. "We've endured much together, but I won't let you put all of us at risk for your crazy visions."

Aric gave her a rueful look and then turned his gaze north, talking to himself in a low murmur.

She turned away and shook her head as she went back through the gates. "That crazy fool will get himself killed," she whispered. "And if he tells the Aesir about the strengths and weaknesses of our army, he will get the rest of us killed."

As Sigrid pulled the gate closed behind her, she lowered her head. She would have to let the council know. There was no telling what they would do to him, but she could not allow one person to jeopardize everything.

"She's not going to let you go," Freya said to Aric.

"I know," Aric replied. His eyes were fixed to the King's Road as it stretched out and disappeared among the volcanoes and lava fields.

"The best outcome will be imprisonment," she continued.

Aric hesitated before asking, "And the worst?"

She gave him a pitying look.

"Right," he sighed. "Can't you... I don't know... can't you just give them all the same visions that you gave me? I'm sure that would convince most of them."

"I'm sorry, Aric," she said as she stood beside him and looked to the north. "This doesn't work like that. You and I were bound together by our experience at Yggdrasil."

"And our journey there," Aric added. "I had so much anger and guilt and grief."

"And I had much to learn about you, the Jotnar," Freya said. "I admit that I have been as guilty as the Aesir of seeing the nine realms as a game board and the other races as mere pieces upon it."

"Games would be a lot more awkward if the pieces had lives and feelings," Aric chuckled.

"If we don't want this game to end with everyone losing, then this piece"—Freya pointed to him—"needs to act sooner rather than later."

—

"Aric's been acting strange," Lifthrasir commented as he walked just behind Lif down a narrow passageway. The corridor was dim save for the lantern that Lif held out in front of her. Her strides were long and confident. Lifthrasir was taller and kept up with ease, though his steps were more hesitant on the uneven slope.

At the end of the path, the stone opened up into a vast cavern. Distant splashing and multiple points of light gave indications of the edges of this broad underground lake. Voices both hushed and boisterous came from the various groups gathered around. Many people sought the vast, open sky outside on their breaks from the daily drudgery around the forges or in any of the supporting roles. However, the intense heat from the lava fields and myriad volcanoes was less than welcoming, so people just as often sought refuge in the cool pools of clear water that filtered into various chambers within the mountain.

"He'll be fine," Lif whispered to him after a long pause. Lifthrasir had gotten used to her silences. In the past, he would have filled the emptiness with a constant string of questions and comments, but spending so much time with Lif had tempered his chattiness. And she, in turn, responded to him… sometimes.

"I'm worried that he's going to do something stupid," Lifthrasir whispered back. The cavern was spacious, but many groups were around and voices carried. As he surveyed the area, he noticed that everyone still congregated in their same groups. He could even hear the Jotnar speaking their own language. Despite all of their time traveling together, Lifthrasir still had not picked up the meaning of any of their words and often wondered if Humans had ever had their own language.

Lif shrugged and walked to an empty stretch of the shore. She removed the heavy tunic and leggings that served to protect against the frequent barrage of sparks and debris that accompanied smith work. Leaving her underclothes on, she took a tentative first few steps into the water. They had been something of a couple for months now, but he still felt a flush in his cheeks as he looked at her. Even in the low light of the lantern, Lifthrasir could see the goose bumps on her skin. After another moment, she crouched down and began to bathe. Lifthrasir took a bit longer to get in the chilly water.

"If anyone can talk sense into him, it's you," he said through chattering teeth. "Sigrid said they had a concerning encounter at the gates. She thinks that he's going to go to Asgard on his own."

"He's been listening more to Freya lately," Lif replied with a shrug as she scrubbed at her soot-covered skin.

"Which is another reason to be worried." He dropped his washcloth and grasped her by the shoulders. "Aric is possessed by some sort of madness. Visions of Aesir, let alone full conversations, are clear signs that he is losing his mind."

"You don't know that." Lif brushed aside his hands. "He's been through so much."

"You mean going to the top of the world and seeing Yggdrasil, fighting a dragon, dying and coming back to life before walking back alone across the frozen tundra?" Lifthrasir did not even attempt to conceal the skepticism in his voice. "For all you know, he got lost in Niflheim and hallucinated the whole thing."

Lif stared daggers at him, her arms akimbo.

"Yeah, I've seen him use the staff against the blighted creatures," he acknowledged, holding up his hands. "There are many things in this world that are beyond me, but you have to at least consider that Aric is not of sound mind. And if his actions threaten the safety and success of our army, then we must think of the greater good and stop him, if only to protect him from himself. The Aesir won't take kindly to a Human coming to them, telling them what to do. They'll either imprison him themselves or interrogate him and learn everything they can about our army and plan of attack."

"He would never—"

Before Lif could get into a full defense of Aric, angry voices and splashes came from a group not far away. A group of Ljosalfar were circled around a couple of Jotnar. Two individuals, one from each group, were squared off and shouting nose-to-nose. A young male Ljosalfar was sitting waist-deep in the water. Lif and Lifthrasir hurried over, as did several of the other groups.

"—for being so clumsy!" Lifthrasir caught just a bit of what one of the Ljosalfar was saying. She was the tallest of the Ljosalfar, though she still only came up to the Jotnar's chin.

"The runt should watch where he's going," the Jotnar retorted with a growl. Despite the soot covering the light blue fur, its color shone through at the roots as the Jotnar's hackles were raised. In his state of agitation, he looked somewhat puffy and larger than he might have mere moments before. "It's not my fault if I can't see such a puny bug flitting around. I didn't even feel it run into me."

"Run into you? You trampled him with your dirty, hairy feet like one of your stupid aurochs," snapped the Ljosalfar.

"Aurochs are not stupid!" roared the Jotnar as he pushed her off her feet, making her splash down into the water next to the boy.

"Hey, hey now. Calm down, Laufrot." Lifthrasir stepped in and placed himself between the Jotnar and the other Ljosalfar just as they were about to rush the tall, blue guy. His voice was forceful and did get them all to pause, even though his head only came up to the Jotnar's shoulder. "We're all on the same side here. Our enemy is the Aesir, not each other."

"Tell that to him," said Laufrot, the female Ljosalfar. As she tried to get up out of the water, she jerked to a halt. Her feet and one hand were frozen in place. In fact, Lifthrasir noticed, the surface had frozen over with the two Jotnar at the epicenter.

"Alright, that's enough of that, Vog," Jorunn said to the Jotnar as she stomped on the ice to free the Ljosalfar. She had hurried over to the commotion to join Lifthrasir in defusing the situation. Lifthrasir breathed out a sigh of relief, though he tried to hide it. It was fortunate that she had been nearby. Jorunn went on: "I know that we're all a little frustrated in such close quarters and with the constant work shifts. These pools should be a refuge, a place for everyone to relax and refresh. We'll be no good to anyone if we're tired and forge defective weapons or armor. And we'll be worse than ineffective if we go into battle worrying about our own allies in addition to the Aesir on the other side of the battlefield."

"We don't need these weaklings," Vog sneered with disdain at the other races. "Asgard nearly fell to the Jotnar. The dragon is dead, and the wall, even if they rebuilt it, can't be as solid as the old Bifrost Skjaldborg. That was built by Jotnar hands. Their most dedicated craftsmen and laborers could not hope to equal even our least skilled workers. We've done nothing but waste our time and allow the Aesir to prepare for our next attack while we babysit these children." He gestured his arm in a wide arc at the gathering crowd.

"We are not the Aesir," Jorunn replied in a calming tone but loud enough for everyone to hear. "They ruled from up on high and dictated to the rest of us. When we defeat and overthrow them, we will not repeat their mistakes. This is a coalition of equals," she said as she helped Laufrot to her feet. She looked to Lifthrasir next to her and Lif skulking on the edges, taut and ready to leap into action if the threats escalated. Beyond them, the crowd had grown—a mix of Humans, Ljosalfar, Jotnar, and Dokkalfar—and she addressed all of them. "Whatever success we will find will be found together, and whatever failures befall us, we will survive all the better together."

Vog regarded Jorunn for a long moment. He looked around at all of the people, and his shoulders relaxed and his muscles lost their tension. Right in front of Lifthrasir's eyes, the Jotnar appeared to shrink as his once bristling fur smoothed back down. Vog turned his gaze back to Jorunn and gave her a nod before turning and walking away.

CHAPTER 7: THE UNDERGROUND

"You!"

Aska stopped and dropped her head just a little before turning to see the uniformed Aesir soldier addressing her. He had just rounded the corner and was pointing at her. The Eldjotnar was pushing a wooden cart laden with ingots of iron and bronze. "Stop right there. Where are you going with that?"

The soaring halls and broad passages that snaked through the subterranean city of Aldrnari were a flurry of activity. Other Eldjotnar, their fur ranging from ochre to auburn, hurried in all directions, keeping their heads down and avoiding eye contact with the soldier. Roaring furnaces and ringing hammers created a wall of sound in the background.

"What?" Aska shouted, pointing to her ears and shrugging.

"What, sir!" The Aesir stepped in front of her, one hand on the cart, the other on his hip and near the hilt of his sword, though he showed no signs of reaching for it. "I'm Lieutenant Vali, an officer of the Aesir Army. You will address me—and every Aesir—with the appropriate respect."

She released her grip on the cart and stood in what might have been mock attention. Even with her slight slouch Aska was several inches taller than Vali. "Yes, sir."

"Where are you taking these supplies?" Vali asked as he eyed the contents.

"The secondary storage is full, sir," Aska replied. Her words showed the proper deference, though her voice had a slight edge to it. "The supply supervisor wants to start overflow storage in the southwest bunks. The Eldjotnar there have already been cleared out and moved in with the smiths in the western annex. Until we get new halls excavated, they'll be splitting bunks, one group sleeping while the other works their shift." Before he could say anything, she added a belated, "Sir."

"Where's your authorization?" Vali arched one eyebrow at her.

"Of course," Aska replied. With a quick flick of her eyes to her right, she took a step back and bumped into a young Eldjotnar rushing past. Aska's feet tangled with his, sending him bowling into Vali. Although young, this Eldjotnar was stout and barrel-chested, and Vali was knocked back a step or two.

There was a brief verbal exchange between the boy and Aska and between the two Eldjotnar and Vali.

While Vali regained his posture and pushed the unfortunate boy back on his way, Aska leaned over into the cart. There was a brief flash of white light visible only to her. Just as Vali returned his attention to her, she stood and produced a leather-bound folio bearing an official Aesir seal with orders as she had stated written upon it.

Vali took the folio and gave it a cursory examination. Aska forced herself to breathe at a normal rate when his eye seemed to linger a little longer on the seal. Soon enough he folded it closed and handed it back to her. "Very well, on your way then."

"Yes, sir." Aska leaned into the cart and pushed it along at a brisk pace. It was heavy, but the cart bore the weight well and the wheels rolled along the smooth, level path. When she had gone far enough and made several turns in the correct direction, she turned down an empty side corridor and paused before looking back.

"That was close, Aska." The youth who had stumbled into Vali popped out from a hidden doorway.

"Very," Aska replied. "But your timing was excellent, Surtr."

"Maybe we should stop for a few weeks while that one is here," he suggested, his voice quavering just a bit.

"No," she said. Aska placed a hand on his shoulder. "If they see a change in our behavior, that will be even more suspicious. Just make certain that we send some of these supplies to the southwest storage."

"Yes, of course." Surtr swallowed hard as he took hold of the cart. He paused and looked at the folded folio in Aska's hand. "Where did you get orders written up and stamped?"

Aska tucked the sheaf of papers into her rope belt at the small of her back. "I know one or two people who are sympathetic to our cause," she said with a knowing smile. "Now hurry and take these to your mother before any other Aesir sees us."

Surtr nodded and pushed the cart into the darkness of the passageway. Aska slid the façade back into place and stood back to ensure that its seams were not visible. She walked back to the nearest turn and peeked back to check if Vali had followed her. With the hallway full of only Eldjotnar, she stepped back into the shadows alone and pulled out the folio. A brief flash of light shattered as the glamour was released, revealing a simple sheet of linen, blank and virgin.

"Too close," Aska said after a long, slow exhale.

—

"Again!" Aska exclaimed in what could only be described as the loudest whisper Surtr had ever heard.

A dozen Eldjotnar paired off and executed a four-move sequence of attack and defense. Staccato clacking of sticks reflected the imperfect timing of the combatants, though all Surtr could hear was the blood pounding in his ears.

"Control yourself," Aska said as she walked by and pushed him back with gentle yet firm pressure. Over the years, he had grown to become one of the largest Eldjotnar of his cohort and one of the largest in Aldrnari. And despite that size, Aska moved him about as if he were a mere mining cart on level ground. "If you lose control, you lose balance, and then it is a simple thing for your opponent to control you."

With swift and abrupt movements, Aska swept Surtr off his feet, and he found himself sprawled on the ground with a stick at his throat. She offered her hand and he took it.

"Where did you learn how to fight?" he asked once he was back on his feet. "Does your home city also have a secret cave like this to train in? And if it does, who taught you? But if it doesn't, does that mean you practice out in the open?"

"Slow down," she said as he took in a deep breath. "It's best to keep information isolated. The less you know about the others who are training, the less exposed they are in case you are discovered here."

"Well," Surtr mumbled after a moment to think about her explanation, "can you at least tell me how you learned all of this? This doesn't look like anything I've seen the Aesir do. Not that we have ever put up an actual fight. The closest was when Ivar was too drunk to just back down." He chuckled a little at the memory. "He got in a few good hits and dodged some of Vali's before the Aesir lost his temper and slammed Ivar into the ground, breaking his jaw and bruising his wrist."

Surtr's expression soured as he continued, "Vali said Ivar would've suffered harsher consequences, but they needed everyone working for a special shipment that was going out that month. He said that batch didn't need to meet the normal quality standards, they just needed to be done."

"Ah, I suspected as much," Aska said, louder than she had intended.

"Suspected what?" Surtr inquired.

"It's nothing." She waved off his query. "And it's certainly less important than keeping your partner idle."

With a gentle push she sent Surtr back to his partner as they switched roles from attacker to defender. Aska walked through and corrected form and technique as she saw fit. It would be a long time before they would be skilled enough to pose a real threat to the Aesir. In a fight, the advantages of the Eldjotnar were their size and number. Aided by the supplies of the Ljosalfar, Dokkalfar, Humans, and the Jotnar, they might just stand a chance against the Aesir. But how would they tackle Mjolnir? As she pondered that question, she returned her attention to these twelve.

"Pay attention! Be mindful! Not just of what but of why!" She adjusted Surtr's stance and then pushed him, unsuccessfully this time as his base was more solid and his weight was distributed evenly.

"You will each need to be responsible for finding and teaching twelve of your own students." They had all stopped, their eyes on her. "Showing them how to do something is far more meaningful and impactful when you and they know why you are doing that thing. And why are you here?"

"To defeat the Aesir!" they said in unison, their voices firm yet quiet. Although they were hidden, they still had to take care and not make too much noise. But their eagerness was palpable, and they hopped in place, ready to continue. Aska looked at them, the slightest smile curling her lips.

"Again!"

CHAPTER 8: THE NATURE OF ETHLIVALD

An explosion reverberated down through the stone corridor and debris rained down from the ceiling. Brokkr, Sindri, Loki, Surtr, Hertha, and Sigrid emerged from a side pathway carrying torches and lanterns. They hurried forward before the echoes of the blast had faded.

"Damn," Hertha exclaimed before the dust had cleared. Despite the warm, red lights that the group carried, the haze was illuminated from the other side with green, gold, and white. As the air cleared, the light shimmered and faded.

"Good thing we didn't waste all of the sapper charges Surtr found on that," Sigrid said.

"Maybe we should have used the whole load of it," Hertha suggested. "That stash we found wasn't even a third of what we used to take down the Skjaldborg. And what we've got left wouldn't be much use against a hedgerow, much less an actual defensive wall."

"Not even a scratch," Sindri said as he handed a polished smithing hammer, inlaid with delicate silver filigree, to Brokkr.

"Yeah," Brokkr said with a smile as he added the hammer to his toolbelt. "Judging by the results, using more would have been a waste and might've collapsed the tunnel."

"I told you that wouldn't work," Loki said from behind the others. Surtr, Brokkr, and Sindri were still closely inspecting the rock.

"So how are *your* efforts coming along?" Surtr retorted with a sneer.

"Uh… I-I've broken through two of the seals." They all turned to him with astonished and questioning looks. "Well, I can unlock one seal at a time, but it closes back up as soon as I start on the next one," he replied with a heavy breath of exhaustion.

Sindri stroked his beard. "What if we—"

"—set off a sapper charge after you break one seal?" Brokkr finished.

"No good," Loki said. "At least not if I don't want to get blown up too. The seal heals within moments of me leaving. I wouldn't be able to outrun the blast."

Sindri and Brokkr eyed each other, then both turned to Loki.

"If I stay and die, you won't have anyone here who can conjure the three energies," Loki interjected before they could suggest that he sacrifice himself.

The Dokkalfar reluctantly backed off and began muttering to each other.

"Well, what are we standing around for?" Hertha snapped at them. "Get back to it. If we don't figure something out, our assault on Asgard will take forever. They have the fresh water and enough supplies to outlast any siege we could lay upon them."

While Brokkr, Sindri, and Surtr strolled off, Loki let out a long, slow breath as he walked back to the door. Hertha followed after him.

"Here," she said in Jotunmal as she passed him half a loaf of bread and a block of aurochs cheese. *"You need to keep your energy up. You will figure this out. I know it."*

"I wish I had your confidence," he said before taking a bite out of the still warm loaf.

"It's not confidence," Hertha replied, placing her hand on his arm. *"It's desperation. We can do a lot against the Aesir. In an open battle, we could outflank them with our illusions. But against Mjolnir and their entrenched position, the only way we can win will be with an enchanted weapon of our own. This is all up to you."*

—

Loki panted and sweat poured down his brow. His hands were pressed against the runes sealing the Rikrsmidja room while a bright light glowed from his hands. Blue, gold, and white shifted and danced at the point of contact between Loki and the stone door. A faint spark of green tinged the pattern and flared with increasing frequency and intensity. The cycle accelerated until an explosion threw him back and his limp body slid across the floor.

Jorunn rushed to his side and found him gasping in quick, shallow breaths. She cradled him in her lap; his eyelids fluttered. With a jerk, his eyes snapped open and he sat up, coughing with the effort.

"Take it slow." Jorunn rubbed his back as he hunched forward. *"That was a good effort. I think you lasted twice as long as last time."*

"Don't patronize me." Loki shrugged her off and he rose upon shaky legs. *"Your coddling won't help us unlock that seal any sooner."*

"Tell me how to help then." Jorunn followed Loki back to the door. *"I may not have your training or mastery, but I am Jotnar. You said it yourself—we are legion, and*

the power of our people is indomitable."

Loki pounded a fist against the door and leaned his head against the stone, cold despite the sweltering heat of the active furnaces nearby. *"I-I don't know. Ethlivald, Mithlivald, Reginvald... they're all intertwined in the seal. As soon as I undo one, the other two rush into the gap. If I'm fast enough, I can break two. But that third seal just won't open."*

His fingers twitched as he demonstrated the dancing lights of the three magics.

"Wait," Jorunn chirped as she watched. *"Where's the green?"*

"Green?" Loki paused as the blue light pulsed from his right hand.

"When you were trying to break the seal, I saw a repeating flash of green light."

"Do you mean when the blue and gold overlap?" He manifested Reginvald in his left hand and brought the golden aura closer to the blue of his right. They sparked off each other and a green hue lit the room. The green became brighter and more intense until Loki's hands touched and the energies erupted in an emerald flash.

Jorunn rubbed her eyes and blinked several times before speaking. *"I don't think so. It was a softer, warmer green, like—"* She paused, trying to remember what green looked like. The fimbulvinter had lasted so long that she could scarcely recall a time before everything was cast in a colorless, gray light. *"Like the needles of a spruce tree lit by the summer sun."*

"Green, hmm." Loki stared at his right hand as it shifted from blue to gold.

A red light came from the door behind them. *"We Jotnar are the most fluid, most adaptable of the races."* Surtr walked into the room, his hand aglow. *"Long ago, we were one people. Living in Utgard, among the lush green of plants, of nature, our ancestors matched their environment. After generations apart in Muspelheim, we Eldjotnar have grown warmer in hue just as you have become more blue in Niflheim. I don't know much about these 'energies' of yours, but I should think they've changed similarly."*

"We don't have generations to get into the Rikrsmidja!" Loki slammed his fist against the stone door.

"And it's too dangerous to spend any amount of time in Alfheim," Jorunn added. *"Even here in Muspelheim, we don't know how safe we are. Asgard could come at any time, and if we're spread out, it'll be easy for them to take us out piece by piece."*

"So what do we do?" Surtr placed his hand upon Loki's shoulder. *"You have spent time among the Aesir. You have studied their texts and learned from Freya herself."*

Loki traced his finger along one of the runes, feeling the smooth texture of the underlying masonry. *"We need trees."*

"Did you see any trees out there?" Surtr asked with a shake of his head. *"Most of what we've been able to cultivate for ourselves are varieties of mushrooms and lichen."* Jorunn gave him a questioning look before he added, *"The lichen is for our animals. It's not much, but the goats seem to like it well enough."*

After they had stared at each other for several long, quiet moments, Jorunn piped up and said, *"Let's ask the Ljosalfar."*

CHAPTER 9: POWER OF THE PEOPLE

Eik stood next to the doorway and nodded to Groenvetr. A sea of Jotnar, over four dozen strong, filled the room in front of the sealed door of the Rikrsmidja. Every Jotnar who could fit had been brought in. All of the issithar along with any Jotnar who demonstrated the faintest aptitude for Ethlivald had been prioritized. They parted, creating a narrow path, and Groenvetr walked across the room carrying a live plant, the soil held tight by the dense web of roots, bound in a mesh rope netting.

Months in the rocky soils of Muspelheim had left the leaves drooping and pale. The Ljosalfar had brought many plants with them and had attempted to cultivate them here. Their efforts met with little success—the harsh terrain and near constant and unpredictable volcanic activity proved largely inhospitable to the flora of Alfheim. This was the last of the oak saplings they had. All of the others had perished not long after their arrival.

It was not just the plants that had suffered. Each and every one of the Ljosalfar had developed ashy and flaky skin and tremors in their extremities to varying degrees. The demands of smithing and generally being confined underground and away from the fresh air and sunshine were proving to be too much. The far-too-few healers were overwhelmed, and their only other solution—a return to the sun and fresh air of Alfheim—was impossible.

Eik watched as Loki took the sapling in hand. This had to work. They needed to conclude this war now, or her people would not live to see their homeland again.

"Everyone," Loki addressed the room, his voice clear and loud. "All of our efforts, all of our battles to free ourselves from the tyranny of the Aesir hinge upon our ability to fight the Aesir on their level. What lies behind this door is the key to that. With your help, I hope to get us in there and give us that weapon. I need you all, every one of you, to focus on this plant. I need you to join me and reach into our collective past and remember how we used to live, connected to the lush, verdant forests of Jotunheim." A low murmur arose from the audience. All present were generations removed from the days before the Aesir-Vanir War, when the Jotnar were one people who lived in a luxuriant, prosperous realm. "The true Jotunheim, not the frozen wastes of Niflheim."

The crowd shifted at the reminder of what was at risk if they lost. Exile to the inhospitable, icy realm would be their best outcome. It was likely that this time, the Aesir would escalate their reprisal and simply eradicate any and all who took up arms against them. Loki raised his palm to his face and rubbed at his knitted brow, his eyes squeezed shut.

"Look upon this sapling and remember!" He slapped his hand upon the plant and imbued it with a bit of Ethlivald. The light flared, and a hint of recognition entered the people's minds. They focused their collective gaze on the shimmering image and concentrated.

A silence fell over the room as everyone reached out with their minds and hearts. Some joined hands; others grasped the shoulders or touched the backs of their neighbors. Groenvetr stayed with the young oak. She whispered to it, a hushed melody rising in her throat as those closest to Loki touched him, bridging the connection.

> High above the sun warms Ymir
> Across the horizon its rays come near
> Catch the light, light, light
>
> Life sprouts where the sky meets the ground
> Our branches reach up and our roots stretch down
> Reach the sky, sky, sky
>
> One by one across the land we tame
> A tree, a copse, a forest, from seeds we came
> Flourish and grow, grow, grow
>
> Water from the skies, strength from the soil
> A bounty to be reaped by our toil
> Cheer the life, life, life

With one hand touching the plant, Loki stretched out his right towards the sealed door. As he got closer, his hand glowed blue. Loki clenched his jaw and furrowed his brow. He curled his fingers into a fist; the muscles in his arm flexed and twitched, and the light burned brighter.

Groenvetr sang louder. Eik heard the familiar melody and added her voice, singing in harmony. As their voices rose, echoing and filling the room, the light began to shimmer. Ever so slightly, the aura around Loki's fist shifted. It was subtle but it was there. The blue shifted to teal. As Groenvetr and Eik repeated the song for the third time, Loki joined in. He did not have all of the words yet but found a vestigial ring of familiarity in the lyrics. Upon the fourth repetition, the other Jotnar joined in.

The leaves on the young oak began to perk up and the roots sprouted out of the netting and reached down to the ground. Its trunk expanded and grew thick and heavy. Loki and Groenvetr remained connected to it, but now it had taken root into the ground, breaking through the stone flooring. As its branches reached the ceiling, the glow of Loki's hand fully shifted and became a rich, pine green.

He unfurled his fingers and placed his open palm against the seal. Once again the runes glowed and began oscillating through their various colors. This time, Loki was able to match each change, color for color: green, gold, and white. Faster and faster the patterns flashed until there was a nova of blinding light punctuated by a deafening crash.

The light extinguished, and Eik could hear nothing and see nothing except for the pulsing afterimages of the silhouette of the door. At last, the room came back into focus and the light of the braziers and torches were all that remained of the brilliant display from mere moments ago. Eik saw that the door had been torn open and the oak had entwined with the door jamb. Inside, she could see the ancient forge of the Rikrsmidja sitting at the center of the room. Runes of power, etched into every surface, glowed—as potent now as they had been millennia ago.

CHAPTER 10: WEEPING AMONG THE WILLOWS

"You have nothing to gain and everything to lose." Gunnar strode back and forth in front of the assembled villagers.

The Ljosalfar township of Groenborg was lofted up in the forest canopy twenty feet above the leaf-littered ground. Wooden walkways, bound with sturdy hemp rope, spiraled around trunks fifty feet across and crisscrossed, connecting from tree to tree. The living trees themselves entwined with these structures until the delineation between fabricated and natural structures was completely blurred.

The main floorboards of the great hall began at the tops of the boles and rose up into the canopy. Smaller rooms and annexes were constructed around sturdy branches in the crown. Ceilings blended into the dense leaves overhead. Branches had been guided in their growth through the generations to create small, individual dwellings as well as great halls. With no central square or gathering place, all of the residents had been pulled from their rooms and were gathered along the pathways nearest the great hall.

"We have done nothing wrong," an elderly Ljosalfar woman spoke up. Her lanky frame and full head of curly hair gave the impression of a stately oak tree. Even the hue of her skin reflected the rich color of the wood.

Gunnar snapped her fingers. One of the Aesir soldiers placed a satchel of wheat grain onto the planks at her feet. "So you say, Laufsdottir. And yet we found half a dozen more sacks of Veizlakr grain than you should have." She scooped up a handful and brought it to her nose. After a deep inhale, she kicked over the sack and poured the entire contents out onto the wooden planks; errant grains spilled over the edge down to the forest floor far below.

"No!" Laufsdottir jerked forward but was held back by her friends.

Gunnar eyed her before casting her glance around the villagers gathered around on the myriad bridges and walkways around.

Laufsdottir regained her composure and stammered out, "We've had a great bounty this season. Everyone had set aside a portion of their allotment so that we could create a special tribute for this year's Wodensdaeg Festival."

The valkyrie scrutinized the villagers. Her penetrating gaze forced most to avert their eyes. She could see equal parts hunger and fear in their faces. Her small complement of Aesir soldiers stood around the five other sacks of grain. They were all armed, and the metal studs of their leather armor glinted in the dappled green light. "Very well," she said after holding her audience in silence for so long. "Since these were to be part of your Wodensdaeg offering, we"—Gunnar gestured to the soldiers—"will simply bring these back to Asgard and deliver them to Odin, personally."

Laufsdottir twitched but made no move to stop the Aesir. The soldiers pushed several of the villagers forward to pick up the extra grain and then marched them along the path towards the primary cargo lift.

—

"We found no poppy," Skogul reported to Gunnar once the grain was loaded onto the Aesir wagons and the Ljosalfar laborers had left. The caravan moved at a steady pace with soldiers flanking the column. Gunnar, Skogul, and Hilder walked several lengths behind, speaking in private.

"They may not be the culprits, but they are complicit," Gunnar replied. "This is the third village we've found with contraband of some form or another."

"And they had taken pains to conceal it," Skogul added.

"You have done well to discover their hiding places." Gunnar nodded. It was the highest gesture of praise that she was wont to give.

"They know that we are searching and are covering their tracks," said Skogul.

"Or they were telling the truth," Hilder opined.

Gunnar arched her brow at the valkyrie. "The rations for every village are precisely calculated by Lord Freyr. There should be no excess."

"I am merely keeping our eyes open to the possibilities." Hilder inclined her head in deference to her commanding officer.

"Another possibility is that the bandits have no central lair," Gunnar said. "If they are constantly on the move, then they would not have left residue of their poppy making in any of the villages."

"We have scoured the woods surrounding the villages as well," Skogul said with a note of defensiveness in her voice. "With the amount of powder they use in their ambushes, there have to be trace amounts left wherever they're producing it."

"Unless they're not doing it here," suggested Hilder.

Gunnar stopped walking and addressed Hilder eye to eye. "What do you mean?"

"There is the possibility… Have we considered—"

"Spit it out, soldier!" Gunnar snapped.

"This scheme may extend beyond Alfheim," Hilder blurted.

Gunnar stared at her in silent contemplation.

"Poppies grow in Midgard as well as Alfheim. They could be harvesting and grinding them there. And thus far, we've only found about a third of the stolen supplies here. So unless we missed some"—Skogul shook her head with certainty—"there is a great deal unaccounted for."

"But no caravans have been attacked in the other realms," Gunnar countered.

"The forests of Alfheim provide the most opportune conditions for their tactics," Hilder replied after a moment's consideration. "They could not hope to take any of the caravans with Aesir guards by force. This poppy tactic has the best chance among the trees here."

"And it puts our focus in Alfheim instead of the other realms." Skogul picked up on Hilder's line of reasoning. "The culprits are likely hiding in one of the other realms. The caves of Svartalfheim are more central, or they might even lurk in the sleepy farmsteads of Midgard, hiding in plain sight."

"If that's the case," Gunnar added, "the bandits may not even be Ljosalfar at all, leading us to misdirect our resources and scrutiny here instead at the true culprits."

"Or it may be some inter-race alliance," Hilder concluded. "A conspiracy that broad could not have been hatched easily. There are only a few places where the various races interact."

"Still, I find it highly improbable that an alliance of such disparate peoples could have formed at all," Skogul mused aloud. "They are kept apart and dependent upon us explicitly so that this could not happen. With our control over the supply chain, they shouldn't have access to extra tools or provisions that would allow them to pull off these heists, much less travel across realms."

"They would not be so brazen as to conspire within the walls of Asgard," Gunnar exclaimed. "It must be one of the hub cities like Knorrborg, Calder, or Sunnan Kaupstad. I leave it to the two of you to track this down. There cannot be many who can elude two of Asgard's valkyries."

—

"The food and cloth I understand." Eik glanced over the cart at Oydis as they moved it along the hidden path. "But what use is all of this ore?"

"Don't you worry about that," Oydis replied over her shoulder. She had the straps over her shoulders as she pulled from the front. The dancing light of the forest streamed through the broad oak leaves as a warm breeze blew in from the west. "We don't have the tools to work the ingots into anything practical, but I know people who do."

"I must admit that I've been curious about what you've been doing with your share of the spoils," Eik said. "Usually we just split up and go our separate ways. But those valkyries would've found one or both of our tracks if we hadn't had Alva and Ljot following and masking our steps."

"Indeed," Oydis acknowledged. "To that end, we should wait a season or two before we raid again—let our trail fade and keep the Aesir spinning like a vargr chasing its tail."

"Now that they know our tactics, they will scour Alfheim for us and for any trace of poppy powder," Eik challenged. "We won't be able to hide in any of the villages."

"It is as you say, Eik." Oydis turned her head and gave a mischievous smile. "How would you like to visit Svartalfheim?"

—

Three days later, Eik and Oydis arrived at a secluded cove along the western shores of Alfheim. Waiting for them was a small skiff crewed by four Humans. Two of them hopped ashore, took possession of the supplies, and passed them over the gunwale to the others.

"Looks like a good haul this time," the captain said to Oydis after opening the crates and inspecting their contents. "This will go a long way in Svartalfheim."

"Thank you for accommodating us on short notice, Captain Gustav." Oydis took his proffered hand, and he pulled her up into the boat. She alighted, causing only the subtlest rocking.

Eik, however, set the boat rattling; her shaky legs could not stop moving. While the cove was protected from the larger swells of the open ocean, the gentle rocking was enough to throw her equilibrium into chaos. Mere moments after coming aboard, Eik was sent sprawling to the deck. Oydis was surprised to see her, who demonstrated deft balance and footwork leaping throughout the leafy canopies of Alfheim, so ill at ease.

"Just try to relax, Eik," Oydis said while gently guiding her to one of the bench seats. "And keep your sight on the horizon," she added quickly, seeing the growing signs of nausea on her friend's face. Though dark-skinned, Eik had a pallor that might rival the complexion of a Dokkalfar.

"Not to worry." Captain Gustav pointed to the dark shape out on the open sea. "The ship will be more stable."

Just then, a gust of wind blew and rocked the skiff a bit, and the clouds high above moved a little faster. "Unless that storm catches up to us," added the captain.

"Hel's taint," Eik muttered through the hand clasped over her mouth, holding back the vomit.

CHAPTER 11: HAMMERFORGED

The staccato chime of an active blacksmith echoed throughout the vaulted cavern. Runes of power—carved into the living rock of the walls, ceiling, and floor—all converged upon the smithy at the center of the chamber. Three short, stout figures attended to their duties at the massive anvil next to the forge. The runes flared with light and energy at every blow. Light from the furnace flickered and bathed the room in an orange glow while a smoky, sulfurous air permeated every corner. The Dokkalfar smith Ivaldi wore simple wool garb under a heavy leather apron. His pale complexion was barely visible beneath the thick layers of grime and ash that covered him from head to toe. Unlike his two attendants' tight braids, Ivaldi's beard and hair flowed wildly in a halo of ashen locks.

"Sindri, hold that ingot in place, damnit!" The younger Dokkalfar's hair was braided into two ropes, one high and the other low in the back, and his beard had not yet come in. The muscles of his arms twitched with every strike of the hammers, fighting to hold the tongs secure and still.

"Come on, Brokkr, put your back into it!" Ivaldi roared. "Once the first set of enchantments have been put in, that weak strike won't even make a dent in the fired metal."

"Yes, sir!" Brokkr gritted his teeth and threw his whole body into the next blow. The hammer crashed down in cadence just after Ivaldi's strike. A shower of sparks and flecks of coke residue erupted from the impact and splashed against Sindri. He turned his face away but held steady. A smile appeared beneath Brokkr's tidy beard.

After a while, the impact of the hammers fell into a steady rhythm and the three Dokkalfar sang to the beat:

Deep in the heart of Muspelheim
Lava burns the hottest
Lava burns true

Deep in the heart of the mountain
Hammers strike the hardest
Hammers strike true

Deep in the hearts of Dokkalfar
Iron in our veins is purest
Iron in our veins is true

We forge armor to protect us
We forge weapons to tame the beasts
We forge the tools to shape the world

Sindri held the white-hot iron ingot atop the anvil; the tips of the tongs began to glow with the heat. Ivaldi and Brokkr alternated strikes—two light taps on the anvil and then a heavy blow on the ingot. They sang the song over and over while they worked. As the metal block cooled, Ivaldi waved off Brokkr, and the echoes of the din faded.

Boelthor, the Jotnar king, stepped forward from just beyond the doorway into the room, his hemp-woven tunic draped over his tall, lithe frame. Living leaves sprouted from the collar and cuffs in a billowing trim. Boelthor's brow creased with effort as he drew upon his inner strength and inscribed runes of Ethlivald into the metal. Green light matching the emerald color of his fur-covered body flared with each stroke of every rune. The block of iron twitched and appeared to resist, almost as if it were fighting against the process. To Ivaldi's eye, something within the ingot reacted to the Jotnar's power, giving the metal a life of its own.

Each minute was an exercise in agony for Ivaldi. He could see Brokkr and Sindri shifting from foot to foot as well. Those small movements faded as time dragged on until the two were leaning together, gaining stability through the delicate balance of their bodies propped against each other. Just when Ivaldi thought the two were about to fall asleep and topple over, a final emerald flash lit the room and Boelthor collapsed to his knees.

"Now!" Ivaldi barked.

Brokkr snapped into action. He lunged and threw open the furnace valve. Molten rock flowed into the firepot and bright amber light blotted out the last, lingering vestiges of visible Ethlivald.

Sindri snapped up the ingot in his tongs and practically threw it into the hearth and shut the hatch. Once again, the room was cast in darkness.

Ivaldi manned the bellows. With each pump, the heat and light of the furnace grew so intense that it escaped from the edges of the hatch and shadows danced across the walls. And yet, for all of its intensity, the bright orange glow could not cover the tinge of green at the heart of the ingot.

Nearly forgotten in the flurry of activity, Boelthor pushed himself up on shaky legs. The smiths regarded him with some reverence but made no move to help. Their attention was on the furnace, ready to act when the time was right. With his strength somewhat recovered and his work done, Boelthor swept out of the room amid a rustling of leaves, leaving behind a lingering floral scent amid the heavy odor of smoke and ash.

Ivaldi did not stare directly at the blinding light coming from the hatch. He watched the edges of the shadows cast upon the walls. The moment the emerald hue finally vanished, he threw open the hatch.

With practiced movements Sindri reacted, closing the valve while Brokkr reached into the hearth with the tongs and pulled out the white-hot steel ingot and placed it on the anvil. Ivaldi resumed hammering, with Sindri taking Brokkr's place. The deafening ring of the metal resounded in the chamber. The familiar amber sparks and ash erupting from each impact now carried the telltale green of Ethlivald.

"Keep up with me now, Sindri." Ivaldi could detect the slightest delay in the young Dokkalfar's rhythm. He should be fresh, having held the ingot on the previous cycle. Ivaldi's own hammer had twice the heft. And while Brokkr and Sindri would be taking turns, Ivaldi, as the master smith, would have no respite until they were done.

"Yes, sir!" Sindri shouted with his next swing back on cue.

Njord entered as soon as the pounding stopped. The leader of the Vanir was clad in woolen raiments bearing intricate embroidery. Golden thread accented the patterns along the seams and hems and complemented the hue of his skin. Njord's raven-black hair lay flat and straight down his back, ending just below his shoulder blades. He repeated the ritual Boelthor had just performed; white light flared instead of green with every rune inscribed. A burst of emerald and white erupted when a Mithlivald rune crossed one of Ethlivald.

The process repeated again, with Buri taking his turn. His flaming red beard and mane matched the firelight. While the cut and fit of his tunic were neat and orderly, the braids of his hair were loose and casual. Though nearly a head taller than the Dokkalfar, Buri shared their build, broad shouldered and square jawed. He approached the ingot with purpose and an unwavering stride. The strokes of his runes were quick and sure. Golden sparks burst continuously as each new rune crossed the ones laid down before by Boelthor and Njord.

Sindri snatched the ingot away just as Buri finished the last marking and tossed it back into the furnace.

"That's one round done," Ivaldi said as he wiped the sweat from his brow.

"How many more times do we have to do this?" Boelthor asked as he and Njord stepped back into the room.

"Until it can't take anymore," Ivaldi replied with a gruff and weary tone. Brokkr and Sindri shot wary looks at him as the three leaders glared. "Uh, your highnesses," Ivaldi added belatedly and bowed low.

"We are creating a tool that will be indelibly connected to all of the powers of Yggdrasil," Sindri said with more formality. "A tool such as this will be a match against the most powerful creatures that plague the land. But with all three magics, it can also be used to tame the land and make it whole and fruitful. And to do that, we must fold into the metal as much of the three energies as it can handle. And only the intense heat from the magma of Muspelheim can melt the enchanted metal enough for us to shape it. Once we have saturated the metal with Ethlivald, Mithlivald, and Reginvald, these will be the most powerful tools to ever exist."

Brokkr shifted uneasily. "Of course, they will each require one final sacrifice…"

Buri and Boelthor exchanged glances.

"We are well aware," they said in unison.

"Bestla and Borr will lead your people well." Njord placed a hand upon each of their shoulders. "With your sacrifices, the future generations will have a peace and prosperity beyond our ken."

"Aye," Boelthor said, meeting his gaze. "It falls to you to see this through to the end."

"Without you, we never would have come to this agreement," Buri said, his own hand upon Njord's shoulder. "Though this was my vision, you tempered my zeal and brought us together, united." He nodded in deference to Boelthor. "And together we shall bring forth a new age, an age of civility and prosperity, under our rule. No longer shall we cower to mere beasts."

As if to mock them, the mountain shook violently. Some small rocks broke loose from the ceiling, but the runes held strong and everything in the smithy remained intact.

"The dragons are at it again," Buri spat.

"Thankfully they only mate once a year," Boelthor said with a wink. Njord gave a little chuckle while Buri shook his head.

"The sooner we finish, the better," Sindri said as he pulled the glowing ingot from the furnace and placed it on the anvil. Ivaldi and Brokkr hefted their smithing hammers as Boelthor, Njord, and Buri left the room.

———

Months passed before the telltale shape of the head of a warhammer emerged from the forge. Runes of power had been etched into the metal throughout the process. In the cool, dark gray metal, they seemed to ebb and flow beneath the surface. Borr, Buri, Bestla, and Njord stepped out from the shadows of the chamber's doorway. Bestla carried the great spear Gungnir, and Njord carried a gnarled shaft of dark wood as the four approached the cooling block of iron.

"Father…" Borr started but could find no other words.

"Look to Njord and Bestla," Buri urged, clasping his son by the shoulders. "You shall carry out this, our legacy."

Bestla looked to the spear in her hand. The runes brightened as if it had heard Buri's words. Soft green light played against the warm amber glow from the idle furnace. Bestla's hemp-woven tunic and pants were styled as Boelthor's had been. Soft leaves billowed at the hems. The sleeveless cut spoke to the warmth of the region and to the smithy itself.

And yet, in spite of the heat, Buri wore the full raiment he would hold court in. Borr's jaw clenched and he gave a stoic nod. There might have been a rasp in the deep breath he took, though no one betrayed any recognition of it.

"Are you ready?" Njord asked Buri.

The Aesir looked at the Vanir king and gave a single nod before taking four long strides to the anvil at the center of the smithy. With no pomp or ceremony, Buri lay down upon it as Boelthor had done months earlier.

Ivaldi placed the head of the warhammer upon Buri's chest with the eyehole aligned vertically. Brokkr and Sindri were absent; their services were not required for this step. Borr placed his hands upon the hammerhead, invoking the power of Reginvald. Njord stood over the supine figure of his friend and ally. With no hesitation, he drove the wooden pole into the hammerhead. The runes etched into the metal flared to life and arcs of energy spidered out, filling the room. Bestla, pushed back by the initial explosion, fought against the seismic waves and placed her hands upon the shaft. At her touch, the wood came to life; leaves sprouted and rootlike tendrils shot through the eyehole and wrapped around the block of iron and the man beneath. Njord used Mithlivald to bring the untamed growth under control. Once an equilibrium was reached, a brilliant flash of white light erupted and Buri vanished, leaving only the great hammer, Mjolnir in his place.

Njord lifted the hammer above his head in both hands as the light and power dissipated. There was a lingering taste and smell of ozone that permeated the air in the room. "We name you Mjolnir." He turned to Borr, holding the weapon out at chest level, his palms facing up. "Borr shall wield your power."

The young Aesir reached out a tentative hand. A spark crackled as he grasped it, causing him to pull away. On his second approach, he gritted his teeth and pushed through the pain to take hold of the hammer.

"And Bestla shall carry the spear, Gungnir," Njord continued, stepping behind the two. "Together, we three shall awaken this world from its nightmare of monsters and chaos. This is the dawn of a new age, an enlightened age."

"At least that's how it was done in the texts that I read," Loki said as he finished retelling the story of Mjolnir's creation.

"We have to sacrifice someone?" Sigrid asked, her brow arched as she exchanged glances with the others in the room.

"The bigger problem is getting a piece of Yggdrasil." Loki shrugged. "I don't even know if it's possible to perform the binding ceremony without a piece of the World Tree."

"Aric!" Frode exclaimed.

Loki, Sigrid, and Hertha looked at him while Surtr, the Dokkalfar, and the Ljosalfar leaders shrugged.

"Aric carries a wooden staff with him. He's had it since he returned from Yggdrasil." He gestured to Sigrid and continued, "We saw him wield it against tainted lindworms in Hoddmimis Holt. It reacted with an intense burst of power. It must be from Yggdrasil."

Sigrid's face went pale, and Loki asked, "Where is Aric?"

CHAPTER 12: OVER THE RIVER

"Do you miss him?" Aric asked, turning to address Lif. Virgin snow crunched under their feet. The slight, flat dip in the landscape marked the road beneath the otherwise pristine white blanket covering the countryside. Bundled head-to-toe in furs and carrying packs laden with supplies, Aric already missed the volcanic heat of Muspelheim. With his walking stick, the gnarled root of Yggdrasil, he tested a small stone bridge. It felt icy but sturdy enough for them to cross.

As he went over, Lif trotted down to the creek below. She dropped her pack, her unstrung bow, and her quiver holding two dozen arrows. With practiced ease, she drew the Jotnar knife that was tucked into the crude rope belt cinched around her waist. Half a dozen chops later, she had her waterskin thrust through the hole in the ice.

Aric sighed with a smile. He drank the remainder of his own waterskin before tossing it down to Lif. She handed the full skin back to him on the far side of the bridge, her kit returned to its previous position on her back.

After a dozen steps, Aric looked at her and tried to pick up the conversation, "So, Lifthrasir…"

Lif shrugged and tilted her head away. It was about as much as he expected from her, but Aric noticed her lips curl down at the corners for a split second.

"We're doing this for him," he said, looking straight ahead. "We're doing this for all of them." Aric caught Freya's nod at the edge of his peripheral vision.

"You still see her?" Lif's sharp eyes had not missed the subtle tensing of his jaw, neck, and shoulders.

"Yes." Aric exhaled a long, wispy breath. "She's still here. She's the reason I even understand… have any idea about what's going on with the blight and why we need the Aesir's help."

Without looking, he knew that Freya was smiling. Aric looked anyway. She was not smiling; her brow was furrowed and her eyes were narrowed and locked on to the forest to their left. Aric saw that Lif had dropped her pack and had her bow strung with an arrow nocked at the ready.

"Use the staff," Freya said, causing Aric to hesitate as he reached for the sword at his side. "Trust me," she urged when his fingers held fast, hovering inches from the hilt.

Both of Aric's hands grasped the staff tight when a dark shape burst from the tree line. It was an amorphous blob of inky shadows, surging forward in lurching spasms. Aric was not certain if it was running or even had legs at all. His eyes were unable to make sense of the shape bounding towards them, larger than a vargr yet smaller than a lindworm. An arrow struck the thing in what Aric could only assume was its head. Another and another followed, though they did little to slow the creature's charge.

Aric's right foot shifted back. Just as he was about to tell Lif to run, Freya shouted, "Hit it!"

That snapped Aric to attention, but he was frozen in place. Aric had faced dragons, vargr, and lindworms, yet this strange thing made him feel so small and afraid. He could hear Freya's voice, but his mind would process no other information as the thing bore down on him.

Something tugged on his cloak and he heard Lif's voice. Still he could not move. The shadow was almost upon him when he saw Freya's ethereal hands reach out and grab the staff where his hands were. Aric's body moved, but not under his control. With the staff cocked back, his feet propelled him forward.

Aric's eyes did not close despite his desperate, urgent desire to shut them. The gnarled root swung with incredible speed and plunged deep into the darkness. In a frozen moment of time, he felt the impact. Then all of the action flooded forward as the shadows vanished in a flash of light, revealing a reindeer with blood, bile, and unidentifiable ooze frothing from its nose and mouth.

Aric had not even processed the terrible sight before him when Lif vaulted over his shoulders at the exposed beast, sinking her knife deep into its skull. The animal collapsed with Lif on top of it as Aric fell back and landed on his ass.

"It's worse than I thought." Freya stood over the rotting corpse. Behind it, Aric could see the trail of corruption seared into its path and the burst haloed around them, left from when the staff had dispelled it. "Njord's power is fading."

Aric grabbed Lif and pulled her away from the putrid mound of flesh and bones before dry heaving and coughing up some water.

"I first felt it when we were walking among Yggdrasil's roots. And then the corruption on those vargr." Freya reached her arms forward, as if it was still there lingering in the air. "I can feel something from the World Tree in them… and less and less of my father."

Aric's attention was pulled away as he felt a tug on his sleeve. Lif was looking at him, her expression somewhere between concern and curiosity.

"I—I'm fine." Aric wiped his mouth with his sleeve. "I just need a moment."

He accepted Lif's help to stand up. His eyes followed hers to see the three arrows in the animal's skull decay and crumble before their eyes. The flesh and bones of the stag followed until there was nothing left but the churned snow and dirt and the foul stench in the air. After a few deep breaths Aric looked around, scanning the nearby tree line and the surrounding horizon.

"What was it doing alone, all the way down here?" he asked.

"Better to move on before we discover it wasn't alone," Freya replied. Aric noticed that for an apparition, she was breathing hard. Calming his own breath, he wondered if hallucinations even breathed. Did spirits?

Lif was already back on the road, and he hurried to catch up, Yggdrasil's root held tight in his left hand, a slight crack at the head where it had struck the stag.

CHAPTER 13: THE BURNING BLADE

"Is that it?" Hertha eyed the six-inch-wide and four-foot-long blade of the massive sword. Including the hilt and pommel, the weapon was nearly as tall as the diminutive Jotnar. It was a simple, utilitarian-looking thing, unlike any Aesir weapon she had ever seen. "Is it done?"

Frode, Sigrid, and Surtr were at her side. Brokkr had brought them all as soon as he and Sindri had completed the weapon.

"Are you... not impressed... by our work?" Loki was slumped against the far wall of the room; his breathing was labored and shallow, and sweat beaded his brow.

Sindri ran an aurochs chamois cloth along the length of the blade, polishing the metal to a mirror shine. His gloved hands worked with care as he wrapped the upper half of the hilt with leather. Intricate runes and knotwork filigree adorned the fuller, running past the cross guard into the hilt. The details and etchings flowed through every part of the sword, unbroken as if it were one solid piece of steel.

"This is the enchanted weapon that will stand against Mjolnir?" Hertha asked as she leaned in for a closer look. It was not until her eyes were inches away that she saw the additional runes shimmering below the surface, as if the metal itself was translucent. "At the battle of the Bifrost Skjaldborg, I could feel Mjolnir's power from across the plain. This appears to be less impressi—Argh!"

At her touch, the patterns on the sword flared to life. The room filled with intense heat and energy. Frode and Sigrid fell back, overwhelmed. Surtr appeared unfazed by the heat but was physically pushed back by a wave that radiated out from the sword. Sindri jerked the blade away from Hertha. As soon as contact was broken, the energy dissipated and she collapsed to her knees, clutching her hand.

"What happened?" Sigrid asked, kneeling beside Hertha. Frode was slower to recover.

"What makes Aesir weapons, and Mjolnir specifically, so powerful is that they can channel Reginvald energies from their wielders." Sindri set the sword onto a cradle. "Mjolnir and Gungnir had shafts made from Yggdrasil's wood, connecting them to the energies of the World Tree itself. For those weapons, the danger isn't in draining energy from the user. The danger is in too much power flowing through them, overloading the wielder's mind and body."

"We don't have that luxury," Loki added. "Without Yggdrasil's wood, the Ethlivald, Reginvald, and Mithlivald enchantments will draw their power from whoever holds it."

Making eye contact with everyone in the room, Loki added, "All of it."

"So it will kill whoever uses it?" Surtr gave the twins a withering glare.

"Well, if it's used for a short amount of time, it won't kill them right away," Brokkr said with a sheepish grin.

"We have to get that staff from Aric," Hertha said through labored breaths. "The piece of Yggdrasil will circumvent that, right?"

"Well..." Loki was hesitant in his reply.

"Well, what?" Hertha showed little patience for understanding the finer points of the powers of the World Tree.

"There's no guarantee that we can bind them together later." Loki recalled the forging process as recounted in the texts. "I'm sure they left out some of the steps intentionally."

Hertha continued to stare at him with a look of anger and frustration.

"They didn't want anyone else to have this kind of power," Loki replied. "All I know is what they wrote down. I don't fully understand how it all works, but having a piece of Yggdrasil might give the user a chance of surviving the power drain."

"We were able to improve upon the ancient smithing process by adding carbon to forge steel instead of simple iron," Brokkr added with a self-satisfied smile. "The steel blade should prove more durable and sharper than those ancient weapons. Mjolnir is, at its heart, a tempered and hardened lump of iron—"

"All things being equal, this sword can cleave Mjolnir in two," Sindri said in simple terms. "With or without the wood, this sword is superior."

Hertha and Surtr exchanged looks. Her legs wobbled as she stood and examined the finger that had touched the weapon. The fur was burned away at the point of contact and the exposed skin had puckered from the heat.

"I will do it," Surtr said with conviction. "Mjolnir and the Aesir will be destroyed by my hand."

"What?" Loki stepped forward. "Without me, we wouldn't even have this weapon."

"Or us," Brokkr and Sindri said. "We would gladly sacrifice our lives to end the Aesir reign."

"You wouldn't even be here if we hadn't convinced you to come," Sigrid said.

"And then the army would be armed with sticks and stones," Sindri retorted.

"There are no trees in Muspelheim to even supply sticks," Eik said with a laugh.

"They killed my mother in front of me!" Surtr roared.

The debate halted and the hall quieted.

"We've all lost people to the Aesir," Hertha said, her voice soft yet firm. Her eyes locked with Surtr's for a long moment before they went to Brokkr, Sindri, Sigrid, Eik, and Loki. "I have more of a claim against Thor and the Aesir than anyone here," she continued. "I was at the Bifrost Skjaldborg when we toppled it. I was there when Nidhogg darkened the skies and laid waste to the Vigrid Plains. Who among you have even stared down an Aesir in single combat?"

Loki stepped forward, his brow furrowed and expression dark. "I killed Baldur."

"After stabbing him in the back," Hertha sneered. "I was there, I saw it."

Loki growled and took a step towards her.

Brokkr, who had been engaged in a hushed, fierce discussion with Sindri, intervened before he could do or say anything more. "This cannot be a rash, emotional decision. We have one weapon, one opportunity to topple the Aesir for all time."

"So what would you suggest?" Surtr asked without taking his eyes from Hertha.

"I bet you'll love it." Sindri winked at Brokkr.

———

Hertha was breathing hard; sweat beaded all along the short fur that covered her body. Despite the months she had spent living here, Aldrnari still felt like an inferno compared to Jotunheim. She had forgone leggings, wearing a simple, sleeveless tunic belted at the waist that draped down to mid-thigh.

"Come on, Hertha!" Sindri shouted through cupped hands. "I've got two days' rations bet on you!"

"What?!" Brokkr exclaimed. "You bet against me?" He raised his hammer at the last minute to block her sword strike.

The Dokkalfar had several superficial scrapes and bruises on both arms from the fights over the course of the week. His stocky build might have seemed a disadvantage against his many taller opponents, but Brokkr's skill, quickness, and familiarity with the hammer beyond mere smithing had surprised his opponents.

Hertha had also been underestimated due to her shorter stature. Most, however, were aware of her ferocity and prowess on the battlefield from the stories of her time leading the Jotnar Army in their nearly successful campaign against the Aesir. In fact, their routing at the intervention of the eldritch dragon, Nidhogg, made her exploits even more celebrated. She had not only fought against Thor, she had survived a creature from the days before the Great Awakening and had led the surviving Jotnar Army to relative safety.

The reputation of such a venerated fighter did not discourage people from competing. In fact, many had thrown their lot in for the mere chance to test their mettle before marching on Asgard. There were so many that, to simplify things and for the sake of efficiency, each group had been limited to choosing just two champions to represent them in the contest.

A week of challenges, pitched battles, close contests, and spectacular upsets had led to the last four fighters: Hertha, Loki, Brokkr, and Surtr. The raucous, cheering audience was packed around a cleared circle ten yards across in the main hall. As the two shortest fighters circled each other, the crowd pushed in closer, those in the back attempting to catch sight of the action.

Brokkr feinted right before pivoting and coming in low left. Hertha sneered, her blunted training sword already there, ready for the block. She locked the blade and hilt against the point where the head of the hammer met the shaft and threw a straight punch into the blacksmith's unguarded jaw. He let go of his weapon and stumbled back several feet. Hertha was already in pursuit, and the dazed Brokkr avoided her sword slash by inches as he rolled to the edge of the circle. Several nearby spectators jumped back as they dodged the attack as well.

"Hey!" Brokkr shouted in anger as he stared at one of his braids that now lay on the ground. "You cut my beard!"

It seemed that Hertha had struck a sensitive nerve, and the Dokkalfar drew a second hammer from his belt and lunged forward with renewed vigor. She was taken aback by his ferocity but never lost her composure. With practiced movements, she deflected or blocked every strike. When his steam ran out and the fight paused, she realized her right arm was shaking, the sword still ringing with the repeated hammering.

"How did you make it this far in the competition?" Hertha said with a smirk. Her voice was strong, and she even flourished the sword while passing it from her right hand to her left. Despite this outward bravado, she hoped the action masked her shaking out her right arm and flexing her fingers.

"You of all people should know not to underestimate your opponent." He returned the smirk and pointed to her sword.

While the competition was meant to be a practical test of realistic combat, they had all been armed with blunted weapons. Hertha's blade was still made of steel, and in her skilled hands it remained potent enough to cut Brokkr's beard. Looking at it now, she saw a series of fractures running down its length. She grasped it; with very little effort, the blade snapped into several pieces. The original three-foot-long sword was now a mere foot and a half from pommel to tip.

"And you should know that a shorter weapon can be even more effective," Hertha said as she dashed in.

The shorter weapon was quicker and more maneuverable, and its altered profile led Brokkr to attempt to block where the full-length blade would have been. Taking advantage of that mistake, Hertha broke through his guard and had the edge of the sword at his throat. She gave him a little nick for good measure.

With a chuckle, he slid the hammer back into his belt and offered his hand. "Yeah." Brokkr blew out a long breath. She could barely hear him as the crowd cheered at the outcome. "You don't need a big, clumsy weapon when a precision instrument will do the job." He gave her a wink as his eyes flicked in Surtr's direction. "But you can't underestimate brute force either."

"That you can't," Hertha agreed as she dropped the broken sword and embraced Brokkr. "We'll see how his strength and reach match up against Loki's cleverness."

Surtr paced around the cleared ring. He moved with measured steps, as if he were making a map of the area with his feet. Loki eyed him with detached interest. His mind was already planning how he would approach Thor again. Having fought with and against the Aesir, he viewed Surtr as a naive boy from a sheltered, backwater hole of the nine realms. That was not to say that he was not physically impressive. Even among the Eldjotnar, Surtr was singularly imposing, but Freya and Sif had demonstrated time and again how to defeat larger opponents. They had taught Jarnsaxa how to stand her ground while sparring against Thor.

The memory of his sister came suddenly and caught him off guard as he considered his current position of leading an army against the Aesir. Would she be proud of him or disappointed that it had taken her death to shake his infatuation with the golden splendor of Asgard?

"You do yourself a disservice by underestimating me," Surtr said from the opposite side of the clearing.

Loki took a moment before responding. "What?"

"I said that you should not dismiss me as a threat," the Eldjotnar said with a growl in his throat. "I may not have fought vargr or armies as you have, but

I have poured all of my free time and extra energy into readying myself for vengeance against the Aesir."

"I'm certain that you have," Loki replied absently, a hint of boredom playing across his face. "The sad goats of Muspelheim must flee in terror at your very presence. And I suppose many a stalagmite has been cut down by your mighty arm. But keep in mind, rocks don't hit back."

"Enough talking," Sigrid said as she stepped into the center of the circle. "Are you both ready?"

Surtr hefted a weighty practice sword in each of his massive hands and nodded. Loki bounced on his toes, holding a one-handed training sword with a casual air. He eyed Hertha, who was watching from the front row of the surrounding crowd, before he bobbed his head once at Sigrid.

"Fight!" Sigrid shouted before stepping back among the spectators as they burst into a roaring cheer that was magnified within the cavernous chamber.

Loki sprang forward, eager to finish this fight and save his energy for Hertha. He knew that her small stature hid a ferocious spirit and highly tactical mind. The sooner he was done with Surtr, the more preparation time he would have for that bout. A flash of steel startled him, and Loki quickly turned his sword and stepped aside. Surtr had been ready. With a flick of his wrist, the point of his sword had come up and cut off Loki's charge before he had taken three steps. The Eldjotnar's long limbs gave him superior reach, and his reflexes were formidable for someone so large.

A smile crept up at the edges of Surtr's lips. *"You fight like an Aesir,"* he spat out in Jotunmal. *"So stiff and disciplined, no imagination."*

On his second attempt, Loki feinted to his left before coming in low after slapping Surtr's blade to the side with his sword. But before Loki could bring his sword back on the return swing, Surtr had stepped forward inside the Jotnar's effective range and jammed him. Suddenly a burst of blue energy erupted and knocked Surtr several paces back against the crowd. Loki smirked at him, the telltale glow of Iss Ethlivald dancing across his free left hand.

"Well, that was different," Surtr said, his abdomen coated in an inch-thick layer of ice. *"However dumb it may have been."* The air around Surtr shimmered, and all who were not Eldjotnar stepped away as the radiating heat intensified. Steam came off the ice as it sublimated and then shattered. A red aura illuminated Surtr's silhouette as the Eldjotnar variant of Ethlivald radiated from him.

"You talk too much," Loki retorted as he stepped forward, his weapon pulled far back, a heavy swing chambered.

Surtr sneered as he brought his own sword to block the obvious attack. To everyone's surprise, the Eldjotnar's blade shattered upon impact. Loki followed up with a flurry of strikes. Even with a broken and shortened weapon, Surtr was able to fend off most of the attacks, though Loki landed several glancing blows. None of those hits were definitive enough for Sigrid to call an end to the match.

The sneer on Surtr's face had long since faded. After the sixth blade slap against his arm, he caught onto the pattern and stepped into the next strike, changing the rhythm of the fight. This gave him the opening to trap Loki's weapon in the crook of the blade and hilt of his sword. With his left hand free, the Eldjotnar grabbed his opponent's weapon. Arcs of red energy coursed out of the point of contact, and the metal began to warp and melt. Blue light flared at the hilt as Iss Ethlivald fought against the intense heat of the Eld Ethlivald. The energies clashed as the light grew in intensity, blue and red turning to white.

Just as it appeared that the blue of the Iss Ethlivald was beginning to edge out the red, Surtr jerked the blade away, wrenching it free of Loki's grip. Loki was powerful but was no match for the Eldjotnar's superior physical strength. In that moment of distraction, Surtr followed up with a powerful swing of his right fist. Loki was knocked to the ground, dazed. There was no hesitation as Surtr stepped on his chest and thrust the blade in his left hand at Loki's throat.

"Victory!" Sigrid stepped in to end the match.

"Well fought," Surtr said as he dropped the practice sword and offered a hand to his downed opponent.

"Yeah," Loki replied as he reluctantly accepted the help up and rubbed at his jaw. "I admit that I underestimated you."

"As we have all been underestimated by the Aesir," Surtr added. He turned and addressed the crowd. "The Aesir underestimated the Jotnar even as they brought low the mighty Bifrost Skjaldborg. And they continued to do so as they allowed you to unite us all into this army."

The crowd cheered as he arced his arm out towards them.

"Your tactics proved to be useful on the battlefield." Surtr now addressed Loki and Hertha. "But I trained specifically to fight Aesir in single combat. I have been working since I was a child to exact revenge against them. Trust me, I will bring out the full potential of our weapon against Mjolnir. Take care of the army and leave the rest to me. I swear upon the memory of my mother that I will not fail you."

A fiery energy combusted from his raised fist. From the far side of the room, the enchanted sword appeared to flare to life in response.

"It is my destiny to wield that sword in battle." Now he held Hertha's gaze as he said, "Please, allow me to give my life's energy to that sword. I will not let you down."

Silence permeated the chamber as all eyes turned to the diminutive Jotnar. She had stepped forward into the clearing after Surtr's victory. Hertha's fists were clenched tight. Loki was expecting her to punch the Eldjotnar. But when she extended her open hand, everyone let out an audible breath of relief. Surtr clasped her small hand, enfolding it within his broad, meaty palm.

"If you die before killing Thor, I won't say, 'I told you so,'" Hertha said, pulling him closer as they shook hands.

CHAPTER 14: THE NEW NORMAL

Brunhilda had been in a foul mood since returning from the north. The near continuous flow of blighted creatures had proven impossible to circumvent. Having failed to identify the creatures' origins, all they could do was fight against the increasingly frequent attacks.

The wet, stomach-churning crunch of tearing flesh and breaking bone heralded the end of this particular encounter. Nearby, Brunhilda caught the telltale flourish of Reginvald energies sparking from the heavy iron head of Mjolnir. Oozing tendrils of corruption writhed in their death throes for several minutes after their bestial hosts had expired. The viscous slime tainted the spelled armor worn by Thor and the rest of the Aesir. Runes etched into the metal glowed and flickered as they fought against the dark power. And though it was midday, these flares were the brightest lights, the dense clouds having blotted out the sun for months now.

In the unnatural twilight, even the looming ruins of Halvard towering above Calder Lake were barely visible. The contrast of the snow covering the charred rubble helped to distinguish it from the virgin white fields that stretched out to the northern forests. Corpses of vargr, lindworms, and even normally docile animals like stags and rams littered the field.

With a roar, Thor swung Mjolnir in an arc and struck the skull of a vargr launching it into the air, hurtling off into the distance. Brunhilda, along with the other Aesir nearby, turned to look at the spectacle. They all pretended not to notice as Thor lost his footing on the blood-soaked ground and stumbled amid the rapidly decaying corpses. Although he did not fall, his imbalance betrayed his state of inebriation.

"It's shameful to see him this way," Asta commented under her breath.

Wiping off some of the gore from the battle, Brunhilda replied,

"Especially in front of the Einherjar."

The Humans who had sheltered within the walls of Asgard during the Jotnar Uprising had been training under the tutelage of Lady Sif. Between the devastation of Baldur's war, the fiery carnage of the dragon Nidhogg, and the vargr savagery led by Fenrir, the Aesir ranks had been decimated. While far below the skill of even the most novice Aesir soldiers, the Humans, dubbed Einherjar, had accepted the call to arms with enthusiasm. Now, after this latest victory, they rallied around Freyr, who had taken on the responsibility to train them while Sif had been focused on rebuilding Asgard's defenses and organizing the Aesir Army. And Thor had not been sober since Odin's death.

"They wouldn't have lasted more than a handful of moments against Suttungr's Jotnar, but they've proven useful against these infected animals," Asta said, watching as they cheered their victory, oblivious to Thor's antics. Freyr led the Einherjar in the familiar Aesir victory song.

> Now is the time to fight
> And it's always time to drink
> Grab your sword, raise your flagon
> Sober men come home on the undertaker's wagon
>
> Oh, the nine realms span far and wide
> May your tankard ne'er run dry
> Raise your sword, grab your flagon
> Drunk warriors fear not even dragons
>
> When the time to die nears
> Adventure ever awaits
> Grab your sword, raise your flagon
> For one last drink and one last shaggin'

Brunhilda's piercing eyes went from the Vanir lord to her own battlefield leader, Thor—the spittle frozen into his unkempt beard, his shaky legs, and the visible clouds of his panting breath despite the relative ease of this fight. She thought back to that battle at Halvard so long past, her first encounter with Baldur disguised as the Jotnar, Suttungr. Her eyes had not been so keen or insightful then. She had not seen the telltale signs of magic in his glamour. More than that, she was disappointed that she had not recognized Baldur— his fighting style, the way he spoke, how he carried himself. She had been blinded by the rush of combat, by the thrill of battle. She had underestimated the Jotnar, and Hilder and Skogul had paid the price.

She wondered what else she had been blind to. Loki came to mind. Disguised as Skrymir, he had joined her mission to obtain the legendary spear, Gungnir. Once they had it, he had betrayed them and killed the

Humans, Skuld and Aric. But it was not until the Battle of the Bifrost Skjaldborg that he revealed his true identity. As if discovering Baldur had been leading the Jotnar Uprising as Suttungr was not enough, seeing Loki again took them all by surprise. She and others had seen both Loki and Baldur incinerated by Nidhogg's fiery breath years before.

In that one moment, the world that she knew had ceased to make sense. Now, toxic creatures poured down from the north, corrupting everything in their path. They had thought that Fenrir was the source of this plague, and rightly so. After his defeat at Thor's hand, they had had a month of tranquility that lasted the duration of Odin's funeral celebration.

"Brunhilda?" Asta tapped her on the shoulder.

"What?" Brunhilda snapped from her reverie. "Yes, you're right. Thor has been constantly drunk since Lord Odin's death."

"He should follow Freyr's example." Asta pointed to the Vanir prince leading the adoring Einherjar. "The Humans have flourished under his tutelage. I would even say that he has flourished now that he's out from under his sister's shadow."

"Freya did cast a long shadow. She and Odin were headstrong and stubborn in equal measure," Brunhilda responded. "But it wasn't an enemy that killed Odin. Thor delivered the killing blow."

"Odin's death was in glorious battle against a worthy opponent," Asta said with a shake of her head. "He found a way to break Fenrir's defenses. That creature returned from the dead with a cloak of darkness that protected it from all of our weapons. After decades of boredom, we are challenged once again. We've faced down threats unseen since before the Great Awakening. Thor should be relishing these days of combat, leading Asgard forward to even more glorious victories."

"Perhaps it's just as well that Thor has not stepped up as a leader." Brunhilda motioned for Asta to keep her voice down. "Freyr is handling the Humans well, and Lady Frigg has taken to Asgard's throne with great success. The mantle of leadership suits her. She has a composure and thoughtfulness that Odin lacked."

Asta gave her a penetrating glare.

"Odin was a clever and successful warrior," Brunhilda added with a look of defiance. She began to enumerate on her fingers. "But seeing what happened with Baldur, the Jotnar Uprising, Nidhogg, and Fenrir, I think we can agree that his leadership has led to some truly disastrous times for the nine realms."

Brunhilda thought back to Frigg's coronation and how she had presided over Odin's funeral. Her speech was uplifting and celebratory while being grounded and authentic. At the time, it had hit all of the right notes and gotten the crowd to rally together, cheering the call for the extermination of the Jotnar. It was clear that Baldur had inherited his way with words from

Frigg. Of course, Brunhilda, along with most of Asgard, had been in a drunken stupor for most of that time and remembered little of the details. Unlike them, Thor had yet to emerge from that fugue. Not that it impeded his fighting ability. In the heat of battle, one could be excused for mistaking the spittle and vomit in his beard for the viscera of his vanquished foes.

"Are you drunk too?" Asta looked at her with an eyebrow cocked.

"No, I…" Brunhilda hesitated. She knew that Asta had been growing more and more concerned about Brunhilda's doubts and questions regarding the hierarchy of the nine realms. "I'm just worried about Thor as well."

Brunhilda understood how Thor felt. Losing those closest to her right before her eyes had challenged her perspective on the glorious battlefield death ideal that their culture upheld for so long. It had been easy for her to say that the Aesir celebrated death on the field of battle. They had been nearly immortal.

She had not known how to deal with that creeping doubt. Speeches and revelry were for others, and so she had drowned her doubts in innumerable tankards of sweet honeyed mead during the festivities of Odin's wake. When they had finally lit the funeral pyre and set the grand and ridiculously ornate longboat adrift, Brunhilda at last sobered up. The timing was fortuitous as Frigg had decided to carry on Odin's final edict and send the Aesir Army to eliminate the Jotnar once and for all.

But that was when the blight returned. Those corrupt animals spreading their rot descended upon Asgard like an avalanche. No longer just vargr and lindworms—rams, stags, reindeer, even aurochs were infected and among the horde rampaging southward. At least these enemies Brunhilda could kill without guilt or remorse. They were a plague upon the land and had to be culled to protect everyone.

"Where's my mead?" Thor shouted while holding the horn of a decapitated ram in his left hand. He had stopped short of trying to drink from it as the flesh sloughed off along with the black ichor. An Einherjar rushed forward with a wineskin, and Thor exchanged it for the ram's head.

Freyr had a senior Einherjar trumpet a series of notes on the warhorn, and the Humans snapped to action, following their leader into the nearest tavern. Meanwhile, a cadre of fostra rushed out from the Skjaldborg gates. The valkyries looked to each other in consternation, knowing it fell to them to safeguard the fostra as they attended to the fallen warriors of the Aesir Army. In conventional circumstances, fostra could trust not to be harassed after a battle. But animals did not attend to the civilized conventions of warfare, and these tainted monsters so much less so. Even their corpses still posed a threat. And so Asta and Brunhilda joined with their sisters as they proceeded to sweep through the muddy, churned, and fetid Vigrid Plains. They stabbed and hacked at anything bestial that still moved while the fostra separated the dead and the wounded into different wagons. Everybody would be taken back, and all weapons and armor would be salvaged and repaired.

CHAPTER 15: BURYING THE DEAD

"You were warned!" Gunnar pointed to the crowd of Jotnar surrounding her. There was the slightest sheen of sweat on her brow as she stood over a particularly large Jotnar. Though now a crumpled lump on the windswept tundra with blood freezing in a puddle of icy blue, she had stood at twice the height of the valkyrie. Gunnar's breath was a little labored from the exertion. Her sword remained sheathed at her waist; its golden hilt gleamed in the bright light of the arctic summer sun. However, the metal covering the articulated knuckles on the valkyrie's gauntlets dripped with azure blood that sparked and bubbled, tinted with golden light as it reacted with the spelled armor.

"Let go of me, Flakka!" Knute hissed. "They killed Anga. They killed my only daughter!"

A crowd of Jotnar encircled the valkyrie and the dozen Aesir soldiers in her retinue. A young, brawny Knute with tensed muscles strained against a fellow Jotnar holding on to his arm.

"There is nothing to be gained by having both of you beaten to death," Flakka replied under her breath. Knute's ire subsided as he lost the struggle against her iron grip.

"This gathering of Jotnar is forbidden," Gunnar continued, oblivious to Knute's and Flakka's whispers. "Your needs are met by the generosity of Odin, and your survival was afforded by Aesir benevolence. Stay in your place, report for labor when called, and we will have no problems. If you don't"—she pointed to the Jotnar body lying on the ground—"the punishment will be swift and terrible."

"All of this is your fault," Knute spat at Flakka when he finally pulled free of her grasp.

"No." Flakka snatched his tunic and held it tight. "I told you that it was too early to meet like this. I needed more time to—"

"Do you have something to add?" Gunnar at last acknowledged Knute and Flakka. "Perhaps you require another example to penetrate that dense fur of yours."

As she stepped forward, Flakka averted her gaze and tried to pull Knute back. But he stood his ground and met Gunnar's eyes. "We do not"—Knute did not shout or raise his voice, but he did put particular emphasis on the next few words—"recognize the authority of Asga—"

Gunnar struck him with the back of her gauntlet-clad hand before he finished. Despite being a head taller than the valkyrie, Knute was laid low by her almost casual blow. Blue rivulets dribbled from a cut on his lip as he rose from the ground. When he had gotten to one knee, Gunnar kicked him in the jaw, sending him sprawling in the other direction.

"Please." Flakka threw herself in front of Knute, shielding him. "We are profoundly and humbly sorry for this transgression. Our old ways and traditions have deep roots. We only wished to pay tribute to Yggdrasil and thank her for helping us turn this small corner of Niflheim into some place that we could call home again."

"You should thank Odin," Gunnar snapped. "Thank him for sparing your entire race after the war."

The gathered Jotnar shifted and looked from the Aesir to each other. A calm settled in the air as the wind died down. Slowly and deliberately, the soldiers slid their hands down to the hilts of their swords.

"Y-yes," Flakka stammered and bowed her head. "We do truly appreciate the food and supplies that Lord Odin bestows upon us." She placed her hand upon Knute's chest and pressed hard as he was about to speak. Her eyes went to several of the prominent Jotnar, sensing their tension. "The generosity of the Aesir is truly boundless. We are your humble servants, for now and for always." And before Gunnar could interject, Flakka added, "My lord."

"Back to your villages." Gunnar signaled to her soldiers. "Now."

The Jotnar moved off in small clusters towards their respective settlements while the soldiers pushed the stragglers along. Flakka had Knute's arm around her shoulder as she helped him to his feet. There was a deep gash across his forehead that was bleeding down over his eye. Flakka signaled to two other Jotnar, who picked up Anga's body and followed. Their small band marched back north, towards Gastropnir.

"You should have let me die," Knute wheezed out as Flakka set him down gently on his bed. "A life of oppression and servitude to the Aesir scum is worse than death. At least in death I would return with Anga to Yggdrasil and new life could spring from our bodies."

"Hush," Flakka said in low tones. Her eyes flicked to see the Aesir soldier lingering at the threshold. Their armed escorts had kept an unrelenting pace, giving no consideration to Knute's wounded state or the body they had to carry back. "If we anger them, they may not permit us to bury Anga and instead force us to burn her body. They know how much more severe of a punishment that would be to us."

"You—you're right," Knute coughed out as the other Jotnar laid the body in the center of the one-room hovel.

"Stay in your place and stay out of trouble," the Aesir soldier said, her voice firm though otherwise stoic. "If you step out of line under my watch, you will find that Gunnar was being gracious. You may attend to your dead, but if I hear one word of Jotunmal, I will not hesitate to mete out Asgard's punishment."

With that, she left and slammed the door closed behind her. The bright light of the sun vanished in the windowless hut, leaving the room bathed in the dim blue light of the two translucent ice columns jutting down from the ceiling. Knute rubbed his eyes, squinted, and groaned as he rose from the bed.

"Slow down," Flakka said as she supported his arm.

They moved over to the wrapped body. Removing the fabric from Anga's head, Knute reached out and touched the battered but otherwise pristine face; she could have been asleep and recuperating for the lack of decomposition. Although the trek back to Gastropnir had been a week long, the body remained preserved by the cold of the blood. Even the Jotnar did not fully understand why their blood chilled the environment and froze when spilled outside of their bodies but they themselves were warm beneath their short, dense fur. This made funeral pyres much less effective, requiring extremely hot, intense fires accelerated by using bellows or covering the bodies with pitch or combustible oils. And yet—though no Jotnar would desecrate a burial site—Aesir had found that buried Jotnar bodies rapidly decomposed, almost as if the ground digested or reabsorbed the nutrients of the flesh and bones.

After a long moment of silence, Flakka pulled Knute up and covered Anga's face again. She moved to the door and opened it, letting in three waiting Jotnar, his sons. They came in and each laid a hand upon Knute's shoulder before placing a hand on the body with bowed heads and closed eyes. Without a word, they and Flakka lifted Anga and carried her out of the room. Knute stood and followed shortly thereafter.

The tundra at the eastern edge of town served as the barrows for the Jotnar of Gastropnir. Even without the raised mounds, the graves would be clearly visible, covered with the bright blossoms of the purple saxifrage. Many other plants had taken hold and flourished on the older barrows. The dense, flourishing alpine forests had taken root upon the dead Jotnar. Since the relocation to Niflheim, generations had been buried in the hardened soil surrounding every town in Jotunheim.

Only the five Jotnar were in attendance. Despite the hard-packed and frozen permafrost, the small group made quick work digging the grave. It was nine feet long, three feet wide, and six feet deep. As a people, they were not the type to shy away from this kind of hard labor, even with their limited tools. Two Aesir soldiers stood a dozen yards to the side, stoic and unmoved by the proceedings.

The Jotnar heeded the threat laid by the Aesir soldier and chose to say nothing lest their words be mistaken as Jotunmal. Several long moments passed with no sound except the rising howl of the arctic winds sweeping over the icy plains. And yet Knute could not contain the flood of emotion and began to sing; he was quiet at first, but as the others joined in, his voice grew bolder.

Yggdrasil gives and Yggdrasil takes
[Choir] Takes takes takes
Ymir dreams and Ymir wakes
[Choir] Wakes wakes wakes

Our lives are shared and blessed
'Twixt Yggdrasil's boughs above and Ymir's dirt below
Reaching for the sky and falling back we go
Our journey is long and burdens eased
[Choir] Eased eased eased

Yggdrasil gives and Yggdrasil takes
[Choir] Takes takes takes
Ymir dreams and Ymir wakes
[Choir] Wakes wakes wakes

'Ere we rise too far above the land
And we sprout fruit of our own
From babe to elder should we have grown
'Fore too long we retire as planned
[Choir] Planned planned planned

Yggdrasil nurtures us and Ymir buries us
[Choir] Buries us us us
[All] Buries us us us

Flakka eyed the Aesir patrol. Although they gave the Jotnar a wide berth, they were walking the perimeter at a slow and deliberate pace.

"We have lost much." Knute's voice was soft though powerful and carried out across the air of the frozen taiga as the chanting drifted away on the wind. "Anga was a loving though stubborn and strong-willed daughter." His voice cracked but held steady as he continued. "And even though she has left us, it's not a loss…" He took a shuddering breath. "This is a renewal." He gestured into the hole. Despite the care and effort of its excavation, roots could be seen reaching out into the grave. "The union of Ymir, the land, and Yggdrasil, the World Tree, gave us form and breathed life into us"—his eyes flitted to the Aesir and back—"into all of us. And so when our time above is over, we return to her embrace. Down in Ymir's rich soil may Yggdrasil's roots take succor from our bodies as we have from hers."

"*Heita* Yggdrasil," chanted the Jotnar in unison.

Knute flinched. For even from this distance he could see the Aesir soldiers grip their spears tighter and eye them at the mere utterance of the Jotunmal word. They were unlikely to do anything now, but they would be certain to report this to the valkyrie, Gunnar.

"We have our place in the nine realms," he continued, a little louder than before. He glanced over at the soldiers. "Ours is to live in harmony with and honor Yggdrasil. Jotunheim is within us and through our connection with the World Tree, we will cultivate the land here as our home. The sweetness of our lives carry us back in death."

With that, he cradled the bundled head while others lifted the body by braided cord tied around her chest, waist, and ankles. They moved her until she was suspended above the gaping chasm and then slowly let the rope out, lowering Anga's body down into the grave. Knute tossed in a handful of purple saxifrage flowers. In turn, the others did the same. Together, the Jotnar filled the grave. As if on cue, a light flurry of snow began when they were done, covering the ground with a fresh dusting of white.

—

"The song sounds much better in Jotunmal," Flakka said to Knute when they were alone in his meager dwelling.

Knute said nothing as he sat heavily upon a chair made from a raised mound of dirt with an aurochs hide draped over it.

"Take this," Flakka said as she placed a wrapped, palm-sized object in his hand.

"What—" Knute started as he unwrapped a corner of the parcel. It was a set of iron carving tools: assorted chisels, files, and rasps. For a bone carver, they would be very useful and much more efficient than the brittle stone and bone tools that he had. "If I'm caught with this—"

"Then don't get caught," Flakka whispered as she covered it up again, having heard a sound from outside. She went to the door, listened, and then indicated to Knute that it was safe to open the package.

"Where did you get these?" Knute asked while examining the heft and quality of the tools.

"Why? Do you need more?" she asked with a wink.

"You can't go back out," Knute said with a start. "They are being more vigilant than ever. There's no cover out across the tundra. You'll be spotted for certain."

"Don't concern yourself—I am quite capable of taking care of myself," Flakka said with a dismissive wave.

"Damn you!" Knute hissed. "Can't you see even now that this isn't about just you? Your actions have consequences. We have to stop all of this at once."

"If we stop, then they win," Flakka snapped back.

"You sound like that new whelp." Knute stroked his chin. "Suttungr, I think his name was. But I don't care about any of your crusades anymore." He shoved the package back into Flakka's hands and backed away as if even being near it would taint him. "It's not worth it. Gunnar spoke the truth. We are provided for—we have what we need to survive."

"There is so much more to life than mere survival," she replied, the package crumpled in her balled-up fist. "Survival is for animals. We are meant to thrive, to live our own destinies."

Knute did not respond. He looked away, the muscles in his jaw tensed and his hands balled into fists.

"Do not give up on the cause," Flakka whispered. "We can only succeed if we are united with the other realms. Anga understood that better than—"

"It is those alliances that make us most vulnerable," Knute snapped. He stood and marched towards Flakka, jabbing his finger at her chest. "The last time we allied with another against the Aesir, the Vanir sold us out and left us to languish in exile here. And the mere prospect of another such alliance killed Anga. Take whatever deals you have brokered and feed them to Garmr. From now on, we trust only ourselves."

Flakka pushed the toolset into Knute's hands and backed away. She held his gaze with a pensive look and said, "You're right. What you said before. This is about more than just me and more than the deaths of one or two people." Her hand reached out to the crossbar on the door and lifted it. "You may be scared and want to accept things as they are, but the nine realms are filled to bursting with people who want more, so much more. And I will be out there helping them to achieve that better life."

With that, she opened the door and exited, leaving Knute holding the bundle, staring out at her shrinking silhouette.

CHAPTER 16: THE FUGITIVE

"What are you doing?" A voice came from behind Lifthrasir just as he was about to reach the giant stone doors at the entrance of Aldrnari.

"I have to go after her—I mean, them," Lifthrasir stated flatly as he turned to see Jorunn with her arms crossed and a knowing look in her eyes.

"The others won't like that," she replied with a shake of her head. "Hertha was livid when Sigrid told her what Aric was up to. She threatened to send Jotnar soldiers to hunt them down and drag them back."

"After all we've been through together?" Lifthrasir said, aghast. "These are our friends. If anyone should go after them it should be us, not strangers, not soldiers."

"This is about more than you and me. If they warn the Aesir about the Alliance's plans, about the coalition and all of the weapons…" Jorunn searched for the right words. "Odin won't wait for us to be ready. They will march here and lay waste to Aldrnari and everyone here."

"It won't come to that," Lifthrasir said, his fists clenched. "And even if the Aesir captured and questioned them, they would never betray the Alliance. But that doesn't matter because I will bring them back."

"'Bring them back by any means necessary,' I believe were Hertha's exact words," Loki said. He and two other Jotnar emerged from the corridor and took up flanking positions by Jorunn. They were packed for light, fast travel. And they were armed.

"And it isn't a simple matter of betraying us to the Aesir," Loki continued. "We need that stick he's always carrying. It's a part of Yggdrasil. We need that piece of the World Tree if our weapon is to stand a chance of destroying Mjolnir and defeating the Aesir."

"He has been going on about Yggdrasil and the corruption and blight, the destruction of the nine realms for as long as I've known him." Lifthrasir's voice cracked. He pivoted, trying to keep the Jotnar from completely surrounding him. "You won't be able to stop him or take that walking stick from him without a fight."

"Calm yourself," Jorunn said in a slow and cautious tone while resting her hand on the hilt of her sword as Lifthrasir reached for his own. "Aric is my friend too. But his rantings about Yggdrasil are pure delusion. We have been in Muspelheim for nearly a year, and there hasn't been a single blighted creature seen in all that time."

"Aric knows more about Yggdrasil and what's happening up there than anyone else." Lifthrasir tried to sound confident despite his own misgivings. "He's not just trying to fight a war." He hung his head for a moment before standing tall. The ring of metal echoed loud as he drew the sword from its scabbard. "He's trying to save the whole damned world—"

There was a loud thump. Lifthrasir's eyes rolled up and his lids fluttered before he dropped to the ground like a sack of grain. The Jotnar who was on sentry duty stood above the unconscious Human.

"Thanks for the help, Vara." Loki nodded to the Jotnar guard.

"With all of the commotion you were making, I had to come see what was happening," she replied, picking up Lifthrasir's sword. "Looks like I got here just in time."

"What do we do with him?" Loki pointed to the unconscious Lifthrasir.

"If we leave him here, he'll just go after us and try to warn Aric," Jorunn mused.

"We can imprison him," Loki offered. "There are plenty of cells here where the Aesir kept troublemakers."

"Relations with the Humans are strained enough." Jorunn shook her head. "That could throw our alliance into disarray, and we haven't even been tested in a fight yet."

Vara moved the sword to Lifthrasir's neck and said, "How about—"

"No!" Jorunn's voice echoed in the chamber and down the hall. "The boy was just trying to help his friends… my friends. We can do this without anyone dying." She looked around for a moment before her eyes lit up. "He's packed and ready to go." Jorunn lifted his satchel. "He must've told some of the others his plan. They won't miss him."

"You cannot be suggesting that we take him with us," Loki groaned as he rubbed his eyes. "This reminds me of a similar situation I was in not long ago. It did not end well for the guards," he said, managing to look proud and ashamed at the same time.

"It's our best option," Jorunn replied. "Aric and Lif already have a significant lead, and we've wasted too much time here already." She pointed to Vara. "After we've gone, you'll report to Hertha, Sigrid, and Surtr that you saw Lifthrasir running off north, following us."

"Hertha will be furious that we let him slip past us," Vara said, fear evident in her voice.

"Just tell her you saw him slip out of a hidden lava tunnel far down the pass. You didn't want to abandon your post in case it was a distraction meant to lure you away," Loki suggested with a wave and a shrug as they broke into a brisk march. "There are dozens of tunnels all throughout these mountains and it's impossible to guard them all and know which one he used."

CHAPTER 17: CORRUPTION

"Einherjar, shore up the right flank!" Freyr shouted over the animalistic shrieks and the sickening crunch of metal striking oozing, rotting flesh. From a hundred yards away, Brunhilda could hear his orders. And she watched as a battalion of Humans, bedecked in utilitarian Aesir armor, rushed to support the collapsing line.

The pale granite of the Bifrost Skjaldborg behind their ranks was darkened with layers of corruption at its base. Humans and Aesir stood side-by-side as they fought a pack of dark animals that might have, at one point not so long ago, been vargr. As terrifying as it was to see these hordes of mindless beasts attacking Asgard, Brunhilda found herself somehow more unsettled at the sight of so many Humans trained and armed, fighting shoulder-to-shoulder with the regulars of the Aesir Army.

At least Freyr was there to lead them in the field. Under his command, the Einherjar flourished within the regimented order of the army. Those who had found shelter in Asgard during the Jotnar Uprising had become even more devoted to the Aesir. And Brunhilda's victory over Nidhogg at the battle of the Bifrost Skjaldborg had enshrined the Aesir's status for the Humans as the rulers and protectors of the nine realms. Because of this devotion, the Einherjar fought with a greater fervor than Brunhilda had seen from the Aesir in decades. But as a dozen were torn asunder by the pack, she was all too aware that they lacked the skill and hardiness of true Aesir warriors.

A flash of energy marked Thor's arrival at the breach. His power, and that of Mjolnir, flattened an area fifty yards across. The blast was indiscriminate and flung Humans as well as vargr dozens of yards away. And though the last of the corrupt vargr were slain by the attack, the spelled armor protected the

Einherjar enough to save them from the same fate.

"That's enough!" Brunhilda grabbed Thor by the collar and pulled him back. She could smell the alcohol vapor escaping out of every pore. He stumbled as she dragged him along, but though his equilibrium was impaired, she saw that his grip on Mjolnir remained steadfast.

"You are dismissed!" Brunhilda shouted to the others who had begun to crowd around. "Victory is ours again today. Go, return to Valhalla and celebrate. A feast awaits you in the great hall. You all did well, you've earned it."

Einherjar soldiers looked on with concern, glancing from Brunhilda to their commander, Freyr. He kept his composure despite the ludicrous image of Thor being dragged off like a disobedient child. He opened his mouth to issue orders, but Thor interrupted.

"Yes!" Thor raised Mjolnir in one hand; his other pushed at Brunhilda while she struggled to keep her grip on his collar. "We've earned our feast. We've earned our drink!"

"Not you, sire," Brunhilda whispered to him. "I think the fostra might recommend more rest and less drink for you."

"Nonsense," Thor snapped. "After every great battle, we drink together!"

The Einherjar cheered along with the Aesir soldiers as Thor pulled free from Brunhilda. She exchanged a look with Freyr, who simply shrugged and led the soldiers in step with Thor. There would be no debriefing today.

Brunhilda shook her head as she watched them depart. She, Asta, and the other valkyries who had participated in the battle turned back to their duties and walked the battlefield, stabbing fallen enemies and searching for wounded allies. They would celebrate on their own in Folkvangr.

—

"Something must be done," Brunhilda said as she entered the armory where Sif was inspecting their inventory.

"The runes aren't holding their power, and the Reginvald and Mithlivald energies remain in flux." Sif tossed another sword into a cart among the ever-growing pile of damaged weapons and armor. Every piece of equipment in the cart held the taint of corruption from the touch of blighted animals.

"It's worse for the Einherjar equipment." Brunhilda gestured towards an even larger pile of scrap in the far corner. "The Humans are unable to channel any of those energies to bolster the runes and enchantments that were forged into the metal. When are we getting more?"

"More?" Sif scoffed. "Where do you think these come from? There have been no caravans to or from the other realms since the Jotnar attack on Asgard."

"But the enchantments are added here, are they not?" Brunhilda asked.

"They are," Sif acknowledged. "However, the base pieces come from Muspelheim and Svartalfheim. And even if we had more in reserve, something is disrupting our connection to Yggdrasil. Our enchanters are having difficulties wielding Mithlivald and Reginvald consistently. It's a delicate procedure, and if there are mistakes, then the metal becomes brittle and worthless. Truth be told, I don't fully understand the mechanics of it myself. Freya attempted to explain it to me once and, by Odin's beard, she said that I fell asleep while standing and with my eyes open."

"Freya was never the most engaging of speakers," Brunhilda said with a sympathetic pat on her shoulder. "That gift went to her brother. But for all of his ability to rouse the troops and inspire the Humans, I would much rather have Freya here now."

Sif gave a surreptitious look around before sighing and nodding. "Agreed. Even with all of these Einherjar, they won't be of much use without proper, functional kit."

"And it causes even more problems when Thor hits them with a blast from Mjolnir." Residual energy crackled from Brunhilda's gloved hand.

"My ears are still ringing." Sif pressed the heel of her hand over her ear.

"Can't you do something about him?"

"I've only seen him like this once before." She paused with a vambrace in her hand; corrosion radiated out from various bite marks that punctured the metal. "After the Fenrir battle… the first Fenrir," she clarified, seeing Brunhilda raise her eyebrows.

"I remember." Brunhilda nodded. "It seemed particularly odd that he wasn't more celebratory about it. Baldur dying while fighting a dragon, Nidhogg no less, seemed an especially worthy death for a descendant of Borr."

"It wasn't Baldur's death that affected Thor so much." Sif's voice was tinged with emotion.

Brunhilda patiently waited while Sif took a few deep breaths.

"Her name was Jarnsaxa."

Brunhilda gave a quizzical look.

"Do you remember the two Jotnar who saved Baldur from the vargr during his Rite of Vinnask?" Sif asked.

"Ah, yes." Brunhilda nodded and averted her gaze.

"He wouldn't admit to it now, but everyone could see that he was enamored with her." She stared at the vambrace for a long moment before dropping it in the pile. "They were… infatuated with each other. Fortunately, back then, Odin was there to snap him out of his drunken stupor. I fear that Frigg is coddling him now."

"She has the nine realms to contend with," Brunhilda offered. "Realms that are currently being overrun by bandits, a fleeing Jotnar army, their deserters, and monsters—monsters spreading a terrible blight."

"These animals are mindless creatures. I'm certain that Thor would sober up and focus if the queen would allow him to hunt down Loki," Sif answered.

"Assuming that they haven't all been slaughtered by these rampaging beasts," Brunhilda mused aloud. "He and the Jotnar Army must have fled down to Svartalfheim to resupply and regroup."

"The skeleton crews we left after recalling our main forces would have offered some resistance, but I fear that the Jotnar most likely overwhelmed them."

"If they get access to the forges in Muspelheim—"

"When Suttungr was revealed as Baldur, they lost their leader, the one who pushed them into this conflict," argued Sif. "They're on the defensive. I agree with Thor. We need to strike now and destroy them completely. With the Skjaldborg rebuilt, the Einherjar can defend Asgard from the beasts."

"You don't know these Jotnar." Brunhilda's voice turned contemplative. "I moved among them, saw their sense of community and the tenacity of their spirit myself. Loki, Skrymir as I knew him, is a natural leader. His passion for his people will not allow him to sit passive and wait for us to act. He may not have known that Suttungr was Baldur, but I doubt that revelation will deter him from picking up the mantle and continuing the Jotnar Uprising."

"It matters little. Whether they shelter somewhere or attack Asgard again, whether they are armed or not, Thor will hunt Loki down and kill him and everyone around him," Sif countered. "Queen Frigg's orders are the only reason he hasn't left already."

"Even that is barely enough for Thor not to go," Brunhilda said with a shake of her head.

"And where am I trying to go?" Thor stumbled in through the armory doorway. His body was leaning to the right, Mjolnir the only thing propping him up. He might have held on to the door but for the horn of mead in his left hand.

Brunhilda and Sif made eye contact. Before they could reply, Thor let out a loud belch that reverberated throughout the room.

"We merely thought it would be a good time to speak with your mother," Brunhilda blurted out.

"She should be informed about the latest attack and how our supplies are holding up," Sif added, indicating the pile before her. "The stockpile is dwindling, and Freyr has informed me that we are running low on the raw materials needed to repair or replenish our stores."

"Where is the caravan from, Muspelheim?" Thor asked after swallowing the remainder of the mead and then dropping the horn onto the pile. "Perhaps they sent some of their excellent mulled wine along with the weapons."

"Yes." Sif took him by the arm. "We will inquire with Muspelheim about their mulled wine."

As Sif escorted Thor from the room, Brunhilda locked eyes with her and nodded.

CHAPTER 18: CAUGHT

"How would we even fix Yggdrasil?" Aric asked, squinting at his walking stick. The dim twilight persisted even in the late morning. Though it was difficult to see, Aric's fingers found the imperfection and traced the hairline crack in the otherwise smooth, solid wood. With a shake of his head, he turned his attention back to his little wooden sled. It was next to a fallen tree that lay in the middle of the clearing. The packed snow was the only remaining evidence of their camp. They had not dared to light a fire and had sheltered in the leeward side of the log. Aric tightened the last few leather straps holding their gear and patiently waited for Lif to finish her ablutions.

"There are three kinds of magic in the world." Freya reached out her noncorporeal hand, fingers raised. "Reginvald is what the Aesir used to kill the eldritch monsters and tear down the old world to carve out the nine realms during the Great Awakening. It is used most often to break things down and shape them according to the will and vision of the user. We Vanir wield Mithlivald to mend what is broken and to nudge and direct the natural flow of Yggdrasil's awesome power. That raw, natural energy is what we call Ethlivald. The Jotnar are Ethlivald personified. When there are many in the same place, or when a powerful one gets riled enough, they can—"

Aric sprang to his feet at the sound of a twig snapping at the north edge of the clearing. At the same moment, a dense, icy mist rolled in from the south and he spun around to face it. With the staff in his left hand, his right reached for the sword at his hip. Two shards of ice flew out from somewhere within the fog and lodged into the downed tree trunk just to the left of him.

"Let's not do anything stupid, Aric," a familiar voice called out from the murky shadows of the tree line. "You've used up your allotment of stupid things several times over."

"Jorunn." Aric blew out a small cloud of vapor as he lowered the staff and relaxed his stance. "When did you—"

"Sorry, Aric." Lifthrasir's hands were bound in front of him with rope, and he was standing between two Jotnar, Erda and Vog, to Aric's far left. Erda held the end of the rope so that Lifthrasir could not flee.

"We've come to bring you back," Loki said as he emerged from the fog at Jorunn's right. Pointing to Aric's staff, he continued, "And we've come for that."

Aric's gaze drifted to the staff and then he jerked it behind him, away from Loki. His other hand again slid towards his weapon.

"This doesn't have to turn violent." Jorunn, her sword sheathed, took a few steps forward with one open hand towards Aric and the other standing down Loki.

"We're almost ready to march on Asgard." Loki approached just behind Jorunn. "If you warn them now, that will only extend the battle and cost more lives… on both sides. It's in everybody's best interest to have a quick, decisive victory. The Aesir are in it for themselves, to hold on to their power over the nine realms, over all of us. We represent everyone…" He paused and seemed to reconsider his last word. "Well, everyone else. If the Aesir come to parley with us in good faith, they will be welcome at our table, as equals."

Aric shook his head. "It doesn't matter who wins the war if we don't find a way to stop this cataclysm from the north. And that will take everybody working together—"

"Just tell us where Lif is. The sooner we find her, the sooner we'll be back in Muspelheim." Loki motioned with his hand and one of the Jotnar moved forward, sword drawn. The other held on to Lifthrasir, who squirmed against his captor.

"Aric." Freya tried to get his attention.

"I see them," he whispered to her.

"Not the Jotnar—"

The ground trembled, and everyone hesitated as the tremors drew closer and more urgent. An explosion of rock, dirt, and snow knocked everyone off their feet as two inky black creatures, roughly the shape of lindworms, burst out of the ground near Lifthrasir. He rolled away as the Jotnar holding him was caught in the creature's crushing jaws.

"Erda!" Jorunn shouted as Vog scrambled out of the way, avoiding the second creature.

Jorunn and Loki hurried to their feet and rushed forward to close the distance to Aric. All three quickly fell into a practiced, defensive stance, their personal skirmish forgotten. Loki unleashed an ice blast in an attempt to get the lindworm to drop Erda. Instead, the Ethlivald disappeared into the dark tendrils. A moment later, the shadow's silhouette pulsed and grew larger. It seemed to be unaffected, but it certainly noticed the attack.

If floating, disembodied points of light could look hungry, the shadow's eyes were that. It launched itself at Loki. He reacted on instinct, bringing his arms up and erecting an ice wall. That slowed the creature for a moment as it bounced off with a shuddering impact. The lithe body of the lindworm thrashed as it regrouped and reared up. Lowering its wedge-shaped head, the creature charged and shattered the wall. Debris and ice rained down as it broke through. Aric, Jorunn, and Loki were thrown in separate directions, away from the beast's attack.

"Cut me loose, Vog!" Lifthrasir shouted to the Jotnar who had grabbed his rope after Erda was devoured.

Just as Vog opened his mouth to respond, the second lindworm darted in and bit off his arm. Lifthrasir, his hands still bound, rolled away from its thrashing tail. Seeing the writhing mass of shadowy tendrils stalking the Jotnar, he shouted at the creature, trying to get its attention. At the same time, he reached his bound hands into the snow, looking for something he might use to aid him.

"Cut yourself free!" A dagger flew through the air and stuck to the trunk of a nearby tree. Lifthrasir's heart perked up at the sound of the familiar voice.

The lindworm opened its mouth, about to bite down again on Vog, when two arrows hit its eye. The creature reeled away in pain before rounding on Lif, who was up in the barren branches of a nearby tree. It charged headfirst, unfazed by two more arrows that disappeared into the inky mass of its body. A sharp crack echoed through the clearing when the lindworm struck Lif's tree. The jolt knocked her from her perch and she fell into the snow with a muffled thud. After a brief moment to shake its head, the beast reared up over Lif.

"Lif!" Aric shouted from the other side of the clearing. He sprinted the twenty yards to her while the larger lindworm's attention was focused on Loki.

"Catch!" Lifthrasir, having cut his bonds, threw the dagger to Lif.

At the same time, Aric swung the walking stick with all of his might and struck the monstrous thing in the head. With a burst of light, the darkness swirling around the lindworm vanished, and Lif thrust her blade up through its jaw into its brain. She rolled away as the lifeless corpse came crashing down.

Aric had only a moment to catch his breath and ensure that she was alright before turning to see Loki and Jorunn futilely engaged with the other lindworm. It shattered every ice barrier Loki erected with ease. And it had doubled in size.

"It's absorbing the Ethlivald," Freya shouted even though Aric was the only one who could hear her.

"But he's only using it to create ice structures," Aric protested even as he saw the lindworm pulse and grow.

"It looks as if it's feeding off of the energy from the Jotnar," Freya guessed. "You have to get Loki to calm down."

"I'm sure that'll be easier to do without a giant shadow creature attacking him." Aric ducked under a swipe of the thing's tail. Before he could swing the staff to hit it, the tail whipped back and batted Aric away.

"Aric!" Jorunn screamed.

He crashed into a tree and dropped the staff. Aric crumpled to the ground, certain that he had cracked a rib or two. Yet he surprised himself, springing back to his feet. He gingerly touched his ribs and took two deep breaths with no noticeable pains.

"Hey!" Freya snapped her fingers in front of Aric's face then pointed. "Monster first, dumbstruck awe at the power of Mithlivald later."

"Right." Aric focused on the creature in time to see its tail whip around and hit Loki, sending him to Aric's right. *The lucky bastard*, Aric thought as Loki landed in a snowdrift, sending up a plume of white.

With his left hand on the hilt of his sword, sheathed at his hip, Aric's empty right hand reached for the staff. In a brief fit of panic, he took his eyes from the lindworm and scanned his immediate surroundings. He plunged both hands into the snow.

A groan from his right caught his attention as Loki emerged from the snow. He hauled himself up, leaning heavily on the staff. The lindworm caught Jorunn with a glancing blow and then reared up to finish her off. Loki leapt into action, the staff his only weapon.

"No!" Freya shouted.

Aric's eyes lost focus. The last thing he saw was the staff glowing blue, charged with Loki's Ethlivald power. Upon impact, the shadow tendrils exploded in fractals and swirls, incomprehensible patterns that scrambled Aric's mind.

Freya was inches from his face, shouting; her words were muddled, barely audible through the ringing in his ears. He did not know what had just happened or even how much time had elapsed.

The ringing abruptly stopped. Looking down, he saw that the staff was in his right hand and the sword was in his left. A quick survey of the area showed that the trees in their immediate vicinity, though already dead, were now desiccated and rotted husks. The air smelled of ozone, and the blanching bones of a lindworm were surrounded by a ring of corrupted snow. Jorunn and Loki were twitching and lay catatonic nearby, as Lif and an unsteady Lifthrasir stripped off their tainted armor, careful to touch only the unstained parts.

"Yeah, I'm alright," Aric answered what he thought Freya was asking. He rushed forward to help Lif and Lifthrasir. Aric's fingers tingled at the touch of the corrupted armor. Pinpricks just under the surface of his skin caused him to jerk his hands away.

"Don't touch that," Freya whispered. Her eyes were closed, hands clasped around Aric's. Through her ephemeral fingers he could see the taint evaporate.

Loki appeared to be in the worst shape. His fur was patchy and his exposed skin was covered in burns. If Aric had had more presence of mind, he would have noted that the burns were old and had scabbed over long ago.

"They're alive, but they need help," Lifthrasir said with his hand resting on Jorunn's forehead, trying to hold her still.

"Asgard is about two days away." Aric repeated Freya's words for the benefit of Lif and Lifthrasir. Looking at Loki and Jorunn, he added, "Perhaps three while carrying these two."

Lif turned her head towards Erda and Vog. One had been torn apart by the other lindworm. The other had bled out from her wounds; a pool of frozen blue blood surrounded the body.

"What happened?" Aric rubbed his eyes.

"I don't know." Lifthrasir looked up, his hand still on Jorunn. "From where we were, all we saw was… I don't know how to describe it. But we couldn't see past it. We didn't even know if you were still alive until it all disappeared and you were the only one standing…" He trailed off when he noticed that Aric was not looking at him.

Freya looked away. Aric thought that she looked pale, paler than normal. Her arms were wrapped tight, hugging herself. Her lips parted as her eyes met Aric's right before she vanished.

"Freya!"

Lif and Lifthrasir turned their heads to where Aric was looking but saw nothing. His legs wobbled, but Lif was there to catch and steady him.

"I—I'm alright," Aric said as he shifted his weight to the staff. "We need to get them to the healers in Asgard. They're the only ones who can help."

CHAPTER 19: ALLIES

Surtr ran his hand along the blade. He could see sparks and feel the tingle of the energy drain. Sweat beaded his brow and the muscles of his arm twitched as he maintained contact. The light display died when his fingers reached the heavy leather wrapped around the hilt, and he breathed out a long sigh.

"*Don't waste all of your life energy before we fight the Aesir,*" Hertha called out from the doorway.

"*I have to get used to the feeling.*" Surtr's eyes were closed as he flexed his fingers and slowly balled them into a fist. "*If I can't handle the energy drain, if the battle is the first time I hold it, there's no telling how I will react. It would be a failure to my mother and all of you if I collapsed into a useless heap in front of the Aesir.*"

"*You?*" Hertha scoffed. "*You proved to be more than capable of dealing with unfamiliar magics when you fought Loki.*"

"*That was different.*" Surtr stood to his full height and his fur bristled, making him look even larger. He towered nearly two feet above Hertha's small frame. "*Loki wasn't using Reginvald. And he wasn't trying to kill me.*"

"*At least we hope he wasn't.*" Hertha chuckled. She looked at him and was reminded of Hrym, Suttungr's right hand in the early days of the uprising, though Surtr was far more thoughtful and calculating than that lumbering oaf had ever been.

"*I know that you've never actually been on a field of battle, but I've seen you in the training area, practicing with the others. You are the biggest one here, but that's not the only trick you have.*" Hertha jabbed her finger into the Eldjotnar's barrel chest. "*There's a discipline that serves as the foundation of your attacks. It's great that you aren't taking the Aesir for granted. But when you face them, you cannot hesitate. They will see that as a sign of weakness and exploit it, push against it until you break. They have spent millennia fighting. If you give them the slightest opening to learn your powers and weaknesses, you can be assured that they will not hesitate."*

"I can't believe that you all fought over who gets to die," Sigrid said as she and Eik strode into the room. "Once we get to Asgard, the Aesir will have no problem helping us figure that out."

"Indeed. That tournament felt like something the Aesir would do." Eik shook her head disapprovingly.

"You dare—"

"Calm yourselves." Sigrid held her hands out and open. "We have to work together or we'll have no chance."

"You're right." Hertha closed her eyes and rubbed at her temples. "Tempers are running high. We've been confined in here too long with people who have never interacted before. There's a lot to process and adapt to. Everyone is on edge."

"We're breaking up more and more fights," Sigrid said, pinching the bridge of her nose. "If we don't march soon, I fear we will fall to so much infighting and make the Aesir's task all the easier."

"And Loki and Jorunn have been gone too long," Surtr said with a note of sadness in his voice. "They have likely failed, maybe even been taken prisoner by the Aesir."

"Meaning that Asgard will be ready for us," Eik added.

"Meaning that we have to march on Asgard now," Hertha barked.

They all looked at each other in silence.

Sigrid spoke first. "You're our military leader. We will follow your recommendations."

"We are ready." Eik saluted to Hertha.

"I will see Asgard topple to the ground and the Aesir felled by my sword," Surtr said, placing his hand on the fiery sword with care.

Sigrid laid her hand on Surtr's shoulder. "We will topple Asgard together."

CHAPTER 20: REUNITED

"Pabbi, Pabbi!" The young Una ran up to the lanky figure of Aric as he pulled along their wagon with a few burlap sacks on it. She coughed twice as she leapt up into his arms. Aric released the wagon handles just in time to catch her.

"Calm down," he said as he nuzzled his face into her belly, causing her to giggle. "I've only been gone a day."

"But I wanted to go with you," Una whined and wiped her nose on Aric's shirt near the nape of his neck. "I'm feeling a lot better."

"And you're better because you were able to stay home and rest with Mamma." He kissed Dagmaer on the cheek. She had arrived shortly after Una, having walked instead of run.

"Not much in this month's delivery," Dagmaer commented as she looked in the bags.

"The gods provide what we need," Aric said as he tossed Una in the air. "Isn't that right?"

She giggled in what might have been agreement.

"Did you at least tell Hege that our axe cracked and we need a replacement?" Dagmaer asked as she pulled out two bags of oats, a small satchel of dried fruit, and a jar of honey.

"Of course I did." Aric reached into his tunic pocket and pulled out a whetstone.

"Really?" She gave him a look of exasperation. "What are we supposed to do with that? It's not dull, it's broken."

"I know," he said sheepishly.

Dagmaer rubbed her forehead. "Let me guess—somebody needed it more?"

"Bergen has been waiting two winters for one. And we can still use our axe to split wood," Aric said. "We just need to get it started in a seam and then hammer it through with a rock."

"But how will we chop down the trees?" Dagmaer took hold of the wagon and began to pull it towards their humble shed.

"I'll help!" Una said, raising both of her arms in the air while still in Aric's arms.

"We will make it work." He gave Dagmaer a meek smile and tousled their daughter's hair. He could tell that she sensed the tension between them. They did not argue often, but Una would hurry to mitigate things whenever it happened.

Una smiled and squirmed out of Aric's grasp. He let her go and watched as she raced to the shore. A moment later, she returned with two bulky pieces of driftwood hugged to her chest. One piece was so large that its end dragged along the ground, leaving a rut in its wake.

"The Aesir always provide," Aric said after he had rushed over to take the wood from Una. He kissed her on the top of her head as she ran back to pick up a few more pieces. Dagmaer merely shook her head and carefully put the supplies away into the shed.

"I never thought I'd see you again, Aric." Brunhilda had a slight smile, but her arms were crossed and she was flanked by royal guards. The Bifrost Skjaldborg loomed at their backs.

"They carried a few weapons. But that one"—the guard captain indicated Aric—"had this." The captain presented a gleaming valkyrie sword to Brunhilda. She barely acknowledged the walking stick, short knife, and short bow with a full quiver the other guard held out. Even before she touched the sword, she recognized it.

"And I certainly never thought that I would see you again," Brunhilda addressed the weapon. A warm and genuine smile came to her lips.

Aric shrugged. "It's been a rather strange path that life has taken since you came into my life."

"I admit that I am curious as to how you survived, let alone found your way to Asgard." She was talking as much to the sword as she was to Aric. From the corner of her eye, she noticed the walking stick. Its dark, gnarled wood was distinctive. Brunhilda was well aware of its resemblance to the haft and shaft of Mjolnir and Gungnir, though she could not fathom how Aric might have come to possess it. A Human would not be able to reach the lowest branch of the World Tree, to say nothing of the strength required to tear one free from it.

"I am relieved to see that you have survived," Aric said, snapping Brunhilda's attention back to him. "I had heard stories of a fiery, redheaded warrior who slayed a dragon."

"Your doing?" Brunhilda gave Aric a questioning look. "Nidhogg's arrival at the battle of the Skjaldborg was…" She paused for a moment to consider those events. "It was a mixed blessing. The beast killed many on both sides, but in the end it was enough to disrupt the Jotnar offensive."

Aric dropped his head, eyes closed. "I am grateful that you were able to stop it before it caused more devastation across the nine realms."

"Indeed, I believe your actions ultimately saved Asgard," Brunhilda said. She paused for a brief moment, and her expression soured. "But your travel companions have put us in a very sensitive predicament."

"These Jotnar are my allies, my friends." Aric tried to step forward but was restrained by Humans wearing Aesir regalia. Lif and Lifthrasir were next to him, held by other guards. Meanwhile, Loki and Jorunn were bound to makeshift litters, unconscious yet still writhing in pain, tainted by the blight. "Please, they need your help. The world needs your help."

"Loki is fortunate that Thor was not here, on duty at the Bifrost Skjaldborg, when you arrived," Brunhilda said with a shake of her head. "Not only would he have left you outside, he would have torn Loki apart limb-by-limb, and then he would have cut his head off and spat down his neck. It was all I could do to not do that myself."

"Listen, I don't know what he did to deserve that kind of ire, but—"

"He was Skrymir!"

"What—" Aric's mouth hung open. He shook his head and knitted his brows. It was a long, uncomfortable silence while Aric mumbled to himself, vocalizing similarities between Loki and Skrymir that he just now recognized. He stared at the unconscious Jotnar he had carried so far. "How—" Aric's voice cracked and he wobbled on his feet. "How is that possible?"

"Loki appears to have the power to create illusions—glamours—to disguise himself. He revealed his true identity during the Battle of the Bifrost Skjaldborg," Brunhilda said, her expression darkening. "Right before he beheaded the Jotnar leader, Suttungr, who had been Baldur all along."

"Yes." Aric recovered his composure, though he still wore a befuddled expression. "We'd heard about Baldur from some of the Jotnar who were there."

"And so you have aligned yourself with them? After what Hrym and Skrymir did to us at Yggdrasil?"

He took a long pause to calm down and breathe in through his nose and then out through his mouth. "You Aesir baffle me. I used to believe that you were infallible, that you had a plan for the nine realms and all of us. But you don't just deceive us, you play games and trick each other."

Brunhilda gave Aric a quizzical look. "Baldur was always mercurial. At one point, he was infatuated with a Jotnar who had—"

"Skuld was Freya."

"What?!" It was Brunhilda's turn to be dumbstruck.

They stood for a moment, looking at each other in silence.

"Are you sure?" Brunhilda asked. "Have you ever seen Freya? Do you even know what she looks like? Where is she now?"

"She's here." Aric placed his hand to his chest.

She peered to one side as if Freya might be hiding behind him.

"Somehow she bonded with me, I think. She's the reason I'm here. I never would have survived the long journey back across Niflheim without her strength."

"How?" Brunhilda stammered. "That's not possible. I mean… It's only ever been done with objects. Buri bonded with Mjolnir." She ran through what she knew of the history of the nine realms. "Boelthor merged with Gungnir."

"Freya said that her father has done it before," Aric offered.

"Yggdrasil," Brunhilda said with a slow realization. "I guess I've never thought of the World Tree as a 'living being.' But it is perhaps the very origin of life in the nine realms."

"That's how Freya explained it to me. Ever since I left Yggdrasil, she has been appearing to me. Freya has told me so much about the history of the world," Aric said, and a stern edge crept into his voice. "The real history, not the lies and fabrications that the Aesir tell to the other races."

"Freya is no impartial observer," Brunhilda cautioned Aric. "Her own ambitions and agenda have laid waste to many facts and people in her wake."

"You needn't convince me of that." Aric shook his head. "I have learned that I cannot trust any of you."

"That is perhaps the most important lesson," Brunhilda said with a chuckle. "Can you see her now?" She scanned the empty field that sprawled out to the west from the shield wall.

"Well." Aric rubbed his eyes and looked around again. "Something happened on our journey here. We encountered two monsters—lindworms cloaked in shadow."

Brunhilda interrupted with an outstretched hand. "You know what a lindworm is?"

"We've lost many to them in our long journey from Hoddmimis Holt."

"Journey to where?" Brunhilda asked.

"To—" Aric stopped himself. "That's not important right now. I know that the war isn't over, but I've come with more dire warnings."

"So you've had run-ins with the blight," Brunhilda acknowledged. "And you've taken up an alliance with the Jotnar."

"This isn't about…" Aric took a long, slow breath. "The blight is the real threat."

"Their rebellion has upset the fragile equilibrium of the nine realms." Brunhilda placed her hand upon Aric's shoulder. "Just tell us where the rest of the Jotnar are. Frigg and the council have declared that the Jotnar are to be exterminated."

"Forget about the Jotnar!" Aric shouted.

Brunhilda was taken aback by his outburst.

"I'm sorry." Aric took a breath. "Freya said that you needed to know about Yggdrasil. This 'blight,' as you call it, is coming from the World Tree. Njord is losing his bond with it, and the monsters are threatening to break free and plunge the nine realms back into the darkness of the days before the Great Awakening."

Brunhilda looked Aric up and down. He had changed a great deal from the frail and broken man she had encountered in Murtrborg so long ago. She took a few steps forward and held him by the shoulders and whispered to him, "I sympathize with you. After our trek to Yggdrasil, I've also come to reevaluate the Aesir worldview."

"Then help us," Aric pleaded.

"That is not my decision to make. Things are more complicated at this moment." Brunhilda leaned her head forward and closed her eyes as her forehead touched his. "But I will do what I can."

The guards shifted, uncomfortable with the level of familiarity their commanding officer was showing to a strange Human in the company of Jotnar. With one stern look from Brunhilda, they snapped to attention.

"Take them to Fostra Eira." She gave the order to the Einherjar captain. "I shall inform Lady Frigg of this and see if I can find Thor before he finds Loki."

—

"Where is he?" Thor's slurred roar boomed through the halls of the palace in Asgard. "Why was I not told that Loki was captured?" He picked up one of the royal guards and threw her across the room. She tucked as she hit the ground and rolled up to her feet rather gracefully, Brunhilda observed as she approached the prince.

Frigg sat upon the throne in the great hall. Her hand idly stroked Geri while the other wolf, Freki, stalked the other side of the room. Both had their ears perked up, muscles in their haunches taut in reaction to the outburst. The ravens, Huginn and Muninn, cocked their heads. Muninn cawed as if answering Thor. Freya eyed her son's tantrum for a moment, her face stoic and unmoving, before returning her attention to the matter at hand. Freyr, along with two Einherjar, had been giving a report on the casualties and loss of supplies in the latest battle when Thor had burst in.

"Answer me!" Thor bellowed as Brunhilda ducked under a loping swing of his fist. She parried a second punch and nudged Thor just enough to turn him around. With a firm push on his lower back, she sent him stumbling towards the door. The guard whom Thor had not thrown was there with the door already held open. With a quick bow to Frigg, Brunhilda hurried after Thor before he could react and recover.

The Einherjar had enough tact not to stare as the guard closed the door behind Brunhilda and Freyr resumed his report.

"Let go of me!" Thor mumbled into the rough stone of the wall. His face and chest were pressed into it with Brunhilda holding his right arm pinned to his back. "How dare you disrespect me like this!" Even if he had been sober, she had the leverage to keep him in place.

"Calm down, sire," Brunhilda whispered into his ear. "I'm not going to release you until you've exorcized this tantrum."

To her surprise, Thor gave a quick jerk, forcing her to dislocate his shoulder but also giving himself enough slack to slip her grasp. As he stepped away, his arm fell limp to his side for just a moment before a pulse of light rushed down his arm and the muscles pulled everything back into place. Brunhilda adopted a fighting stance between him and the door, ready for his attempt to get back to the audience chamber.

Instead, Thor took up a slightly more upright stance and rolled his shoulder while flexing his fingers. She could not be certain if it had been the pain or the flash of Mithlivald that had sobered him up, but he appeared more calm and collected than he had been moments earlier.

"Tell me where he is." His voice was even and calm; no hint of a slur remained. It frightened her more than the prospect of fighting him. With a deep breath in through his nose, he rose to his full height, shoulders rolled back, fists clenched. Through the material of his sleeves Brunhilda could see his muscles twitch. For a moment, she thought that she could reason with him.

"Sire, I ca—"

"Now!"

Brunhilda eyed him. A drunken Thor was one thing. A sober and enraged Thor was perhaps more than she could handle. She almost longed to be back at Yggdrasil, staring down the fiery tempest that had been the eldritch dragon, Nidhogg. Yes, it had been a monstrous beast covered in iron-hard obsidian scales with teeth like swords and claws as long as spears, but the worst that could happen was an honorable and legendary death. Thor would likely pummel her with his bare hands and cast her down from the Bifrost into an ignominious, watery grave. She could feel the Reginvald crackling from his fists. Thor would break every bone in her body, heal them, and break them again to get the information.

"Come with me," she said with a sigh, and raised her hands in surrender.

CHAPTER 21: VISITATIONS

"He doesn't look like much of a threat." Thor stood over the fitful body of Loki in the infirmary bed. Brunhilda could feel the muscles tense as she placed her hand upon Thor's arm. After all of the fearsome beasts she had faced down, she knew that there was precious little she could do if he decided to harm the Jotnar. Despite the large, expansive windows that adorned two of the walls, the outside light was dim. Braziers in the corners of the room and torches mounted at regular intervals along the walls bathed the dozens of beds in a nurturing, warming glow.

"When they brought him in, he was convulsing and frothing at the mouth," Fostra Eira said from the other side of the bed. "It was similar to the conditions of Sigurd and the other Aesir soldiers injured during that Fafnir incident, although the burns and scarring covering his body and face are far from recent. Apparently the Humans were able to stabilize Loki and the other one long enough to get them to Asgard." She gestured to the female Jotnar in the next bed. Eira paused and seemed to think of something. "They were not forthcoming with how they accomplished such a feat. There are clear traces of Mithlivald. No Human should be able to wield that power."

"Aric..." Brunhilda paused when Thor raised an eyebrow. "The Human male mentioned something about Freya imbuing him with her spirit and life energy."

"Freya perished in a Jotnar ambush while returning from Halvard three years ago," Thor said. Brunhilda thought she heard a hint of sadness in his voice.

"He was with me at Yggdrasil," Brunhilda continued. "No mere Human could have made the trek back without aid of some kind. He claims to see visions of her, telling him about the corrupted animals rampaging throughout the nine realms."

"So the monsters aren't just in Asgard?" Thor mused aloud. "Where were they when they were attacked?"

"They were at least two days south and west of Asgard," Brunhilda answered. "He would not say from where he came, but it's likeliest they're in Svartalfheim or Muspelheim. The caves would provide the most secure locations to fortify against…" Her eyes flicked from Thor to the wounded soldiers in the other beds. "Against attack."

A dozen beds, of which only half were occupied, filled the airy room. All of the Aesir and Vanir injured in the last battle had responded well to the Mithlivald treatment and had been released the previous day. Only four Einherjar and the two Jotnar remained.

"Where are the Humans?" Brunhilda inquired.

"After we treated them, I had the Einherjar take them to the prison cells," Eira replied. "They only had minor injuries. However, our Mithlivald techniques are taking longer to work against the corruption on the Jotnar. We think that it's somehow feeding off of their connection to Ethlivald."

"Sire." Brunhilda pulled on Thor's arm, but it was like trying to move the World Tree. "Loki will be here for a while." Fostra Eira nodded in confirmation. "We should speak with Aric and find out what happened."

Thor jerked his arm free from Brunhilda's grip and pointed to Fostra Eira. "You will inform me as soon as he is awake. I don't care what time of day it is or what else is happening."

"I report to the queen." The fostra did not bother to look at him as she moved to the door.

"Please," he called after her, his voice strained and cracked.

Eira paused, her hand on the jamb as she looked back, first to Thor and then to Brunhilda.

Brunhilda could not tell if Thor was full of rage or sorrow, but she knew that this was very personal for him. She gave Fostra Eira a sympathetic, pleading look.

Eira pinched the bridge of her nose and let out a long breath. "Yes… yes, alright. I will send word to you if he regains consciousness."

"And that's how I ended up here." Aric and his old gythja, the matron of Murtrborg, stood on opposite sides of iron prison bars. Lif and Lifthrasir were resting in a far corner of the cell on a pile of straw.

"That was quite a tale," was Hege's taciturn reply. Aric had expected a stronger reaction to what he thought was an epic tale that rivaled the sagas sung during the Wodensdaeg Festivals that she used to preside over in their provincial little hamlet. Perhaps he lacked the flair and showmanship of the mummers, he thought with a bit of disappointment.

Looking a bit deeper, Aric could see how the world had etched more lines on her face and dimmed the brightness in her eyes. He could only imagine what she must have gone through in her own journey to this time and this place.

"What of you, Gythja Hege?"

"Please," she said with a raised hand. "It's just Hege now. Titles like gythja feel like they belong to another world. Those of us who fight with the Aesir are called Einherjar. The rest are simply laborers, helping to rebuild and maintain what's left of Asgard, of the nine realms."

"Humans fighting alongside Aesir?" Aric ran his hand through his hair. "I've seen some amazing things since leaving Murtrborg, but this is quite possibly the most unbelievable thing that I've heard of."

"Lady Sif herself attended our first training session." Hege beamed with pride. "And Freyr leads us on the field of battle. In fact, even though we stay in Western Asgard City, we've seen most of the pantheon, even Lord Odin and his retinue when he and Lady Frigg rode out to fight the blighted Fenrir."

"Amazing," Aric said with a note of awe in his voice before remembering these gods were not as powerful as he'd been brought up to believe.

"But you"—Hege reached out to Aric through the bars—"you saw Yggdrasil. The World Tree birthed us all, including Odin and the Aesir. And you were there. I fear I would never be able to survive that journey."

"I had a lot of help." Aric looked away, and his gaze drifted to the opposite corner of the cell, finding nothing. Freya had not made an appearance since the lindworm attack that had nearly killed Loki and Jorunn. He cast his gaze down to his hands and the gnarled staff, grateful Brunhilda had returned it to him and allowed him to keep it in the cell. The power that once coursed through his veins had become so familiar he could not tell if it was still there or not. Aric had had no chance to test it as they had arrived at Asgard with no further encounters.

"Indeed." Hege's hand rested on the bars of Aric's cell. "Allying yourself with Jotnar… I never would have thought that possible. You were always so devout."

"You heard my tale." Aric crossed his arms across his chest. "If you had seen what I saw, you would understand. As you said, we all came from Yggdrasil, we are all her children—"

"It's that kind of seditious talk that we cannot allow," Thor thundered as he burst into the prison. "The Jotnar have upended the peace and stability of the nine realms. They are responsible for this calamity."

"Sire," Hege said as she knelt and averted her gaze.

Aric just stood there. He had seen Jotnar, fought vargr, and faced down a dragon the size of a small mountain. This Aesir was simply another person.

"Brunhilda," Aric called out when the valkyrie walked in next. "Are

Jorunn and Loki recovering—"

"Silence!" Thor roared and slammed his fist against the bars. A flash of light erupted from the point of contact. Sparks cascaded down while Thor held on, muscles twitching and knuckles pale. "You have no standing here! You will address only me, and you will tell me exactly how you know Loki and why you were traveling with him."

Aric stumbled back and landed on the straw-covered floor with a dull thud. He did not know how, perhaps through his bond with Freya, but he recognized the clash of energies, the runes etched into the bars pushing back against Thor's outburst of Reginvald. "Thor," he whispered. Recognition dawned on his face. This was the first son of Odin. Freya had been Skuld when he knew her. She was only a goddess in his visions. This was his first time seeing one of his gods in the flesh, in all of their splendor.

"It's alright," Brunhilda said and laid a hand on Thor's shoulder. His body relaxed a slight, nearly imperceptible amount. He made no move to step away from the bars, though his hands, balled into tight fists, dropped to his sides.

Aric took a deep breath as he stood tall and brushed the straw and dust from his body. He locked eyes with the god he had once revered.

CHAPTER 22: TO ARMS

"For generations, the Aesir have kept us isolated and pitted us against each other. Their stories paint each of us as freaks and monsters." Hertha swept her arm over the crowd before she clenched that hand into a fist and pounded her chest.

An army a hundred thousand strong—made up of Humans, Jotnar, Eldjotnar, Ljosalfar, and Dokkalfar—was gathered, standing at attention, armed and armored.

"Jotnar are giant savages or feral beasts only good for hard labor," Hertha shouted.

Surtr led the Jotnar and Eldjotnar in a roar of boos.

Hertha turned to Brokkr and Sindri. "Dokkalfar are tiny vermin that skulk in deep holes in the ground, digging up gems and ore."

Brokkr and Sindri banged their tools together while their people did the same and shouted.

"Ljosalfar are spindly beings who flit and float among the leaves, coaxing lumber from the trees," Hertha said as Eik stamped her feet on the ground and the other Ljosalfar mirrored her.

Hertha gestured to the crowd of Humans. "And Humans are simple and grimy mules tilling the fields."

The soldiers joined Sigrid and Frode in a raucous din.

"While we toil away, eking out a meager existence, they lavish themselves in excess and opulence." Hertha's voice boomed out through the massive hall. "They may have led the charge of the Great Awakening, but they did not fight alone. We all contributed, we all sacrificed to bring about a brighter future."

The roar of affirmation was deafening. Many of the soldiers beat their swords against their shields or stomped their feet as they shouted. Hertha stood at the front of a dais, flanked on either side by Surtr, Frode, Sigrid, Eik, Sindri, and Brokkr. She raised her hands to quiet the assembly.

"Odin and the Aesir have kept us isolated and separated because they fear our strength when we are united. They are not invincible. We have proven that they are vulnerable. They no longer have Gungnir. And though they may still have Mjolnir, we have our own weapon!"

Hertha gestured to her right, where Surtr stood. His broad frame and height contrasted to her silhouette. In one smooth motion, Surtr gripped the hilt of the sword on his hip and drew it from its sheath, raising it high above the crowd. The blade turned a vibrant crimson and all fell silent, awed by its power. Only Hertha noticed the grimace on his face and the quaver in his arm. She gestured with her arm, and Surtr lowered the sword and placed it back in its scabbard. He let out a long, slow exhale as he fought to maintain his composure.

"Our Allied Army will tear down Asgard brick by brick!" Hertha drew her own sword and raised it high.

With that, the battalion lieutenants signaled and the trumpeters blew the deployment call. A thunderous din arose as one hundred thousand pairs of armored boots shuffled and began the slow, purposeful march north. It was not the disciplined and coordinated synchrony of the Aesir Army or even that of the Jotnar Army under Suttungr. But there was something appropriate about this to their coalition. Hertha could not help but smile at the unity even as she understood that most of them, if not all of them, would die in the assault against Asgard.

CHAPTER 23: INTERROGATION

"W-what happened?" Loki groaned, his words slurred and just above a whisper in volume. There was a metallic taste and wooly feel in his mouth as he struggled to part his dry, chapped lips. The smoothness and softness of the materials enveloping him felt comforting and oddly unsettling. "Where am I?" His eyes were slow to open and even slower to focus. A golden light coming from somewhere nearby saturated his field of view with a dreamlike quality. There was something strange and yet familiar about his surroundings that he could not quite grasp as his mind searched for something solid to ground itself upon.

"He's awake," said a voice from somewhere off to his right. There was a distinct dryness to her tone.

"Shall I—"

"Yes, yes," a second voice chimed in. "I promised that I'd let him know."

Loki turned his head to see who was speaking. The blurred silhouette in the approximate shape of a woman came closer. Before her face came into focus, the edges of his vision darkened and then went completely black. Loki slumped back into the mattress and drifted off.

—

"Get up, you cur!"

Loki came to with a start. He was being shaken by a pair of very strong hands squeezing, crushing his shoulders. A burst of Ethlivald erupted from his hands as he struggled to break free of his assailant's vise grip. Even through his heavy-lidded eyes, the familiar flash of golden light tinged with blue shocked him fully awake as his power was repelled. That light dissolved into a rich orange hue, and in the background his ears picked up the soft crackling of several fires.

"That won't work." One of the hands went to his throat.

As his vision at last focused, he saw the blurry silhouette of his attacker's head ringed with a bright crimson aura. The hands squeezed tighter and slammed Loki back down. The force might have been more painful if there had not been a downy soft mattress beneath him.

Loki pawed at the hand cutting off his airway. He tried to speak but only managed to cough out something unintelligible.

"Sire, please," a familiar voice called out from behind Thor. Brunhilda stepped forward and placed one hand upon his and the other on his chest. Thor's grip relaxed as he allowed her to push him back.

"Thor? Brunhilda?" Loki's voice was raspy and strained. He looked around the room and recognized the intricate and ornate detailing that could only exist in Asgard. "What happened? How—"

"Where is your army?" Thor barked. Brunhilda was exerting a fair bit of effort to hold him back. "How many of you are there? Tell me quickly, and I shall give you a quick death. Hold anything back or lie to me, and I will make certain that the tales of you being tortured, bound underground with a snake dripping venom on you for eternity, come true."

"Same old Thor," Loki said with a stronger, more defiant tone. "Always rushing headlong with little understanding of what is transpiring around you." He sat up, cautiously at first. Feeling stronger and more confident, Loki swung his legs out and stood.

Brunhilda moved one hand to the hilt of her sword even as she kept her other pressed against Thor.

"The age of the Aesir is over. We have shown the other realms that you are vulnerable, that you can be defeated." Loki's fur bristled and the air temperature dipped as his strength and determination surged. "We are taking back ownership of our own destinies."

Thor pushed past Brunhilda with ease and grabbed Loki by his tunic. The Aesir's muscles barely strained as he lifted the Jotnar up off his feet.

"Jarnsaxa would be ashamed that she ever had anything to do with you," Loki sneered.

Thor flinched at the name. The scowl on his face softened, though he maintained his hold.

"No matter what you do to me, this tide has risen and will not be stopped."

Brunhilda placed her hand on Thor's arm and lowered Loki back to his feet.

"We no longer recognize your authority." Loki's eyes locked with Thor's. "You will get no more labor from any realm. We have turned all of your mechanisms of oppression against you. Our uprising is armed and supplied with the materials and resources you forced us to produce for Asgard."

"They are in Aldrnari." Thor threw Loki back onto the bed.

"Sire?" Brunhilda had a quizzical expression.

"His clothes are permeated with the soot and ash from the forges of Muspelheim," he replied with a dismissive wave of his hand. "Aldrnari is the only city there large enough to house the numbers required to threaten Asgard. Its forges would be needed to produce the weapons and armor they'd need."

"Our location doesn't matter," Loki hissed. "The fight will be here. Our peoples are united. All who you have oppressed. Together we have learned that you kept us isolated because you feared our strength. And so we have learned not to fear you."

"I have also learned much since the days you were welcome in Asgard," Thor sneered. "As much as you resist, as much as you fight against us, we Aesir had the vision to fight against the eldritch monsters, to bring order to the realms. We beat back the chaos once before and shall do so again."

He turned and strode away. As Thor approached the door, the Aesir prince paused and turned his head. "Throw Loki in prison and prepare him for execution. His death shall be slow and painful. At long last, we shall avenge my brother's murder. I'll see to it personally after I lead the army and crush this absurd rebellion once and for all."

CHAPTER 24: THE SOUTHERN OFFENSIVE

The long columns of soldiers spilled from the main gate of the Bifrost Skjaldborg. Every active member of the Aesir Army was in formation, marching in step, with all of the Einherjar bringing up the rear. Dozens of valkyries raced ahead of the battalions astride their mounts. Some rode horses while others rode Svelbjarg rams. Thor's chariot, pulled by a pair of enormous goats, was at the head of the army.

He rode in silence. His face was dark and hardened as his mind lingered on his mother's words.

"Why have you marshaled the army and the Einherjar?" Frigg's voice was strong and resonant in the troop courtyard as she strode towards Thor. He had mounted his chariot while his attendants were making fast the harnesses on the goats set to pull it. All around, Aesir soldiers were in full kit and making ready for a forced march. The Human soldiers looked less prepared as they fidgeted with their gear and weapons, unfamiliar with combat beyond the relative safety of Asgard. Frigg was trailed by the entire council of Asgard and their retinue. Brunhilda was at her side. "It's folly to leave Asgard so exposed, so vulnerable."

"You have entrusted the military decisions to Thor, my lady." Sif answered for Thor as he made final checks on his supplies and equipment loaded aboard the chariot. He placed Mjolnir in a secured spot and strapped it in place. "Thor has called for the assembly of the army in pursuit of the fugitive Jotnar nation and their mutinous collaborators from the other realms."

"Their crimes demand punishment, swift and decisive," Thor said, though he did not pause in his preparations. "According to Loki, they are in active sedition against Asgard. All traitors must be dealt with. Our voice is the law of the nine realms, and we mete out judgment on our terms. We do not sit and wait for them to come to us."

"Now see here," Brunhilda said as she stepped forward, "I must echo our queen's concerns." Though still a valkyrie, she was now included on matters of defense. Even in the gloom and melancholy of the past few months, her victory over Nidhogg was still sung about in taverns and courtyards throughout Asgard. "We need you and Mjolnir to defend the city and everyone within. The threat of the blighted creatures remains the most immediate threat."

"Mere beasts," Thor scoffed. "We must not show weakness in front of the lesser races. Our leniency to the Jotnar has led us to this very moment. The Alfheim brigands began their raids not long after the Aesir-Vanir War concluded, when the Jotnar and Vanir were let off with little more than a slap on the hand. Freya openly and willfully flouted Odin's authority as she traveled the nine realms fomenting unrest."

Huginn and Muninn cawed in apparent agreement. Freyr and the other Vanir on the council bristled. "Now see here—" began Freyr.

"Still your tongue before I cut it out!" Thor roared.

"Do not make such wild and frivolous comments about our friends, Thor." Frigg addressed Freyr directly with a nod of deference. He was visibly shaken, though Brunhilda could not tell whether it was from fear or rage. Frigg turned back to her son. "We have no proof or reason to accuse our allies."

"The Bifrost Skjaldborg has been rebuilt and stands strong. And you have the dragonslayer." Thor gestured to Brunhilda with a disdain she had not expected. "With the Hero of the Battle of the Bifrost leading the city guard, defending Asgard should be trivial. Much simpler than killing Nidhogg." Thor did not wait for any response as he whipped the goats into a trot and raised his arm. Frigg, Brunhilda, and the others did not think he was so far gone that he would trample them, but they gave way to be certain. "Army of Asgard, fall in!"

—

Thor shook his head as he thought back on that ludicrous encounter. How blind Odin and Frigg had been to the conspiracies brewing right under their noses. Everyone was against them. Even Baldur had betrayed his own people to lead the Jotnar Army to Asgard's very gate. All of the other races resented the strength and power of the Aesir. None of them could have had the will, power, and vision to orchestrate the masterpiece that had been the Great

Awakening.

Sif rode up next to Thor's chariot. Her horse was a broad-shouldered destrier, armored and packed for the march to Muspelheim. "I support your decision. Asgard will be fine. But you should exercise more tact around the Vanir. After Freya's death, they are more in line with us than ever against the Jotnar. However, as you noted, they did fight against us before. It wouldn't take much for them to see this new uprising as a chance to depose us and take their place in our stead."

"None of them would dare," Thor spat. "Only Freya had the fire in her loins to defy Father."

"Not long ago, I would have agreed with your assessment." Sif paused and gathered her thoughts. "But as you said, Baldur turning on us and leading the Jotnar in breaching the Bifrost Skjaldborg has made us look weak. With a full-scale rebellion brewing and both you and I away, this could be the very opportunity the Vanir would exploit to execute a coup."

Thor pulled back on the reins and drew his chariot and the rest of the army to an abrupt halt. He turned his attention back to the north and swore under his breath. The clarion call of the great Gjallarhorn trumpet reverberated across the valley.

CHAPTER 25: THEY ARE COMING

Lif sat on a small pile of straw, hugging her knees to her chest and gently rocking back and forth while she stared at the gray sky. Through the dense cloud cover, the light of the noonday sun barely reached into the prison cells. Small windows near the ceiling were the only openings to the outside world. Even if they were not barred and too high up to reach, they were scarcely large enough for her to fit through. Lifthrasir sat next to her and held her hand.

"I know this isn't ideal," he whispered and leaned his head against hers. "Just pretend like we're still back in Muspelheim."

She jerked away and stared at him with a grimace.

"Right," he said as he took her in his arms again. "Hoddmimis Holt then. I know that we had only just met, but I could tell that you loved that little valley... despite the smell." He gave her a playful nudge.

Lif rolled her eyes and craned her head around their small cell. It was well kept and overall a very pleasantly appointed prison cell, but there was an open lavatory in the corner away from the door.

"Well, yes, it's not exactly a field of wildflowers in here. And of course that's not the worst part. Thor shouting at Aric that he would 'execute us if we didn't divulge everything we knew about the Jotnar Army' isn't the warmest welcome I've ever received." Lifthrasir gave a long, low sigh. Even he knew this was a dire corner they were backed into. Not only were they unable to do anything to heal Yggdrasil, they were going to be stuck in an Aesir prison when the Allied Army came. He leaned forward and buried his face in his hands. And it was Lif's turn to put her arm around his waist and give him a reassuring squeeze.

"Keep it down," Aric hissed at the couple. "Someone's coming."

Footsteps echoed from beyond the door that led to the prison cells. After a brief jangling of keys in the lock, the door swung open.

"Aric." Brunhilda swept into the hall. "I regret that I haven't had an opportunity to greet you properly."

"Well, perhaps you could let us out of here?" Aric replied dryly.

"It's good to see that you have regained your humor. You were rather dour when we last met." Brunhilda smiled and patted his hand, which was holding on to one of the cell bars. Her smile faded when he failed to react. "Still as morose as ever, I see."

"Well, meeting a god and having him threaten you with execution would sour anyone's mood," Lifthrasir said as he stood and approached the valkyrie. Lif also stood but remained firmly at the far end of the cell.

"Yes, there is much that weighs on Lord Thor's mind. With the other realms in open revolt in the south and diseased animals and monsters attacking from the north, things are not ideal."

"That's why we are here," Aric said, his voice low yet strong. "Freya told us that the Aesir can repair Yggdrasil and stem the tide of these monsters. In fact, they are the only ones who can."

"Yes, you mentioned Freya before," Brunhilda said with a skeptical tone that Aric recognized. Her hand squeezed his, hard.

"Ow, what are you—?"

"I don't feel the presence of Mithlivald. I would hesitate to do any real damage on the chance that you are merely hallucinating. Of course, our fostra could heal you." Brunhilda's free hand idly traced the hilt of her sword.

Aric managed to pull his hand free. "I used to see her. But in our last encounter with a corrupted beast… something happened and she vanished. I haven't seen her since."

"Funny." Brunhilda smirked. "That is exactly her nature. She came and went as she pleased. Freya vexed Odin to no end. Not even Huginn or Muninn could keep track of her when she left Asgard. However, since the ending of the Aesir-Vanir War, there have been no overt hostilities between the two. Though they seemed to take to their verbal sparring with a great deal of enthusiasm."

"You all amaze me." Aric interrupted her reminiscing. "With the power and riches you have, while so many in the world toil and suffer, you still find time for such pettiness. I wonder if just the Aesir or if Humans and all of the other races would fall to such idiocy in your place."

"These are not 'petty squabbles,' as you may think. These conflicts are at the heart of how the nine realms are ruled." Brunhilda gave Aric a look he could only describe as pity. "Or even if the nine realms exist at all. Were it not for Borr's vision—"

"We would all still be in caves, cowering in fear of the eldritch horrors that roamed the land." Aric finished her sentence. "We've had this talk before. And now, just as then, one good deed does not excuse generations of oppression—"

"Please." Brunhilda held her hand up, silencing Aric. "You know that I sympathize with your plight. My eyes are open to your struggles and the struggles of the Jotnar. I have voiced my doubts with Lady Frigg at every opportunity."

"Thank you," Aric replied, a look of pleasant surprise spreading across his face. "Thank you for that. And I'm here to offer what help I can. Together, I'm sure that we can convince the queen to make peace with the Alliance and go—"

"It's too late," Brunhilda interrupted. "Thor has already taken the Aesir Army to strike before you're ready."

"What?" Aric was aghast. "No. How does he—? I never told—"

"You're in Muspelheim." Brunhilda answered the unasked question. "There are few enough places for a gathering large enough to pose a threat to Asgard. And that's the only place with the raw materials needed to supply an army. Do you really think that we know so little of our own kingdom?"

"Then why haven't you already attacked?"

"It's as you say," she said. "Blighted creatures have been attacking. And after the Jotnar attack, we've had to rebuild the Bifrost Skjaldborg before the army could leave."

"Can't you call them back?" Aric said in desperation. "There has to be a way to communicate with them, to stop them."

"I'm sorry, Aric," Brunhilda said as she placed her hand over his on the iron bar. "We just need to let this play out as it will. Lady Frigg will not countermand Thor without more than the word of a Human and a valkyrie."

—

Brunhilda walked the market square, having left Aric and his companions. Her conversation with Aric still nagged at her.

Looking around, she could not help but compare the stilted, formal transactions occurring here to the warmth and boisterous nature of the Jotnar market in Gastropnir. While the Asgardian merchants acknowledged their regular customers, they used that association to hurry along the transaction and conduct more business. Their familiarity seemed more of a tool to facilitate business rather than an aspect of genuine concern and interest. An embrace or pat on the shoulder allowed the merchant to direct their patrons along to other wares or else to make way for fresh customers.

Even though Thor's abrupt departure had left the city in a palpable state of tension, everyone went about their daily business in an almost purposeful ignorance. But even the valkyrie's conspicuous presence did not silence the whispers and murmurs about the public confrontation between Thor and Frigg. Brunhilda thought that she even noticed a subtle hesitancy towards Aesir customers from the Dokkalfar and Ljosalfar merchants.

Brunhilda's ears twitched at the distant chime of alarm bells from off in the west. Several clusters of reserve troops collected their gear and ran off to their specific calls to duty. The people in the merchant square flinched for only a moment before resuming their business. Everything played out as she had seen many times before. And yet this time, there was a strange feeling in the pit of her stomach that she could not ignore. The little hairs on the back of her neck and along her bare arms pricked up.

As her ears focused on the distant sounds of battle, the market square grew quiet and dim. Brunhilda recalled the schedule and remembered that Tyr was the on-duty commander right now. Even with only one hand, the Aesir was more than capable of dealing with a simple blight attack. And yet she could not let go of the feeling that something about this fight was different. There was a familiar sensation. She racked her mind for it, for something. A sound, a scent?

"Valkyrie?" The rotund Dokkalfar merchant had been trying to get her attention for several moments. "Are you interested in purchasing that figurine?"

"What? No, sorry, Felman. I don't..." Brunhilda trailed off, looking at the marble carving of Yggdrasil in her hands. It had exquisite detail, with a lithe Nidhogg curled around its roots and an eagle perched in its canopy. Her fingers traced the branches and lingered on the leaves. For all of the fine craftsmanship, it looked nothing like the actual tree. She did not remember picking it up. It had been involuntary, a subconscious reflex to something that her conscious mind had not grasped yet. Then it came to her. Her nostrils flared and she took a deep breath. A familiar scent wafted on the breeze from the north.

The tree dropped from her hands and the Dokkalfar lunged forward and caught it. Brunhilda spun towards the Bifrost Skjaldborg. She took one step and then a second. In a moment, she was sprinting. Before she had cleared the last building, she heard a spine-tingling howl rip through the air, and then the unmistakable sound of the Gjallarhorn immediately after.

As Brunhilda neared the massive gates at the western edge of the city, she had to push her way through a wave of bloody, wounded Einherjar falling back. She was not wearing her full armor kit, though she had the valkyrie sword in its sheath at her hip. It was reassuring to have her old sword back by her side. The sea of Humans flooding through the Bifrost Skjaldborg jostled her so that could scarcely progress forward without hurting them. For the briefest of moments she wondered if this was what Hrym had felt like amid the aurochs stampede she had unleashed on him in the Battle of Calder so long ago. Instead of his violent reaction, however, Brunhilda weaved her way to the left to avoid the worst of the crowd.

At last, she cleared the gate and saw the Aesir line collapsing under the pressure of the approaching swarm. Her sword rang as she pulled it from its scabbard. Brunhilda furrowed her brow and clenched her jaw tight. *All of our actions have consequences*, she thought with grim determination as her eyes scanned the horizon. Amid the undulating sea of shadow, floating points of light shifted and bobbed along, each pair marking a single creature whose individual silhouette was lost in the dark tidal wave. It was out there. It was coming.

CHAPTER 26: NATURE'S FURY

"Einherjar, to the right flank!" Tyr, the Aesir watch commander, shouted from the center of the line. To their credit, the able-bodied Humans leapt to action even in the face of these nightmarish things, all writhing shadows limned with fangs and claws. They rallied and redoubled their efforts, heartened by Tyr's leadership.

After the loss of his right hand, he had recovered in a short amount of time under the care of Fostra Eira. Though he was unable to fight as before, he had insisted on returning to active duty. Having to relearn combat with his off hand, Tyr had decided to train alongside the Human soldiers under Freyr's direction. Their shared experiences gave the Einherjar a particular esteem for the Aesir commander. And so, as he ran headlong and unflinching into danger, they followed close behind.

More than a thousand shadowy creatures large and small descended upon Asgard like scavengers to a rotting corpse. They appeared to merge and split apart, so Tyr found it difficult to count them for certain. Having led many defenses before, he did not let this fluster him. Although in the past, they had had Thor wielding Mjolnir with them. That power had been key to defeating the larger, more powerful creatures. And with the unpredictable failures of Reginvald and Mithlivald of late, this absence could prove disastrous. For now, however, the Einherjar weapons and armor burst with the magic of their enchantment as they clashed with the blight. With the flourish of warhorns, Kari led a charge of the Aesir city guards from the left flank and closed in as the dark wave broke against the Einherjar shields.

—

Kari and Tyr had just gained control of the first wave of blighted animals when a starkly chilling howl cut across the Vigrid Plains. From the horizon emerged a blurred mass of dark, shifting tendrils concealing thousands of individual creatures. At its lead was a terrifying hound the size of a small house.

"Fall back!" Kari shouted. She grabbed the horn from the downed signal officer at her feet and blew three quick blasts. The Einherjar paused their attack, looking up from their anticipated victory close at hand. Gasps and cries of horror could be heard from among the Humans as they saw the approaching horde. Theirs was not an orderly retreat as many panicked and fled, leaving behind discarded weapons and shields.

"Hold the line! Wait for your signal!" Freyr attempted to calm them and hold to their training. "We can't let the blight into the city!"

But for all of the drills on the practice field, the Humans did not have the experience to maintain their composure in the face of such terrifying foes. While the Aesir soldiers held fast, their years of discipline and training ingrained in them, they were vastly outnumbered. And so even these hardened warriors faltered, if only for a moment, as the new threat drew closer.

Several corrupted animals broke through the gaps in the line and wreaked havoc among the vendors in the merchant square. The marshalling and practice fields emptied as the off-duty soldiers hurried to deal with the incursion. Blight tainted every building and street that the creatures passed through. Alarm bells chimed and horns blew to signal where the animals were heading. The screams of civilians mixed with the bestial howls and the shouts of soldiers.

—

"Nidhogg's taint." Sif came to a halt as the company crested the ridge at the southern edge of the Vigrid Plain and Asgard came into view. A writhing mass of dark shapes obscured the Bifrost Skjaldborg. At this distance, to Sif's eyes it looked as if a nest of ants had discovered a morsel of food.

"Onward!" Thor's voice boomed as he took the lead and started to run. He and the Aesir troops flowed past her for a brief moment before she joined the charge.

In mere moments, the broad expanse of grass flew by. As they drew near, Sif could see that the recently repaired shield wall was truly being tested. Volley after volley of arrows were swallowed by the dark morass. With each wave, the animals crashed into the stonework. Even from so far away, Sif could see the cracks starting to form. The masonry had been hurried, and with the continued hostilities, they had had to rely on the few Dokkalfar who were already in Asgard. That lack of skilled masons was never more apparent than at this moment.

As the rampart buckled and a small section broke away, Sif found that they had nearly closed the distance to the monstrous host. Suddenly, with fifty yards to go, the right flank of the horde wheeled about and the gleaming metal of the Aesir Army crashed into the shadowy host.

The Aesir cleaved into the stampeding herd. Soldiers slashed and fought against the corrupted animals. Though the Reginvald-spelled weapons blazed with energy, the creatures were undeterred.

"The blight is getting stronger!" Sif shouted to Thor. She stepped with purpose into the fray, slashing one animal after another. Sif grew more frustrated and began to curse with each stroke of her sword. Her deft footwork and precision strikes should have left a trail of corpses in her wake, yet the monstrous creatures rebounded and attacked again with vengeance.

A dazzling bolt of energy erupted from the front. The thunderous boom and the telltale smell of ionized air heralded Mjolnir's power. Nondescript shapes flew in all directions away from the epicenter, but the respite was momentary as the creatures flowed in to close the gap created by Mjolnir's power.

"Fenrir's balls!" Thor roared in frustration. He was breathing hard and beads of sweat dotted his forehead. "Is there no end to these vile beasts?"

"Hit them again!" Sif shouted from a short distance to his left.

Thor gritted his teeth and his brow furrowed with the effort. With a roar, he drew upon all of the Reginvald power he could summon from Yggdrasil and unleashed an explosive arc of lighting through the warhammer. The air itself sizzled with the energy unleashed as nine arcs of electricity flowed from the clouds above and connected with the hammerhead. A chain reaction cascaded as the web of lightning leapt from one creature to the next, dispelling the inky corruption and laying waste to the throbbing mass.

Sparks popped and fizzled off the enchanted Aesir armor, leaving all of the soldiers unscathed. Sif let out a long, slow breath. From the corner of her eye, she saw Thor drop the mighty warhammer and teeter on his feet before pitching forward and falling to the ground, his body limp and unresponsive.

"Thor!" Sif rushed to his side as the rest of the Aesir Army seemed to recover from the blinding power they had just witnessed. As she neared, Sif could see the rise and fall of Thor's barrel chest. His breathing was shallow and rapid, but at least he was breathing. Kneeling at his side, she drew upon her limited Mithlivald abilities. As she laid her hands upon him, the energy dissipated. Looking at her hands, she realized that he was not injured; that last attack had overwhelmed his body, leaving him drained. There was little to do except to get him to a bed so that he could rest and recover.

A terrifying howl ripped through the air. In the distance, the rustling of the trees to the north sent a flock of birds up into the air. The aspen and firs shook until at last they gave way to a bounding shadow creature in the shape of a ten-foot-tall hound. In the span of seconds, the beast cleared the distance from the woods to the wall. The defenders had managed to shut and bar the massive gates before its arrival. Many Aesir and Einherjar had been left outside of the wall, but they were all trained and prepared to give their lives in defense of Asgard.

Thor lay still and unresponsive as Sif appraised the situation. She saw that the enchantment on the Aesir weapons continued to fluctuate, leaving them useless for all intents and purposes. And so she reached for Mjolnir. But as her hand made contact with its haft, the weapon remained inert in Sif's hand.

The helhound, Garmr, stalked closer and then was hit by a volley of arrows. Reacting to the attack, it bounded forward and barreled into the gates of the Bifrost Skjaldborg. Although the runes carved into the rock and gates flared with the white light of Mithlivald, the beast's force was so great that the masonry at the hinges fractured, and flakes of granite and marble cascaded off the towering structure. Shadowy tendrils seeped into the cracks and spread, expanding the fissures.

Several archers who had been too close to the edge tumbled from the ramparts as the great wall shuddered from the impact. The rest of the defenders pelted the attacker with everything they had—arrows, rocks, vats of scalding oil. And yet Garmr was undeterred. A thundering growl rumbled from deep within the creature and shook the bones of all nearby. The creature leapt back, ready to ram the defensive wall again.

Sif steeled herself and focused her thoughts into Mjolnir. A surge of pain flowed through the handle up into her arms as she at last bridged the connection to Yggdrasil. A flood of energy surged through her and, with the darkness-enshrouded beast within reach, Sif swung the warhammer and unleashed all of the power she could channel.

Yet at her core she could feel something was amiss. And the impact failed to penetrate the shadowy tendrils.

The helhound flinched but paid little heed to the annoyance; it sprang headlong into the shield wall once again. And once again the white Mithlivald runes flared to life at the impact. But this time the light faltered, and the stone gave way in a shower of granite, mortar, and lumber.

CHAPTER 27: STREETS GILDED IN BLIGHT

"Move!" Hege leapt and tackled the Dokkalfar merchant, Felman, out of the way. A large section of masonry crashed down inches away from them. Debris and dust continued to pelt the pair as they lay motionless for several long moments while Garmr moved deeper into the city.

"Come on, we can't stay here," she said, coughing as she pulled herself up from the surrounding rubble and tugged on the Dokkalfar merchant's torn shirt. Felman accepted the help; he was covered in scratches and bruises. Even though Hege had not been on active duty, she wore a heavy gambeson that had protected her.

All around the merchant square, the Einherjar and city guard who had not been at the Skjaldborg were racing to aid the civilians and contain the corrupted animals. Every Aesir was well trained in war and joined the fray. Though most only served in official capacity for a decade, many would join for the occasional raid on bandits or the hunting of animals. All of the other races were not only untrained, they had also been forbidden from arming themselves. Only the Humans of the Einherjar had been allowed to join the reserve forces.

As a result, West Asgard was a chaotic mess, with noncombatants running in all directions as Garmr and several other animals tore through the cobbled streets.

―

The pile of rubble where the Skjaldborg's gates had stood shifted. Inky black tendrils pushed the stone clear as several beasts emerged from the debris. A vargr leapt to the side just as a flash of golden light sent masonry and metalwork bursting outward. With allies so close by, Brunhilda ensured that the wave of Reginvald had been limited to a very tight radius.

The valkyrie's armor was dented and crushed in many places but had otherwise maintained structural integrity under the crushing weight. She mouthed a silent thanks to the Aesir enchanters for all of their work, though once again she cursed her own lack of Mithlivald. Golden blood trickled from a shallow gash in her forehead and matted down her fiery red locks, and she was almost certain several of her ribs were at least bruised if not outright fractured. Her breathing was labored and pain flashed in her chest as she coughed from the dust.

Brunhilda looked in disgust at the writhing blight left in the wake of the tainted animals. She tore off her left vambrace before the tendrils could crawl onto her skin. With a quick but thorough check of the rest of her armor, she climbed out of the crater that she had made. The ambient sounds of battle surrounded her, but her keen ears picked out the distinctive growls of Garmr in the distance. Steeling herself against her various injuries, Brunhilda rushed out after her quarry.

The shadowy figure of a gigantic hound sat on the collapsed structure that used to be the prison. It let out a howl that cut through to every corner of Asgard, West and East. Garmr then bounded up as it sniffed the air.

From the west, a bolt of energy shot through the air and knocked the canine into a nearby building. Sif dropped Mjolnir and leaned against the low remains of a crumbling wall after the exertion.

"Aric!" As soon as she recognized the building, Brunhilda ran forward and cut through the rubble pile with Reginvald. A second swing of her sword bounced off a large marble slab with a teeth-rattling clang. The vibrations threatened to shake the weapon free of Brunhilda's grip. Having lost the sword once before, she was determined not to drop it again.

Some smaller bits of rocks shifted and Lif emerged. Lifthrasir carried the staff while also supporting Aric as they came up behind her. A large stone arch had held fast and maintained a small pocket where the Humans had sheltered during the collapse. The trio moved away from the rubble, towards the recovering Sif, who was dragging Mjolnir. Aric stifled a shout of pain as he stumbled on the scree.

"Are you injured?" Brunhilda called behind her, though she did not look back. Her eyes were locked on the shadowy beast before her as it recovered from the blast.

"I-I'll be fine, don't worry about us," Aric called out through gritted teeth.

"That doesn't look good," Sif said as she pointed to a piece of wood jutting out from his leg. The red bloodstain was spreading through his pants.

"Here," Lifthrasir said to Aric as he passed him the staff. "Hold on to this, I'll dress the wound."

But as soon as Aric grasped the staff, a surge of white light and power flared from the wound. The wood shaft pushed free as the flesh stitched itself back together. Sif cocked her eyebrow at the clear use of Mithlivald by a Human. Her look of skepticism was matched by looks of surprise on the faces of Aric and Lifthrasir. Lif maintained her usual stoic expression.

A din of growling and shouting combined with the impact of metal on stone and flesh drew everyone's attention. Brunhilda had not waited for their reply or even assessed their condition. Instead, she had charged at the towering, writhing, canine-shaped mass before it could regain its footing. Aric noted that this was not the reckless abandon he had seen when she had fought Nidhogg at the World Tree. Her face betrayed no emotion, and her deft footwork appeared to step between every strike of the lashing limbs. In seconds, Brunhilda had closed the distance unscathed and stood directly under the giant hound's slavering jaws. Golden light blazed from the valkyrie's sword, and she thrust the point up through its head.

Aric flinched at the burst of light. He gasped when he looked again. The light was gone, and inky tendrils held the weapon at bay; Brunhilda strained to push the blade through. Garmr's paw struck in a flash and batted the valkyrie away into a crumbling wall, the clang of armor against stonework marking the intensity of the impact. Brunhilda's body dropped to the ground, unmoving.

Just as the helhound was about to pounce, a rock flew through the air and struck it in the head. Aric and Garmr turned to see that Lif had thrown it and had another rock in her hand. The shadowy mass did not leap so much as it burst towards her like water from a ruptured dam.

"No!" Aric shouted. His hands reacted out of pure instinct and thrust the gnarled staff forward until it impacted a solid object deep within the dark, shifting shape. When it connected with Garmr's body, the shadows burst out in an ethereal cloud away from it, revealing the animal within to be free of the blight, though quite shaggy and unkempt. The large hound was sent hurtling across the boulevard and crashed into a tavern before crumpling to the ground in a furry, shapeless heap.

Aric stared at the staff in his hands. That was not the reaction he had been expecting. Since Freya's disappearance, he had felt weaker, more normal. Aric spun his head from side to side, looking around, expecting—wanting—to see her again, to hear her voice making some snide quip or pithy remark. But he saw nothing of her among the scattered destruction and chaos. Instead, there was a shimmering light coming from his hands. It was the staff itself.

Before he could think on it for long, he caught sight of the shadows coalescing and creeping towards Garmr. The beast's form twitched and spasmed, and Aric thought he could see the fur stand on end and extend out, trying to meet the encroaching darkness. With no real plan, he leapt at the writhing tendrils and swung the gnarled wooden root at the animating shadows. The darkness dispelled in an explosion of light and energy, leaving the air charged with electricity that sent the small hairs on Aric's skin tingling. His muscles seized, overloaded by the power, and he dropped to his knees.

From Aric's immediate left, a deep, resonating growl drew his attention. The pile of fur and muscle shifted and rose as the hound staggered to its feet, teeth bared, muzzle flecked with foam and saliva. It lunged at the distracted and unprepared Aric. Inches before it reached him, a blast of energy seared the air and struck the animal, slamming it into a stone wall. A roiling cloud of dust and a shower of masonry exploded from the impact. Aric wheeled around to see Thor wielding Mjolnir.

From beneath the rubble, something shifted. Thor, Sif, Brunhilda, and Aric looked on in shock as the canine silhouette emerged from the haze. As Thor steeled himself for another strike, the beast's bright eyes darted around, seeming to calculate its odds, and then it bounded towards the smashed gates of the Bifrost Skjaldborg. Though weakened, it shrugged off the swords, spears, and arrows in its path and crashed through the soldiers barring the way. Once clear of the city, it sped off to the north and vanished into the woods.

"You are full of surprises, Human." Thor sounded more annoyed than curious. The massive Aesir towered above Aric. There might have been some respect in the Aesir's face, but Thor did not offer to help him up. So with more than a little stiffness in his joints, Aric rose to his feet unaided.

Feeling returned to his extremities, and he shook his head to clear out the fugue. His hands buzzed with the residual power of the blow. The air felt thick and heavy, and the crackle of energy still lingered. Yet Aric barely noticed any of these other things. His eyes were fixed upon a familiar silhouette standing just to Thor's right. It was Freya, but less corporeal, a mere apparition. Thor shouted something that Aric could not process, though it was enough to draw his attention. His eyes shifted only for an instant, but when he looked again, Freya was gone. He took a cautious step forward and scanned the scene. A meaty hand pulled on his shoulder and brought him back to the present moment.

"I said that your display of power was… unexpected." Thor looked irked. He was not used to being ignored, especially by the likes of one such as Aric.

"Yes." Aric continued to cast his gaze around the perimeter. "I doubt anyone could have foreseen any of this." He pulled himself free. Thor, mouth slightly agape, stared at his hand and then Aric.

Aric took a few cautious steps forward and shifted from the right to the left. A groan and shifting of stone caught his attention. He turned to see Lif and Lifthrasir pulling slabs of rock off Brunhilda's still form. Aric hurried to see to the fallen valkyrie.

"Fostra!" Thor shouted as he followed. All around, soldiers and citizens were emerging from the aftermath and seeing to the needs of those trapped or injured in the skirmish.

CHAPTER 28: THE BRISINGAMEN

"We are grateful for the aid you provided against the blighted animals." While Frigg's words addressed Aric, she cast her gaze upon the larger assembly in the reception hall. Thor, Sif, Tyr, and the rest of the Asgard leadership were in attendance.

"You've witnessed the threat these creatures pose to the nine realms." Aric took a deep breath. He looked around. Three years ago, he never could have imagined himself in the halls of Asgard, let alone standing in front of the Asgardian pantheon and lecturing them. "When we stood in the presence of Yggdrasil and saw the damage upon the World Tree, Freya came to understand the threat posed. She was too late to save herself and do anything about it. But she was able to impart to me the vision and knowledge to bring the warning to you. So that you could address the problem and once again save the nine realms."

"Yes, this latest incursion has given us much to discuss." Frigg was gracious and far more diplomatic than Thor had been. Her warmth and composure gave Aric a kernel of hope. "Please, accept the hospitality of Asgard for you and your companions as we confer." She gestured to the council.

The guards opened the tall double doors behind them while an attendant ushered the Humans out of the room.

"There's not much to it but wait for their decision, I suppose." Lifthrasir broke the silence as the three Humans stood outside of the palace, staring at the doors that had just been shut in their faces. Aric did not so much as acknowledge the boy's words. Instead, he walked away, following the pathways with the speed and confidence of someone familiar with them.

"Aric?" Lifthrasir reached a hand out after him. Lif held him back. He looked at her, and she simply shook her head. She recognized Freya's influence, and her instinct was to allow this to run its course. The crowds and throngs of people moving around the palace were giving her anxiety, and she longed to find some solitude and quiet.

"Slow down," Lifthrasir said, dragging his feet and getting her to pause at last. "We've barely gotten to see anything of this city since we arrived. They sent us straight to the fostra and then put us in those prison cells. Aren't you even a little curious about this place?"

Lif furrowed her brows at him and then looked around at all of the devastation. They had just crossed over the Bifrost Bridge and emerged from the mists that engulfed it. In contrast to the untouched buildings of the eastern half of the city, in West Asgard there did not appear to be a building that had been left unscathed. And even in that state of disrepair, the marble gleamed in the little light that seeped through the dense clouds above.

"Well, yeah." Lifthrasir ran his hand through his hair. "Things are in pretty bad shape here, but there—"

He had pointed back across to the east only to see the guards cross their spears with menace. When walking through the dense fog, they had not noticed the Aesir standing at the bridge's entrance. Staring them down, Lif moved towards the guards only to find Lifthrasir grasping her arm, holding her back. The guards did not so much as twitch in reaction to her action, but Lifthrasir seemed to fear what they might do if they tried to go back across.

"Maybe we should help out here?" He managed to get her to turn around.

Laborers of all races were picking through the debris, looking for anyone trapped or wounded. However, work crews had self-selected along racial lines, with Aesir directing their efforts. Whenever a survivor was discovered, the healers rushed over to stabilize them and ensure their safe transport.

Fostra Eira had a triage area set up in a wide open field in West Agard. Noticing the weapons, armor, and regalia Lif concluded that this area was where the army was housed. Because the buildings were spread far apart and had sustained very little damage, the open space had been one of the first areas cleared that people could find refuge from the devastation. All of the healers were actively engaged in tending to the myriad injuries. Although they seemed to be uniformed and acting as healers, their movements were slow and unsure. Lif noticed some of their hands flickering with white glows and sparks before giving up and tending to the injured as she would. The use of bandages and splints appeared to be unfamiliar to these fostra.

After observing them for a few moments, Lif shook her head in dismay and stalked over to the makeshift infirmary. She pushed her way in front of a fostra fumbling with a splint and went straight to work on the wounded

Dokkalfar he was treating. Lifthrasir trotted along behind her and assisted.

"What are you—?" The fostra were perplexed and looked to Eira.

"Not bad," Eira said as she watched Lif set and splint Felman's broken arm. "Please, continue." Looking to the other fostra, she gestured for them to come closer and said, "Pay attention."

Aric saw flickering images in the shadows, a series of hazy, nondescript silhouettes that, despite lacking any recognizable feature, in his heart he knew belonged to Freya. They beckoned, and he followed, his movements his own and yet not. He felt a power, a sense of something just barely draping over his skin.

Although he was nowhere near the Bifrost Bridge, the air grew cold and still. He was vaguely aware that his breath was visible, misting with each exhale. A cloud of vapor curled out and surrounded him. As he approached the various palace guards, they gave no indication that they saw him. He passed down glittering marble hallways gilded and adorned with ornate filigree in twisting knotwork designs and inscribed with incomprehensible runes. He flew past, not slowing for even a moment.

At last he arrived at the base of a tower; the spiraling stairs at his feet felt at once new and familiar. He flew up two steps at a time. Before long, he came upon the highest landing. A massive oak door was the only thing there. Aric reached out and touched the handle. He heard the faintest of sounds, a series of mechanical clicks and metal sliding against metal, before the door swung open on silent hinges.

The antechamber was well appointed though not as gaudy as the rest of the palace. Braziers lined the room, but none of them were lit. The only light came from the landing's window at Aric's back. While the full moon illuminated things well enough, he moved through the space with the practiced pace of one who had been there many times. A menagerie of animal hides adorned the walls and a boar skin rug lay at the center, its head facing the entrance to greet all visitors. Three other doors lined the circular room, evenly spaced, all four doors marking the four cardinal directions. Aric gave all of this little attention as he moved without pause to the door to the west.

It was darker still here, and yet Aric knew this space. Freya's bedchamber was cavernous, the size of the great hall of Murtrborg to his reckoning. A ten-foot-tall curtain concealed a balcony on the other side. At this point, Aric stopped questioning how he knew so much about this place he had never been to before. The luxurious, four-poster bed on the far side of the room dominated the space. As he moved to the wardrobe and vanity along the wall to his right, he sensed a power in the room around him; the air vibrated against his skin.

His fingers slid along the smooth oak surfaces and traced the drawers and cabinets. At last, his hand came to rest upon a sturdy, reinforced latch. Again, he heard the whisper of metal sliding past metal and clicking into place before it popped open. Aric's fingers tingled as they grasped the edge of the drawer. He slid it towards himself, and a soft, golden glow escaped. As his eyes adjusted to the sudden illumination, the jewel-encrusted necklace came into focus.

"Brisingamen."

Aric jerked at the word. The voice was weak, but the sound felt like it came from within his own head. Focusing again upon the shimmering trinket, he reached out a hand, with more hesitation than anything he had done thus far. In fact, he was actively trying to pull his hand back as it stretched out of its own accord. As soon as his finger touched it, a light flashed within his mind, undimmed by Aric's shut eyes. Visions, sounds, smells, and tastes spanning several centuries surged to the forefront of the Human's consciousness, overwhelming his senses.

CHAPTER 29: SEIDR VISIONS

A haze of smoke and snow flurries whorled around the Vigrid Plains in massive eddies. The Bifrost Skjaldborg was little more than a pile of rubble, with the legendary arc of the Rainbow Bridge gone, plunged down into the chasm between Asgard and the continent. Freya stood, a blazing weapon in her right hand while the bodies of slain Aesir, Vanir, Jotnar, Dokkalfar, Ljosalfar, and Humans littered the battlefield. Other dark shapes lurked in the distance, obscured by the dim light and debris swirling all around. At her feet lay Thor. Although he was facedown, his blazing auburn hair splayed out on the ground like a sculpture of fire. The warhammer, Mjolnir, sat just beyond his open hand, its haft splintered and the once indomitable iron head cracked.

Looking a short distance to her left, she saw a familiar face. "Freyr," she whispered, voice cracking. A flood of emotions welled up in her chest upon seeing her brother also on the ground, unmoving, dead. Tears poured from her eyes. She did not wipe them away and gave them time to flow. After what felt like forever, she shut her eyes and pressed them against her sleeve and wiped the tears and snot away.

"So this is victory," Freya said aloud to the vast emptiness. Her words drifted out on the howling winds that whipped around her. "It is possible to bring down the Aesir." She looked to the bright weapon in her hand, but its searing light prevented her from seeing it clearly. "By my hand it will happen."

Through the shifting smoke and snow, Freya saw the dark shapes shift and move. In a sudden burst, they coalesced and rushed towards her.

Freya's eyes snapped open and she lurched forward. She had been sitting out in the deep woods; a circle of trees surrounded her. The remains of a small fire littered with the caps of mushrooms sputtered and smoldered next to her; swirling tendrils of smoke clung to her body and permeated her clothes. Freya coughed and dry heaved, her body folding over her crossed legs. She crawled on all fours until she was clear of the circle; her head still swam with the visions.

Far overhead, Freya thought she saw a dark shape flit out of a tree and across the sky. But her vision was still hazy, and after she rubbed her eyes, there was nothing there. Freya collapsed onto her back and breathed in the fresh air outside of the circle. When she opened her eyes again, she could not tell how much time had passed, but the fire was extinguished, its ashes cold, and the smoke had long since dissipated.

"All of the races together." From her back looking up, she saw how the tree crowns avoided their neighbors, keeping to themselves. Freya squeezed her eyes shut in an attempt to preserve the fleeting vision. "The Vanir and Jotnar alone were not enough to overthrow Odin and the Aesir. But what can the Dokkalfar, Ljosalfar, and Humans truly add? They have shown no ability to wield Yggdrasil's energies. On the battlefield, they would be slaughtered. The accursed art of seidr only gives fragments of knowledge, never anything clear. Why do I bother with it?"

She raised her hand and stared at it. The memory of the weapon remained elusive and hazy, but its power lingered and she felt the skin of her fingers prickle. "The Dokkalfar and Jotnar were instrumental in the construction of both Mjolnir and Gungnir," she mused aloud. "With Gungnir lost, the balance of power lies with the Aesir. To stand against them, I will need a weapon of at least equal power."

Freya rose to her feet. She looked around and saw her oilskin satchel, hanging from a low branch. With care she opened it up, exposing the shimmering feathers of the fjathrhamr cloak. Her fingers traced the runes inscribed into the feathers as she marveled at Njord's skill in enchanting objects.

"How did you do it, Father?" she asked. "Why did you not write any of this down? I have tried over and over, and I cannot create anything close to the power that you achieved. Without a weapon to rival Mjolnir, I have had to tolerate Odin's smug, self-righteous reign. You left us with no way of breaking this stalemate as the Aesir have squandered the fruits of the Great Awakening."

Freya looked at her open palm. As her fingers curled closed, she shut her eyes, recalling the feel of the weapon in the seidr vision. "The forge still resides in Muspelheim. We sealed it off, locking away the means of creating another weapon. But to craft this sword, I need to access it."

Her eyes snapped open. A look of resolve took over the sharp features of her Vanir face. Freya swung the fjathrhamr over her shoulders. In a flash of light and flurry of feathers, a large, golden eagle emerged. With a stretch and extension of its broad wings, it launched itself up into the clear night sky. The raptor's silhouette shrank as it raced out to the horizon.

CHAPTER 30: THE BEGINNING OF THE END

"Are you sure this will work?" Freyr asked in a hushed voice. The boulevards and thoroughfares of Asgard were all wide and shining. In West Asgard, however, the buildings were far more crowded, and dark, narrow alleyways radiated out in myriad directions. Despite the throngs of merchants and patrons mere yards away, the two figures were well hidden and their voices were drowned out by the ambient noise.

"I have seen it." Freya's voice was quiet yet forceful.

"Through the power of seidr?"

She heard the doubt in his voice. "I have seen Odin's death." Freya put a hand upon Freyr's shoulder. "I know the events that must transpire to make that happen."

"It is said that Odin himself had a vision after his battle with Nidhogg. What if he knows what you are up to? Those damn ravens of his are everywhere."

"That is why we cannot speak of this ever again. I shall follow the path set out for me. And it is best if you do not know any more. It seems to get more difficult to slip away from those birds every time. And if they follow you, that would give them twice the opportunity to discover us."

With that, Freya cast a spell; in a flash of light, a lithe, dark-skinned Ljosalfar appeared in her place.

"It's hard to believe you learned that from a Jotnar," Freyr said, a look of amazement on his face. "I wish that I could do that."

"You did always take after Mother." Freya always found it interesting that her voice changed with the forms that she took. This magic certainly was not as powerful as that of the fjathrhamr that her father had created to turn into birds, but the essence of this glamour seemed to be similar. And she still struggled, unable to re-create it. The loss of the fjathrhamr during the Fenrir incident had significantly limited her ability to travel the nine realms. But the insight brought by their visit to Yggdrasil had opened her eyes to Odin's weaknesses.

"And you always had Father's gift of blunt and hurtful words," he said with a dismissive wave and an exaggerated pout.

Freya frowned. She saw that his poking fun was a vain attempt to mask his hurt feelings. And yet she could not make the effort to assuage him. Freyr's feelings paled against what was at stake. The Aesir had led the charge to tame the world, but under Odin's rule, that great legacy had languished. Nidhogg and Fenrir were the harbingers of more dire threats to come. If she did nothing, Odin's actions would bring about the ruin of the nine realms.

"Stay close to the Aesir," Freya said. "We need to stay in their good graces for as long as possible. Odin will never trust us, but you have a good rapport with Thor and Tyr. I'm counting on you." And with that, she stepped out of the alley and blended into the busy crowds of the merchant square. As a Ljosalfar caravan set off towards the gates, she slipped in with them.

CHAPTER 31: RESTORED

"Thank you, Aric." Freya's voice broke through the cacophony of light and sound. There was a faint ringing in his ears and all of his senses buzzed, raw and overstimulated. That was when he noticed an additional weight on him. The Brisingamen had found its way to his neck. Aric rubbed his eyes, and as the room came back into focus, he saw a familiar silhouette standing over him.

"Freya?" Aric stumbled to his feet and passed through her. Freya remained an apparition as before, and that was somehow comforting to him.

"You have done well to have made it to Asgard, to my chambers, without my aid," she said, looking around and seeing her personal items untouched in the years since her death. "I'm certain I have Freyr to thank for keeping my things safe and secure."

"What… happened?" Aric whispered. "Where did you go?"

"During our last encounter, something about Loki's Ethlivald caused a reaction with the blight and drained my power." Freya passed her hand through the Brisingamen. The luster had faded from it. "It wasn't until you touched my necklace that I had access to enough Mithlivald to restore myself this much."

"There was magic in this?" Aric had no head for this talk of magic and powers. He reached a tentative hand up to the necklace he now wore. This time, the contact elicited no reaction from the cool, smooth metal and gemstones.

"Some of us with the appropriate knowledge and mastery of the energies of Yggdrasil can imbue objects with that power," Freya explained with carefully chosen words as her eyes scrutinized Aric's confused expression.

Aric waved her off. "I don't suppose it matters if I understand any of this."

"All knowledge is important. Though you may not master it or have a direct hand in its worldly applications, that does not mean that you cannot affect it or be affected by it." Freya searched Aric's face for comprehension. "Understanding that there is power in this world and that we are all connected is perhaps all that is required of you," Freya mused aloud.

"Who in Hel's taint are you?"

Aric spun around to see a tall, dark-haired, and golden-skinned figure in the doorway. His head whipped to Freya's apparition and then back to the stranger. Aric was dumbstruck; the resemblance was uncanny. It was as if Freya had a somewhat stronger jawline and narrower hips.

"Freyr!" Freya reacted with an uncharacteristic outburst of emotion. She took several steps towards him but stopped short as he lunged forward.

"How dare you desecrate my sister's chambers!" Freyr was upon Aric. Despite his slight frame, he showed little difficulty grabbing Aric by the neck and lifting him off the floor. "What? A Human?" he snarled. "What is a Human doing in the palace? Are you one of the Einherjar?"

Aric struggled to breathe as he clutched at Freyr's arm.

"Enough!" Freya shouted. A faint burst of light erupted where her hand touched Freyr. He flinched and dropped Aric, then flexed his hand and rubbed at the point of contact while he looked around the room.

Freyr circled to the right and approached with caution. "What are you?"

Aric was coughing and rubbing at his throat as he got back to his feet.

"Speak!" Freyr lunged at him again.

"Freya!" Aric shouted hoarsely as he threw his hands up to shield himself. "What of her?"

"Freya sent me." Aric looked to his left, where Freya was standing. Freyr followed his gaze, but his eyes passed over her head as he swept the room once before glaring at Aric again. "I-I was with her at Yggdrasil—"

"My sister died while returning from Halvard!" Freyr rounded on Aric again. "The Jotnar caught her in a cowardly trap—"

"No," Freya said. "That is to say, I was caught in their trap, but they didn't kill me. I used it as an opportunity to move in secret. Against the Jotnar, Suttungr, and…" Freya paused as she looked from Freyr to Aric and back. "And Odin."

Aric, who had been repeating her words to Freyr, balked at that.

Though his mouth was agape Freyr simply looked at him and nodded. "I was curious about that," he mused aloud. "I suspected her hand in the Jotnar rebellion and was curious when she led the Aesir Army against them."

"I was not lying to you," Freya addressed Aric. "The Great Awakening, the nine realms." She gestured to their current surroundings. "The Aesir have done much to improve the world around us. But after Borr's passing, the Aesir have grown lax and stagnant. The Rite of Vinnask was a joke, a mere formality. At least until Baldur's turn and the rise of Fenrir."

"Hey!" Freyr interrupted. "What are you staring at? Is she… is Freya here?"

"I…" Aric shook his head before turning his attention to Freyr. "Y-yes." Freya waved her arm, and it passed through her brother.

"Well, in a manner of speaking," Aric said as Freyr once again looked around the room. "I can see her and hear her."

"Freya?" Freyr called out before looking around the room. "How could this be?" Freyr glared at Aric and raised his fist. "If you are lying to me—"

"I'm not." Aric stepped forward, uncowed by Freyr's aggression. He saw Freya's hand reach out and he followed suit, touching Freyr's fist. Upon contact, sparks of white, gold, and blue ignited.

"Freya." Freyr stared at the powers of Reginvald, Mithlivald, and Ethlivald coming from the hand of a mere Human. At last he relaxed and then continued in a hushed voice. "Odin is dead. Thor is unstable, though Lady Frigg reigns. What should we do next?"

"The conflict with the Aesir must be set aside." Aric repeated Freya's words as they both looked out the window at the heavy gray clouds. "There are larger problems at hand."

CHAPTER 32: NORTHWARD

"The nine realms are burning, and from the ashes the people are rising up." The Eldjotnar, Surtr, smoothed his auburn fur and gestured to the other leaders at his side. Sigrid and Brokkr at his immediate right wore expressions of dire concern. "But we can only do this together! We have to stand united against those who have held us down and taken advantage of us."

Hertha stood at one side of a divided crowd with Frode on the other. Impossibly, the large Jotnar, Vog, was being held at bay by his diminutive commander. Her bearing and presence dominated the giant who towered over her. Laufrot had her teeth bared, a feral snarl on her lips. Frode struggled but had the help of other Ljosalfar to keep the two apart.

Surtr strode into the gap between the pair. While he looked at each of them in turn, he spoke to everyone. "It was your labor that built the nine realms." He placed his hand upon Vog's shoulder. "Jotnar sweat and blood built Asgard and the wall that separates us from them."

With his other hand on Laufrot's shoulder he connected the squabbling pair. "And it's your lumber that they use to construct the framework for everything. Even the Aesir know to combine our strengths to create a whole greater than its parts." Surtr paused for a moment.

"But they have taken from each of us. We have suffered at their hands." Memories of his mother flooded his mind. Every whipping he had suffered at the hands of the Aesir over the years, every person they had taken from him—all bubbled up and threatened to overwhelm him. After another moment to regain his composure he continued. "My mother spoke up against them. She dared to hold on to the traditions of the Eldjotnar people and for that the Aesir... the Aesir tortured and killed her. They sought to make her an example," his voice cracked but he continued, "an example to scare us into line. They have made examples across the nine realms to scare us into submission. And like them, my mother is an example," he paused as everyone brought up a friend, family, or other loved one who was executed by the Aesir. "They are examples to us to defy the Aesir and fight against them!"

There was a power in his words as they echoed out across the gathered army. In a crowd of over a hundred thousand people, all of them full of nervous energy, only those at the very front could hear his voice, let alone make out his actual words. And yet every one of the people in attendance understood Surtr's message.

He gestured to his left, where Vog and Hertha stood. "Our cousins to the north have shown us the way. They have shown us that the Aesir are not all-powerful, are not unbeatable."

The Jotnar troops nearby eased as the tension slipped away. Hertha removed her hand that had been pressed against Vog's chest and gestured to her soldiers, pointing to those who had fought by her side at the Bifrost Skjaldborg. They led a cheer that whipped everyone into a roar.

"And our might is not confined to the field of battle. Our most recent allies have proven their worth in helping to unlock the secrets of Muspelheim's forges." The Ljosalfar joined in the jubilation. Even Laufrot relaxed and gave a curt nod to Surtr.

"Though the Aesir once used our talents against us, now we have reclaimed our skills and heritage to create a weapon to use against them!" Surtr raised the bright blade above his head, holding it by the sheath. Despite the heavy leather wrapped around it, the runes glowed with the power forged into the metal.

There was a slight pause as Surtr's right hand hovered over the leather-wrapped hilt. Sparks crackled between his flesh and the sword. The Eldjotnar clenched his jaw and steeled himself as he closed his fingers around the handle and drew the weapon, the blade glowing as if it had come fresh from the forge. The runes erupted in an explosion of light that swirled in conflagration and enveloped the radiant metal. The crowd once again burst into a raucous cheer.

Sweat poured from Surtr's brow, and he grimaced with the effort. He quickly slid the blade into the scabbard. It clicked into place, extinguishing the flame and dousing the weapon's blinding glow. Although it had been in contact with his flesh for a mere handful of seconds, he felt as if he had carried the weight of the blade overhead for an entire day. His eyes lingered upon the sheathed sword as he pondered how he would be able to wield it on the field of battle.

With Hertha's aid, Surtr stood tall, regaining his composure despite the fatigue from holding the burning sword. "Asgard is still a week's march away. When they see us, they will see an army like none have witnessed before and quake in their marble towers. They will see our people united, and they will know that their time is over. Let the Aesir fear us then!"

Once more, the army shouted and cheered in affirmation. Amid the jostling, Vog and Laufrot drew close, their eyes locked with intensity. Hertha watched them, ready to jump in. Gyrating bodies moved in and out, threatening to stumble into them and knock one into the other.

After what felt to Hertha like an eternity, the Ljosalfar gave the Jotnar a single, tight-lipped nod. Vog returned the gesture and they parted, joining their respective sides in celebration.

"But for tonight, let us celebrate our accomplishments, our alliance, and each other together!"

All the leaders joined hands in a circle before turning back to the soldiers. They issued orders, and everyone jumped to action as they made camp for the night and broke out in a cacophony of music and songs from their varied regions.

CHAPTER 33: DECISIONS

"Yggdrasil is dying." Aric's voice cracked as he felt the weight of the Aesir and Vanir lords' collective gaze upon him. He stood alone in the great vastness of the august hall. With a quick glance to his right, Aric felt at least a little comfort seeing Freya beside him, though he knew no one else could. Her expression was stern, though it softened just a little as her eyes settled on her brother.

Even after Aric's account to him of all that had happened, Freyr remained skeptical. He had escorted Aric to the audience chamber in complete silence and now sat upon the dais beside Heimdall, Ydun, Thor, Tyr, Sif, and Brunhilda, with Frigg at their center.

"And what would a Human know of the World Tree?" Thor shouted with a slight slur.

Aric thought he detected a little swaying in his posture but decided to ignore it. He raised his staff, presenting it to the council. "I traveled to Yggdrasil's valley at the heart of Niflheim alongside Brunhilda." He nodded towards the valkyrie, who nodded back. "With us were both the Jotnar Skrymir and Human Skuld who, unbeknownst to us, were Loki and Freya in disguise."

"What?!" Thor roared as he stood, sending his chair toppling behind him.

A flurry of chatter erupted among the council members.

"Silence." Though Frigg did not shout, her stern voice caused the chatter to cease. She gave Aric a wave. "Continue."

Thor looked like he had more to say, but Frigg did not give him a second glance. With a great deal of reluctance, he righted his chair and sat back down.

"After our battle with Nidhogg, we were betrayed by Loki. They captured Brunhilda and left me and Freya for dead."

"Brunhilda told us all of that," Thor interrupted again. Frigg shot him a glance and he said no more.

"What you don't know is that after Freya revealed her identity to me and restored my life, I had a moment with Yggdrasil. I believe the spirit of Njord was speaking to me. Not in literal words, but in gestures. A part of its root came off in my hands when I freed Nidhogg—"

"You did that?" Thor erupted, his voice accusatory and his visage a portrait of unbridled rage. "That beast killed dozens of Aesir—"

"But it killed more Jotnar, didn't it?" Aric countered with his own indignation. "It routed their attack. From all reports, Baldur and the Jotnar had destroyed your wall and were poised to overrun your defenders and sack Asgard. I will forever carry the burden of the lives lost due to my actions—actions at the time I thought were necessary to protect the stability of the nine realms and the rule of Aesir law." He paused as he considered where he had stood mere weeks ago as an ally amid those set on tearing the reign of the Aesir asunder. "Despite my misgivings and my loss of faith, I had a little hope that you were the lesser of two evils. It didn't hurt that I had just been betrayed by a Jotnar I had counted as an ally."

"A Jotnar with whom you are somehow allied with again," Thor said with incredulity. "He has already betrayed everyone here at least once. He killed my brother, Baldur. Twice!"

"But if I hadn't released that dragon," Aric continued, "you and all of Asgard would have been lost. And there would have been no one with the knowledge and the power to heal Yggdrasil. I saw the corrupted creatures trapped beneath the World Tree's roots. I saw them pressing forward, pushing against the limits of their prison. The monsters that have been ravaging the nine realms thus far are those same animals. Until now, only the smaller creatures have escaped, but there are bigger and far more deadly threats lurking in the darkness below."

Aric had a haunted look on his face as he recalled the sight. He could often see the writhing shadows and the gleaming pinpricks of eyes penetrating through the black depths in his dreams… or perhaps his nightmares.

"Aric?" Brunhilda prompted when the silence had stretched for too long.

His head snapped up and he looked through her before his eyes came back into focus. Aric shook his head and addressed Frigg and the rest of the council. "Freya appears to me in my dreams and in waking visions." He gestured to his right, though he knew they saw nothing but empty space. "She tells me that Yggdrasil needs your help. Freya can feel her father's energy fading from the World Tree."

Aric raised the gnarled staff as he spoke. There was a faint shimmer that played across its bark. "Njord's spirit is at its breaking point. We need to fight our way through the blight and restore the seal. Freya has had visions—she has seen Yggdrasil splinter apart and break open. We must act now, or the monsters of old will return, and everyone in the nine realms will die."

—

Frigg stared at the Human with great intensity. Any other being would have wilted beneath her icy gaze, but this one stood firm and his unwavering eyes met hers. Odin had spoken to her often of his seidr visions while at Yggdrasil, recovering from his fight with Nidhogg. All of his machinations had been intended to prevent the cataclysm he called Ragnarok. But those actions had resulted in Baldur's deaths, first at Yggdrasil and then later as Suttungr, both at the hands of Loki; the return of both Nidhogg and Fenrir; the sundering of the Bifrost Skjaldborg; and then Odin's own death. Frigg weighed this new information with macabre curiosity. Should she hold to Odin's path and continue the campaign against the Jotnar, or should she pivot and act upon what she now knew?

Although her eyes remained fixed upon Aric, she could feel the other Aesir looking to her, awaiting her decision. Even while Odin lived, she had guided and directed the practical governance of the nine realms. Her husband had been clever and wily, and yet the day-to-day administration of a vast kingdom had lain beyond his ken.

Her own attempts at breaking through the veil of seidr magic had failed. And yet seeing the single-minded obsession that it had cursed Odin with made her even more thankful that she had been unsuccessful.

"You cannot possibly be considering this," Thor bellowed, breaking the silence. "Baldur is dead. Odin is dead. The Bifrost Skjaldborg is in ruins again. We must remain focused upon the defense of Asgard and on our real enemies. Not some story concocted by a Human claiming visions of Fr—"

"The defense of the nine realms is ever at the forefront of my mind." Frigg's head snapped in his direction, silencing him with her glare. "And yes, Loki did kill Baldur, but it was not the uprising that killed Lord Odin."

Thor shrank back at that comment. All in attendance, except for Aric, had witnessed the tragic death of the previous lord of the nine realms. Although the resurrected Fenrir had Odin in its slavering maw, it had been Thor who had swung the final blow that had killed the blighted vargr and Odin.

—

Brunhilda watched Thor's outburst with interest. He slammed his fist down onto the armrest, and an almost impotent burst of golden light flashed upon impact. She looked down at her own hands and concentrated. Brunhilda's brow furrowed, and the sounds of the conversation faded into a dull ringing in her ears. Sweat beaded across her forehead and her jaw muscles twitched as her teeth ground together. After a long moment, her hands flashed. Yet it was only a dim, shimmering aura.

"He's right!" Brunhilda exclaimed as she spun on her heel. The metal of her blade sang out when she drew the sword and pointed it at Frigg. Guards positioned all around the room reacted in an instant and leapt between the valkyrie and the queen, their spears leveled at Brunhilda.

Thor was up out of his seat, his hand on the hunting knife on his belt. "How dare you—"

"No, no." She realized her mistake and brought the weapon close to her body, pointing the blade up. "Look." Brunhilda focused again and barely elicited a flickering glow in the sword.

The guards twitched half a step forward at the possible threat.

"He speaks the truth. Yggdrasil is fading." She pointed with her left hand at the guards' spears, the golden glow flickering, stark and obvious even in the glowing, firelit hall. "It's not just the blight corrupting our weapons and armor. Our connection with Reginvald and Mithlivald has grown weaker of late. We've all been feeling it. Our armory is crowded with carts overflowing with useless metal scraps of equipment on which the runes and enchantments have completely failed."

The imperial guards were the most disciplined of all Aesir soldiers, and though they did not flinch or lose composure at the valkyrie's words, for a brief moment their eyes flitted from the perceived threat of Brunhilda to their own weapons.

"Even all of the Mithlivald runes that our enchanters carved into the Bifrost Skjaldborg failed to withstand the most recent blight assault," she continued. "Our entire defensive strategy without Mjolnir relied on the Skjaldborg's ability to repel any attack. We can see that plan was flawed. It was only by sheer fortune that this occurred while Thor and the army were close enough to return. Our losses would have been far worse if this had happened even one day later. And would we have been able to drive off Garmr at all? That helhound is still out there."

—

To Aric, it felt as if Brunhilda's words were echoing around the chambers for an eternity as he looked to all of the Aesir, trying to get any hint of emotion or reaction. Aside from the guards who remained in their alert position, all eyes were on Queen Frigg, whose eyes bore down on the valkyrie with an intensity that he had never witnessed before.

"Your point is well stated," Frigg said at long last. She rose to her full height, and Aric could almost feel the power radiating out from her. "Yggdrasil is the priority," she said. "I shall make preparations immediately to travel to Niflheim and bond with the World Tree." She stood and addressed Thor. "As my successor—"

"No!" Thor said as he stood. His voice came out loud and raspy. Aric could feel the emotion within. "I have lost my brother and my father. Surely there is someone else—"

"No one remains who has more power with Mithlivald than I." Frigg's voice was powerful and commanding.

Thor was silenced immediately, and Aric noticed that Freyr flinched and looked away. He saw the Vanir's lips twitch but could not read his expression.

"As my successor," Frigg continued and placed a gentle yet firm hand on Thor's shoulder. She guided him to the throne and pushed him into the seat. "The duties and responsibilities of defending and governing the nine realms now rest upon my son's capable shoulders." Thor opened his mouth once more as if to object, but his mother continued speaking. "He bears his father's power"—she laid a hand upon Mjolnir and then kissed him on the forehead—"and my wisdom. May he use both to return peace and prosperity to all creatures, great and small, who reside upon Ymir."

"Please, Mother," Thor tried to interject, but Frigg would not be deterred.

"I wish that we had more time for a proper coronation." She removed the golden circlet that she wore and placed it on her son's head. Its delicate features were nearly lost among the tangles of flaming red locks crowning his head. "All hail Thor, the new king of the Aesir, ruler of the nine realms, and defender of the people."

"All hail King Thor!" the room sounded in unison. All of the Aesir and Vanir in attendance bowed. And at last the guards turned away from Brunhilda and bowed. Only the Aric and Freya remained standing upright. The pair exchanged looks that ranged from relief to concern.

CHAPTER 34: CONSEQUENCES

"Bear witness, Eldjotnar!" Freyr stood atop a makeshift dais in the great hall of Aldrnari. To his left, Nanna was suspended by her wrists. They were bound with iron manacles connected by heavy chains to tall poles on either side of the platform. Even through the fur there was visible bruising and swelling. Dried blood crusted around her nose and from a split lower lip.

"Asgard provides for each and every one of you. You have all that you require to live and work." Freyr paced across the front edge of the platform, like he was chastising a work crew for underperforming. "Your service to us and to the nine realms is the sole purpose of your existence. The harvests and distribution of goods throughout the nine realms are my dominion. I have studied and determined exactly what is required by every subject of the realm. But here you are taking more!" He became visibly angry and raised his voice. "When these institutions are attacked, I am attacked. When they are stolen from, you are stealing from me!"

The assembled crowd of Eldjotnar shifted and surged with nervous tension. Twelve Aesir soldiers stood in front of the dais; the light from braziers around the room glinted against their armor and weapons. Beyond that light, there was an additional glow that came from the runes etched into the metal.

"This is what becomes of those who steal from me!" Freyr snapped his fingers, and Hillevi unsheathed a long knife. She approached and stripped the tunic from Nanna's torso. The blade flared to life with the power of Reginvald.

In the shadows of the back right corner, Aska looked on, restraining the teenaged Surtr. The muscles of his jaw twitched with his teeth clenched. There was a deep and guttural growl coming from deep in his core. Aska embraced Surtr in something resembling a hug and also a grappling hold. She could feel a slight relaxation of his muscles as she squeezed with all of the strength and compassion that she could muster.

"There's nothing that we can do for her now," Aska whispered in his ear, her voice soothing. If everyone's eyes had not been locked to the scene on the dais, they might have seen a faint shimmer coming from her arms as she held Surtr. "All we can do is bear witness to her sacrifice and then continue our fight. Her death will not be in vain."

With her arms still around Surtr, Aska turned her head in line with his and they both stared. He held his eyes open, though tears streamed from his face as his mother's screams of agony echoed throughout the great hall. Then, all at once, there was the wet sound of a blade cutting into flesh, followed by a terrible silence. The air shimmered as the temperature within the chamber spiked. In unison, the guards brandished their weapons in the ready position, although they knew they did not have to do anything more.

Aska heard the muffled scream that Surtr unleashed into her shoulder. His body shook with grief and rage, and still she held him tight. Eldjotnar nearby gave sympathetic looks. Some were tense, their fists balled up tight. Others slouched, heads and shoulders drooping as they turned away from Surtr and from the dais and began to leave.

As the Aesir dispersed the crowd, Aska led Surtr away, making certain that he did not linger, that they appeared to be mere bystanders. She knew the Aesir would be looking for others who had been involved in the smuggling and skimming of materials. They knew that the Aesir's display here today would drive the conspirators to halt their activities. At least for a short while. Or if not that, then they surely hoped to draw out allies and sympathizers they could apprehend and interrogate.

"Come on." Aska led the way. "I know just what you need."

―

An eruption of sparks showered down on Aska as Surtr slammed his hammer repeatedly on the flattened iron ingot. She was grateful for the heavy leather apron that deflected most of them. If Surtr or any other person were paying attention, they might notice the white flashes of light where the bigger, hotter sparks hit her skin. Fortunately for her, that reaction was a passive effect as she had to use all of her might and attention to hold on to the steel. Both of her hands grasped the tongs and vibrated as each impact traveled through them and threatened to shake them loose. Smithing not only required strength, it required skill and control to tease out the best properties of the material and get a usable result. This thing, however, was a wide blob of indeterminate shape. But Surtr continued to pound at it with abandon.

With one final strike, the hammer bounced off the iron and flew out of Surtr's hand. Aska dodged as it struck the wall behind her and clattered to the floor. She let out a sigh of relief and tossed the hunk of metal into the corner atop a pile of four other misshapen pieces.

"Feeling better?" she asked as the exhausted Eldjotnar slumped over the anvil.

Surtr huffed and puffed as he fought to catch his breath. She waited patiently while she massaged her hands, her fingers almost locked into curled claws. His arms moved, slowly and heavily, as if they and not the iron ingots had been the ones beaten out of shape. When he moved his hands, the anvil glowed where they had been.

"No." He walked over to where the hammer lay on the ground.

"Grief is a long road with no end," she said as he bent down to pick it up. "It starts out rough, as if it's made from big, unhewn boulders. At first, it feels insurmountable. But if we can just find a way to start, to move forward, we get used to them, we get used to the bumps. It becomes a part of our journey. Though even with time, it will never again be smooth."

Their eyes met as he stood up, hammer in hand. They regarded each other for a long moment before he lifted his empty hand and pointed at the stack of fresh iron ingots on the far side of the room. "Just get me another one."

With a sigh and slight shake of her head, she grabbed an ingot and placed it into the furnace. Surtr stretched out his right arm and swung it in a wide, circular arc as he prepared for another round.

CHAPTER 35: THE VIGRID PLAINS

"So that's Asgard?" Surtr spat as he crested the final rise at the southern edge of the Vigrid Plains. The gathered host of the Alliance, more than one hundred thousand strong, stretched out in long columns behind Surtr. Though they had nearly ten thousand head of aurochs, everyone, even the leaders, had made the considerable journey on foot. Even three leagues away, the marble spires shimmered in the gray light of the cloud-covered sky. The roiling dense fog accompanying their army blurred the horizon behind them and hid their full number from observation.

"You can see it?" Sigrid asked, squinting.

"I could feel the arrogance and ostentation of the Aesir from Alfheim," Surtr snarled.

"Well, they've seen us," Hertha said as a low and powerful rumble of sound washed past the assembled horde.

"There was never a chance of sneaking up to the Bifrost with an army of this size," said Frode as he wiped the sweat from his brow and joined the others. "Even with this mist."

"Shall we wager if they send an envoy to parley with us?" Brokkr directed the question to Sindri on his right.

"I wouldn't take any odds on that." Sindri replied as he eyed his fellow Dokkalfar's proffered hand. "I'm certain that they are marshaling their forces as we speak, readying their attack as soon as we are within range."

"I should think that we gave them reason enough to warrant caution the last time we clashed," Hertha said, a low growl rising from her throat.

"All the more reason they will strike before we can dig in," Sigrid cautioned. "We have marched hundreds of leagues, while they have had weeks to repair the Skjaldborg and make all manner of preparations."

"And yet for all of their preparations, they will not have anticipated this." Surtr's hand patted the scabbard at his hip. Even through the wood and leather the exposed hilt flared at the contact.

"Let us hope it is enough," Eik said. "Without a piece of Yggdrasil, it will draw its power from you."

"I am prepared for that," Surtr replied. "Their reign is at an end. One way or another, I will never return to a life under their boot."

Heimdall trumpeted a single, resounding note from the mighty warhorn, Gjallarhorn. Although the Bifrost Skjaldborg had not been fully restored after Garmr's attack, its parapets bristled with troops and weapons. A makeshift gate protected the opening, though it was unclear how well it would hold under duress. From the central platform above, Heimdall spotted the approaching army from the south. They were two days' march away, having just emerged from the vast forests of Alfheim.

Thor, Freyr, Sif, and Frigg emerged atop the stairs to join Heimdall and Tyr, who had been on command duty. Aric and Brunhilda were just behind them. The rest of the pantheon arrived shortly thereafter, with Loki and Jorunn bound and escorted by armed guards bringing up the rear.

"It looks as if fortune has provided an opportunity for us," Freyr declared from the central battlement. "The Jotnar and their alliance have delivered themselves to us. We can crush them now and be done with this. Then we can march to Yggdrasil together, without any further distractions."

"No!" Aric pleaded. "This doesn't have to come to violence. Let's use this chance to come to a peaceful resolution."

"It is far too late for that," Thor said as a crackle of energy flowed along his right arm down through the great warhammer, Mjolnir. "Freyr is right. We must take this opportunity the fates have given to us and end this opposition and restore order."

"I can talk to them, stand them down," Loki called out. "If you'll only allow me to—"

"Do you take me for a fool?" Thor roared. "I would not trust you to hold my drinking horn. You have done nothing but lie and deceive the Aesir ever since Baldur came upon you and your sister all of those years ago. You may very well be the harbinger of doom itself."

"No, I—"

"Your kind has done nothing but stand in the way of civilization and progress since the beginning," Freyr rejoined. "It is time for you and yours to be swept aside so that the nine realms may be reforged into the paradise it was always meant to be." He pulled his sword from its sheath and stepped towards Loki. The blade flashed gold before the glow extinguished.

Thor and Brunhilda regarded the blade, now dull and ordinary. The valkyrie drew her own weapon. The golden hilt had lost its luster and the steel was dim in the uncanny twilight. Metal clinked and scraped as the disciplined Aesir line shifted with unease. Thor, Freyr, and Brunhilda looked up and down the battlement; the aura that always shone from their spelled weapons and armor had vanished.

Thor hefted Mjolnir in his hands. He concentrated upon the weapon as his eyes scanned from the haft to the head. The runes flared before they softened to a low, pulsing shimmer.

"Perhaps this is a different sort of opportunity," Frigg said, her eyes upon the dull warhammer. "They won't know that our power is waning. If we parley with them, we can come out of this with the most favorable terms."

"They are a mob," Thor interjected. "Even the Einherjar are more than a match for these untrained 'soldiers.'"

"Without the additional advantages of Reginvald and Mithlivald, our superior tactics and fighting skills will be taxed against their numbers," Sif chimed in. "Even the Skjaldborg will do little to stop a full assault in its current state."

"Every Aesir soldier and every Human Einherjar would gladly take up this challenge to prove their mettle," Freyr countered. "I have trained the Humans, and though they are fragile, they are fierce and have worked hard. They will not let us down—"

"And we appreciate them," Frigg cut him off. She was breathing heavily having rushed up to the ramparts. Heimdall's signal had come just as she was about to depart for Yggdrasil. "But even if we emerged victorious, the losses in a conventional battle of this scale would be staggering. And with the blighted creatures nearby, we would be left with no recourse, no defense against them. I will not win against the Alliance only to fall to wild beasts."

"You would have us debase ourselves and bargain with them?" Thor spat.

"Not you." Frigg placed a hand upon her son's shoulder. "Mjolnir must stay here to defend Asgard." Turning to face Freyr, she looked him in the eyes. "You shall represent us."

"Me?" he said, a hint of surprise in his voice. "I have no interest in speaking to them as equals or negotiating terms of peace."

"You won't be issuing any terms." Frigg waved dismissively. "You have no authority in such matters. It will be your responsibility to receive their envoy and escort them to us."

"But—"

"You were about to leave and had abdicated the leadership of the nine realms to me when they arrived," Thor interjected. "And the military decisions have always been my dominion."

Frigg gave her son a look of deep contemplation. A slight grin showed at the edges of her lips as she inclined her head to him. "As you say, my king.

And what is your command?"

All eyes fell upon the new Aesir king. Thor gripped Mjolnir's haft a little tighter and his eyes turned down, towards the familiar, reassuring lump of spelled iron. The runes flickered again and his brow furrowed. Before the silence had stretched on for too long, Thor's head snapped up and he pointed to Freyr.

"Sif will accompany you with a retinue of valkyries to ensure a sufficient show of force," he said, his voice strong, with no hint of hesitation. "I will receive their envoy and hear their grievances and demands. They are not to be harmed." Thor emphasized those last words to the Vanir prince. While his voice still echoed in the still, cold air, he waved with his hand to send Freyr and Sif on their way, leaving no room for any rebuttal.

Sif bowed and hurried to the stairs to assign the valkyries. Freyr hesitated for a moment, lips parted as if to say something. But under Frigg's withering glare, he closed his mouth and followed Sif.

CHAPTER 36: INTERLUDE

A shower of leaves cascaded down from the broad, expansive canopy of the World Tree. Brown and dead, the once verdant valley had rotted beneath the three years of dense clouds above. From the deep roots to the soaring boughs, the massive structure shuddered. The fissure at the base was wider than twenty men abreast even as it continued to pull apart and splinter the trunk. Scores of dark, corrupted animals raced out as a powerful presence surged up from the depths. Creatures poured out in all directions as the caldera floor filled and darkened with writhing, shadowy shapes.

In the first few months after Nidhogg's escape, this had all begun as a slow trickle. Tentative creatures covered in dark tendrils squeezed their way through the splintered trunk and roots of Yggdrasil. As the crack grew, so did the exodus. This mindless sea of blackness undulated as animals of every variety climbed over and under each other, searching for an outlet. As the inky stampede buffeted against the sheer cliffs, some of the creatures were pushed up into the hidden entrance. In this way, a steady stream of corrupted animals seeped up and out onto the tundra above. It was the only practical egress from the secluded caldera. Despite the pressure from the myriad creatures, this narrow opening limited the flow of corruption out into the rest of the nine realms.

But then the air grew still. Even the whipping winds in Niflheim above quieted. The squirming sea of shadows tensed as all heads turned to face the tree; anything with the semblance of ears perked up. In the next instant, the lull shattered as a shock wave crashed through the frozen tundra. Snow, ice, rock, and other debris were pushed by the high pressure front, which sent all of that material tumbling down into Yggdrasil's valley.

The initial din was the loudest and most powerful, but then the great canopy of the World Tree swayed and crashed to the ground. Rolling aftershocks followed, and the ground undulated in waves like the sea. The tremors grew in intensity until the cliff face in the direction of Asgard splintered. Once solid and unbreakable, the sheer granite cliffs calved great sheets of rock, throwing up clouds of stone and ice in a thunderous cacophony. Crevasses radiated out from that section, down towards the center.

The collapse opened the floodgates. No longer limited by the narrow passage, the tainted beasts rushed out onto the cold, windswept tundra of Niflheim in a mighty sea of dark, inky waves. Despite lacking a driving, central intelligence, they felt the pull of the life and conflict far away. Almost as one, they pulsed and surged south, towards Asgard.

CHAPTER 37: NEGOTIATIONS

"They have the worst timing," Aric sighed to Freya. They were still standing atop the Bifrost Skjaldborg. There was a commotion in the courtyard as the Aesir Army and Einherjar marshaled. To either side of them, the on-duty archers were supplemented by scores of reserve archers. Human assistants carried bundles of arrows and lit braziers. The gates had opened to let out Freyr and Sif and closed again. Their task was to receive the contingent from the Alliance, but the Aesir were always prepared for battle.

"Perhaps they will accept the truce, maybe even join the task to restore Yggdrasil," Jorunn responded.

Aric's eyes came into focus on her, standing just to the left of Freya. His eyebrows were furrowed in confusion until he realized that she was talking to him. "They did not come to sue for peace or to take prisoners. They have come to tear down the order of the nine realms and begin anew," he said.

"So," Jorunn hemmed before letting out a nervous chuckle, "surrender is out of the question?"

Freya shook her head. "They came here to die."

Aric gave her a quizzical look.

"They cannot know that Yggdrasil's powers have waned for the Aesir," Freya responded. "Even if they succeeded and forged a weapon to rival Mjolnir in the Rikrsmidja, they would know that victory was slim. Very few of them would survive such a battle as this."

"Their plan was always to attack," Aric said, shaking his head. "Surtr will not be denied. I don't know what they did to him, but he was ready to fight the Aesir, blight or no."

Freya looked out at the advancing army. Aric could not read her expression but thought she exhibited an air of anticipation. Was she looking forward to this battle?

"I never realized..." Jorunn paused as she watched the legions of soldiers continue to spill out onto the Vigrid Plains. "There are so many of them. How can we hope to reason with them, to hold back that much rage?"

"We can't," Thor said as he laid a hand upon Aric's shoulder and waved to three Aesir guards nearby. "And now your presence is no longer required."

"No, wait!" Aric exclaimed as they took him and Jorunn back into custody.

—

"Perhaps we can get them to help," Sif said to Freyr. "Although I doubt they would survive in Niflheim." The two Aesir rode out at the head of an honor guard of two dozen soldiers. Asgard's standard flapped in the wind, carried by Bodil, the lead valkyrie in attendance, riding at Sif's flank.

"We will not leave these savages at Asgard's doorstep," Freyr spat. "With or without Mithlivald and Reginvald, we should slaughter them all. The Jotnar killed my sister." His voice quavered with barely controlled rage. "They are here, now. Fortune favors us, and we would be fools to not take advantage of this."

"Frigg was very clear with her edict," Sif said, shaking her head.

"She has allowed herself to be swayed by that Human... that simpleton." He scowled thinking about Aric. "He desecrated Freya's personal chambers. I was fooled by the energy that he must have picked up from her things. His presence was an obvious ploy to get us to drop our guard and put us in a state of confusion when this army arrived. And it worked."

"The swarms of blighted beasts contributed more to the current state of the Skjaldborg," Sif observed with a calming tone.

Freyr gave Sif a long, hard look. He turned and looked ahead. "I will do as my queen commands."

—

The Allied Army continued to march closer than the Aesir were comfortable with. Valkyries and the regular army held themselves at rigid attention. As the invading army continued to advance, there came the subtle sounds of armor and weapons clattering and scraping. Despite their training and tutelage, the Human Einherjar shifted in place.

"We should make camp here and lay down our defenses up ahead there." Hertha pointed to a slight rise on the Vigrid Plains. Though that was where Baldur had laid his own siege only a year ago, all evidence of their camp had been cleared away by the Aesir. Conventional tactics dictated an army attacking a fortified position to dig in and prepare for a prolonged siege, build fortifications, and cut off supply lines. With Asgard's precarious position, separated from the continent of Ymir save for the Bifrost Bridge, that tactic was even more sound.

Surtr continued to walk just ahead and to her right. He gave no indication that he had seen her gesture or even heard her speak. His brows were furrowed and his jaws clenched tight as his eyes locked on to the Bifrost Skjaldborg and the gleaming, marble spires beyond.

Just as Hertha was about to repeat herself, Surtr spoke. "This is not that kind of war. There will be no quarter, no retreat, no surrender. After what the Jotnar did, what we do now, there is no going back. We shall never cow to their rule. If we lose, they will have to kill us all. If we win, it will only be by breaking them." He turned his gaze to her. "All of them."

"There's no way to do that," Hertha said in shock. "Even with the Skjaldborg in its state of disrepair, they have no reason to leave its protection. And without Suttungr's siege engines, we have no way to breach it. The envoy coming towards us is an unnecessary courtesy. They have no reason to sue for peace."

"We shall give them a reason." Surtr's hand patted the scabbard at his hip. His movement was deliberate and careful, avoiding touching any part of the sword itself.

Freyr and Sif came to a stop about fifty feet away from the motley entourage. Hertha looked at her companions. Eldjotnar, Dokkalfar, Ljosalfar, and Human standing together was certainly a rare sight. Her step faltered as all but Surtr came to a halt twenty paces from the Aesir.

"We come with an invitation." Freyr held up a hand, an expression of boredom on his face, his right hand resting on the hilt of his sword. "Queen Frigg has—"

Surtr's face was unmasked rage, and with a roar he drew his sword; its light flared a crimson red as he swung it in a tight arc. The Eldjotnar's practiced motion was fluid and blindingly fast.

Hertha was frozen in shock, but Freyr drew his sword deftly to block the strike—perhaps he had been expecting it, or perhaps he was just that good. The blade flashed white when it cleared the scabbard, and yet the moment before contact, the light sputtered and extinguished.

As the red arc continued, it passed through the Vanir's sword as if nothing was there. A gout of bright white blood erupted from Freyr's neck as his head and severed blade tumbled to the ground.

Sif had dropped into a guard stance, her sword drawn. The golden glow flickered; confusion flashed across her face for a mere moment before her combat instincts kicked in. Surtr's return swing cut through her sword, but she had stepped back enough to keep her own head. The valkyries brandished their spears and charged forward.

"Fall back!" Sif yelled and threw her arm up to call off her soldiers. Two valkyries fell to Surtr's burning blade before they could stop. As they turned to Asgard, Thor's voice could be heard from up on high. While his words were indistinct, the volley of arrows arcing across the sky made clear the order given.

Hertha shook herself into action and shouted an order. "Issithar!"

The front line of the Allied Army consisted of her most skilled Ethlivald users, and they lobbed a flurry of ice that intercepted and deflected the incoming missiles. The army broke into a run, with issithar continuing to provide cover from the volleys of arrows.

Gjallarhorn blared, echoing through the crisp, cold air. The gates of the Bifrost Skjaldborg flew open and the Aesir Army poured forth, followed closely by the Einherjar. Nearly the entirety of the able-bodied Aesir and Humans rushed out of the gates.

—

Back in the prison cells Aric, Jorunn, Loki, Lifthrasir, and Lif huddled together as stone chips and dust rained down from the ceiling. Metal clattered against stone above them as armored soldiers ran by to their ready stations and responded to shouted orders.

"It would seem that your little trip has been all for naught," Loki sneered from the corner.

"What?" Aric saw Freya pitch forward and fall to her knees.

Loki started at Aric's reaction and took a defensive posture. Aric ignored the Jotnar and rushed over to the kneeling apparition. Freya clutched at her chest, and for a moment he wondered if she had stopped breathing—then he wondered if she breathed at all in her current form.

"Are you alright?" he asked Freya, reaching out to her.

Suddenly he recoiled. He had touched her, or at least felt something. She was not completely solid, but there was resistance to her form. That had never happened before. He glanced at his hand, then returned his attention to Freya. Lif was next to her, and Aric realized that her eyes were directed straight at Freya. Aric furrowed his brow and turned to look at the others. Loki, Jorunn, and Lifthrasir were standing along the far wall in various states of shock and surprise.

"You can see her?" Aric asked.

"F-Freya?" Loki stammered.

"We see… something," Jorunn said.

"I-I'm alright," Freya whispered as she rose to her feet. Aric stood as well, leaning forward as if to offer assistance. Lif pointed to Aric's neck, and he realized that the Brisingamen was glowing with white light.

Metal rang against metal as the two armies crashed into each other. Flesh and bone tore and cracked at the ferocity of the conflict. Any hopes of a peaceful settlement had evaporated the moment Surtr beheaded Freyr. Even nature itself was resigned to the violence as lightning arced across the sky and thunder boomed above the already deafening cacophony.

The Einherjar pushed their way to the front of the lines. Their leader, Freyr, had fallen without them. They surprised even the full-blooded Aesir and Vanir with their ferocity. In the wan light under the thick blanket of clouds, their armor cast them as a wave of light. In the past, it would have been a brilliant wall of gold. Now, however, this army was a flickering and inconsistent beacon on the field of battle. Emboldened by Freyr's fall and Sif's retreat, the Allied Army surged forward.

Amid the ebb and flow of the fighting, a small pocket of calm opened up with Hertha and Surtr in the middle. "Are you well?" she shouted over the din of battle all around them.

Surtr was down on one knee, breathing hard. Sweat beaded all across the short auburn fur, covering his face and body in a dim, red light. "I-I will be fine." He released his grasp of the sword and the metal reverted to a cold, gray steel.

Hertha rushed to pick up the sword and sheathed it. Once it was secured, she helped Surtr to his feet. He took a deep breath as he regarded Freyr's decapitated corpse. At some point, as his soldiers surged ahead of him, the Vanir's head had gotten trampled or kicked away and was no longer anywhere to be seen.

"Freyr is dead," he said to himself, the words inaudible against the clamor of battle around him. For so long, Surtr had held Freyr as the focus of his angst and ire. And now that he was dead, the Eldjotnar expected a sense of satisfaction… or at least relief. His attention lingered on the body for a long moment, oblivious to anything else. Memories of Muspelheim and his mother flooded his head. A voice gradually pierced his fugue, calling his name with ever increasing urgency. All of a sudden, the riotous bedlam of battle filled all of his senses and he realized that Hertha was shaking him, shouting at him.

"Are you just going to stand there?" she yelled as recognition came to his eyes.

"What?" Surtr shook his head and blinked. Hertha pressed the sheathed sword to his chest. They exchanged looks and he took hold of it. His tears blended with sweat and he wiped his face.

"Come on," Hertha said as she put his arm across her shoulder and helped

Surtr to his feet. "It's far too early in this battle to sit out. I know that your vengeance may be satisfied with Freyr's death," she said with a smirk, "but there are still plenty of Aesir left to kill."

"Don't... worry about... me," Surtr said between panting breaths. "I still have more to give yet." He pulled away from Hertha and stood unsupported, though his legs trembled slightly. "Thor, Frigg, and every other Aesir *hrodi* will feel the touch of the burning blade before this day is over."

Hertha gave a snort and chuckle as she watched him heft his hatchets and totter two steps to the left as Brokkr and Sindri led a contingent of Dokkalfar past. "I certainly wouldn't bet against you."

The pair gave her a hearty guffaw and wink. "I'd give us a fifty-fifty chance of living out the day," Brokkr called out.

"Not even I would bet against us," Sindri bellowed and punched his partner's shoulder. "The Aesir already regret underestimating us. Today is the last day of the Age of the Aesir!"

Hertha gave a guttural shout in reply and broke into a run amid the Dokkalfar battalion. Surtr was left standing alone, staring after them, hands clutching his weapons, the sword in its sheath at his hip, his breathing evening out.

CHAPTER 38: ESCAPE INTO THE CRUCIBLE

"Come on, we can't just sit here and do nothing." Loki grabbed Aric by the hand and helped him up to his feet. The cell was secure and the metal was scried with powerful runes. All of the guards had left to join the fighting above, leaving this motley crew alone. Aric looked at the still kneeling Freya. After a moment, she recovered and stood, returning his look.

"The more we fight, the weaker Yggdrasil gets." Freya shook her head. "We have to put an end to this immediately. The World Tree, the nine realms need us." She stood and shimmered, for a brief moment visible to everyone. "All of us."

"And what would you suggest we do about that?" Loki looked from the barred door to his hands. While the Reginvald and Mithlivald power imbued into the metal appeared to fluctuate in intensity, so did the blue glow of Ethlivald in Loki's hands.

Aric followed Freya's gaze to the gnarled staff in his hands. "I suppose that is my responsibility."

Jorunn, Loki, and Lifthrasir wore expressions of incredulity as Aric swung the wooden stick back. Only Lif took the precaution to shield her eyes. Upon impact, a bright flash of light and energy erupted, blinding the others. Even Aric, who had shut his eyes, was rubbing them as ghost images were seared onto his retinas. But the door was now open, and the group hurried out once they had all recovered.

Without the benefit of their enchantments, the Einherjar and Aesir faced a pitched battle against the overwhelming numbers of the Allied Army. Despite their more rigorous training, the defenders of Asgard could not hold back the tide. Yet even against such daunting odds, the Einherjar were possessed of a singular goal: to wipe out the enemy that had slain Freyr in cold blood and threatened their very way of life.

"Shore up the left!" Hege called out the faltering line to the Einherjar under her command. The Humans from Asgard filled in the gaps left by Aesir who had fallen, coming up against many of their fellow Humans on the other side. Up and down the Vigrid Plains, a flickering golden light came from the mass of soldiers in the east. Together their front was a neat and orderly system that saw injured troops pulled to the rear and replaced before the enemy could break through.

But the enemies kept coming. Hege looked back to the Bifrost Skjaldborg and saw a broad expanse of churned, frozen turf between that impressive wall and the rear of their army. The reserves of the Allied Army were tenfold greater than the Aesir's. Hege knew that this war of attrition would not favor them. In her moment of distraction, a spear breached a gap in the shield wall and punched into her left shoulder. It was her shield arm, and the injury caused her to drop it. As had been done many times over this day, a reserve Aesir soldier stepped up to close the break. Hege was pulled back to the rear.

Once she was with the fostra, she was able to take a breath and look around. More and more she had become accustomed to seeing these aid stations packed with casualties. Early in her service as an Einherjar, she had been amazed to see the healers' Mithlivald in action. Wounds big and small were mended in mere moments and the soldiers were sent back into battle immediately. But as the fimbulvinter stretched on, Hege had witnessed the vaunted powers of her gods wither and fade. Her faith remained steadfast, and yet she could not deny a nagging doubt taking hold in the back of her mind. As she looked around, she could see that even their pristine arms and armor had lost their luster.

Here, the soldiers had been stripped and their equipment tossed into scattered piles. They would not be sent back into battle anytime soon. Movement from her peripheral vision drew her notice, and Hege's eyes fixed upon those piles. The residual blight that infected nearly every Aesir weapon and piece of armor writhed and pulsed as the fighting grew to a fever pitch. Although she could not see the front line from her current vantage point, what she did see shocked her. As Allied soldiers engaged with tainted Aesir soldiers, the corruption spread to them. Bodies crashed together as the armies pushed forward, each side straining to push the other back. In these close quarters, armor, weapons, and soldiers on both sides became tainted with the inky blight. The intensity of the fighting increased as the corruption spread through the melee.

"Find Thor! Find Frigg!" Aric shouted above the commotion. A sea of soldiers and citizens rushed towards the Bifrost Skjaldborg while fostra carried cloth for bandages and cots and stretchers to the forward aid station. Freya had led the way with a short detour to the Asgardian armory. Now, bedecked with Einherjar weapons and armor, Aric, Loki, Jorunn, Lif, and Lifthrasir raced through West Asgard virtually unnoticed.

"There!" Freya called out to Aric. From the ground level they could see Heimdall up on the rampart shouting and relaying orders. Intermittent blasts of smaller warhorns communicated troop formations and movements to the field of battle below. "Heimdall relays orders from the general to the field commanders. Thor will be in the thick of battle, leaving Sif or Lady Frigg directing the army. Either may be reasoned with."

"Loki, Jorunn, and I will try to reach Queen Frigg there." Aric pointed to the rampart before pointing to Lif and Lifthrasir. "You two, find Brunhilda or Sigrid out in the field. Maybe you can convince one or the other to stand down their battalions."

"I should go find Hertha or Surtr," Loki said. "They will listen to me."

"If you go out there, every Aesir who sees you will cut you down before you get ten yards in," Aric countered. "We'll be lucky if the guards even allow us to go up to the rampart, much less approach Queen Frigg."

"Fair point," Loki conceded. "But perhaps it would be easier if I looked like this." There was a brief shimmer of blue and gold energy across his fur. Amid the chaos of soldiers rushing forward and civilians rushing back to shelters, no one else seemed to notice the startling transformation. For a moment, his fur was gone and he looked like a shining, golden Aesir. As the rippling illusion was about to reach Loki's feet, the façade flickered and the glamour shattered in a dim burst of light.

Aric was startled to see this feat, even in failure. Freya waved a hand in front of his face to snap him out of his amazement. She pointed to his hand, and he understood her meaning immediately. He held out the wooden staff to Loki. "Try this."

The Jotnar eyed the gnarled piece of wood; its unmistakable hue and texture spoke to its origin, the World Tree Yggdrasil. He flexed his fingers into a fist before opening them up and reaching for the staff but stopped, inches away. The fur all over his body bristled and energy crackled from the end and arced to the outstretched finger. Loki pulled back with a sharp gasp.

Before he could say anything, Lif grabbed his wrist and placed it directly on the staff. The air hummed with power and Loki's body once again shimmered. Lif pulled her hand away, though a lingering glow stayed with her. No one appeared to notice that a golden Aesir now stood where there used to be a blue-furred Jotnar. Still holding on to the staff, the Aesir version of Loki reached out to Jorunn and touched her, bathing her form in a mixture of gold and white light until she took on the appearance of a Vanir woman. Though they were clad in Einherjar armor, no one would give them a second look out on the field of battle.

Freya paused for a moment, then gave an approving look. "Now go!"

CHAPTER 39: DUELING PAIRS

Sif cut through the ranks of the Allied Army with deadly arcs of her flashing blade. Even though the enchantments on her weapon and armor had become unreliable, her physical skill was without peer and she dispatched with ease all who stood against her.

Because Surtr had not pursued Sif and her valkyries, they quickly regrouped with the Aesir Army. Now, flanked on both sides by a dozen valkyries and backed by the weight of Asgard's defenders, Sif rallied back to the front lines.

"Aesir!" Sif shouted above the roar of the battlefield. "Surtr is mine! Kill the rest." Jotnar and Eldjotnar made up the majority of Allied troops at this part of the front. Sif's keen eyes noted that their armor was sturdy if plain and the way that they held their weapons indicated that many of these Jotnar were experienced, likely veterans of the Battle of the Bifrost Skjaldborg. Despite the tactical advantage they would have had against the untested Humans, Ljosalfar, and Dokkalfar, Sif would not debase herself by attacking races so far beneath the skills of her and her valkyries.

And yet even these seasoned Jotnar fighters proved little distraction as the Aesir commander searched the crowd for the red glow of the blazing sword or the smug visage of that cowardly Eldjotnar, Surtr. Only the lowliest of vermin would attack an opponent during parley.

She replayed that moment in her mind while casually blocking, parrying, and striking at one opponent after another. How had his blade worked so perfectly and powerfully while the rest of their weapons failed? She knew that the Eldjotnar retained a deep connection with Yggdrasil's Ethlivald energies, just like their cousins, the Jotnar. But she had never seen it manifest in that manner before.

She and Freyr had been caught unprepared, and he had suffered for it. She would honor his memory and learn from his sacrifice. Freyr's blade had lost its Mithlivald, but it was unclear if even that power could have absorbed or dispelled Surtr's attack. Sif would have to stay agile, ever moving and slipping under the Eldjotnar's swings as she would not be able to rely on blocking or even parrying the fiery sword for fear of it cleaving her weapon and leaving her unarmed.

"Sif!" Bodil shouted, shaking the commander out of her reverie.

While preoccupied with these myriad thoughts, the Aesir had failed to notice the diminutive Jotnar female who had charged through the crowd and thrust her sword from below Sif's eyeline. With a deft flick of the wrist, she flared her blade and turned the lethal Jotnar attack into a glancing blow. All of the other Jotnar and Eldjotnar were as tall or taller than the Aesir and Vanir defending Asgard, and in Sif's distracted state of mind, she had certainly not expected an attack to come from below.

—

Even as the maelstrom of battle tore up the once tranquil Vigrid Plains, Sif and Hertha carved out a small circle of death around them. Soldiers from either side were quickly dispatched or forced away from these formidable women. As the fighting swelled, the blight continued to spread through the combatants. Its growth was exponential as tainted soldiers infected others and those infected still more.

Hertha stayed low and threw out two feints before lunging forward with an overhead slash. Although Sif had been keeping a low guard stance against the shorter Jotnar, her sword was already in a high guard to parry.

"You fight like Baldur." Sif did not often waste time and energy bantering on the battlefield. Her actions were quick and efficient, but this opponent was proving to be more tenacious than expected. "Did you know? Or did *Suttungr* deceive you as well?" Sif's riposte came with no preamble, and Hertha only just bobbed beneath the blade.

"You Aesir are always playing your little games," Hertha hissed as she unleashed a flurry of thrusting strikes. "With no care given to the ordinary lives affected."

These attacks lacked power; their purpose was to keep Sif on the defensive. However, she had anticipated the tactic and stepped in, taking a glancing blow while executing her own attack. As Hertha's blade slid off Sif's armor, the Aesir's sword struck the Jotnar's left shoulder. If the Reginvald enchantments and Sif's channeling had been working, Hertha would have lost her arm and likely her life. But the well-crafted armor from Muspelheim turned the Aesir blade, which cleaved off only a chunk of the pauldron.

"These are no games, little one. Your death will be very real," Sif snapped.

Hertha bounded two steps back and cut down an Einherjar soldier who had thought to take advantage of the opportunity. "All of this blood is on your hands!" She turned back to face Sif. As they addressed each other, Hertha ran her fingers over the clean cut on her pauldron and then eyed the minor scratch in the Aesir woman's armor. She let out a guttural cry and closed the distance in half a dozen strides. This time, each stroke was considered, deliberate, and executed with her full strength and intention. Sif's sword was almost knocked from her grip as she pivoted to block the first strike.

Sif had to withdraw a short distance with her weight on her back foot. Instead of acting like a feral, cornered animal unleashing another flurry of rushed and weak swipes, this Jotnar fought back with more control and power. Even with this unexpected turn, the Aesir maintained her composure and recognized the underlying techniques of this Jotnar's fighting style.

As the next exchange began, Sif pictured Baldur attacking instead of this Jotnar. Visualizing his fighting style, she predicted the most likely attack pattern and, instead of dodging, she stepped into the line of the attack—but she had ensured that her protected shoulder took the brunt of the lethal thrust while sending her own blade into a gap in the side of Hertha's armor.

As Sif pulled her sword free from Hertha with a wet squelch and stood tall, she pulled out the Jotnar's blade, lodged in her own armor.

—

Thor had leapt down the last flight of steps from the Bifrost Skjaldborg after witnessing Freyr's death. If he could have relied upon Mithlivald, he would have jumped from the rampart the hundred feet down to the ground and healed himself. But this would have to do. The delay meant that nearly the entirety of the Aesir Army and the Einherjar had flooded out of the gates and now stood between him and the cowardly Eldjotnar who had ignored the parley and attacked. Though he knew that his duty was to command the army and see to the defense of Asgard, his rage had taken over and he knew that only he, wielding Mjolnir, could defeat the enchanted, burning blade that seemed somehow unaffected by the waning connection to Yggdrasil's magics.

Forcing his way through, he pushed aside and even knocked down his own subordinates. The Aesir Army surged against the unruly mob that was the Allied Army. If he had not been so intent upon locating the Eldjotnar with the magic weapon, he would have been astonished by the lack of discipline demonstrated by his soldiers. The fighting was mere moments from devolving into an all-out brawl instead of the orderly shield wall that they practiced and drilled into the muscle memory of everyone daily. Instead, he only saw the undulating mass of bodies pushing in from the southwest.

His eyes swept the ruckus from one side to the other as he searched for the one tall, auburn Eldjotnar among all of the other races bedecked in armor flowing around him. In a rage, Thor unleashed a fraction of Mjolnir's power at the mob of enemies in front of him. Heads and limbs were flattened by the shock wave despite the sturdy armor they all wore. And yet they closed the gap without losing any ground, leaving him no clear path forward.

With a roar of frustration, he hefted the warhammer overhead and brought it down with a thunderous crash of Reginvald energy. This time, the concussive wave threw back dozens of bodies, and the arcs of electricity lingered in the air and played across all those caught in the blast radius, friend and foe alike.

As the fallen writhed in agony from Mjolnir's lingering effects, Thor spotted the Eldjotnar he was looking for. His fiery sword was hidden, sheathed, but his size and stature set him apart even from the other large Eldjotnar nearby. Thor started to walk and then broke into a run. His focus was singular, set on his target. There was an arrow stuck in his pauldron that he had not even felt. Allied soldiers struck out at him as he passed. But like his father before him, Thor would not be lured astray from his goal. His sole purpose on this field of battle was the utter destruction of the enemies of Asgard.

—

Surtr rubbed his eyes, blinking away the lingering flash of light and power. The ground-shaking explosion had rocked him back to full awareness. He had seen his fellow Eldjotnar flung off their feet all around him.

And then Surtr saw him. A great mane of flame-red braids, on his head and down his tangled beard, framed the visage across the field. He saw not only Odin's son; he saw all of the Vanir and all of the Aesir. He saw all that they represented, all that had kept him and his people subjugated for so long. This battle would not be over until all of it came crashing down. This day it had started with Freyr, and Thor would be next to fall.

Surtr's muscles felt half-dead; the energy sapped from his body and limbs made him long to lay down and curl up into a ball. And yet seeing all of the progress their army was making against the Aesir redoubled his resolve. Under his breath he swore that each and every one of them would fall to his blade.

—

Surtr and Thor charged at each other across the Vigrid Plains, shrugging off the inconsequential barbs of arrows and crossbow bolts that happened to find them. Golden white light and energy pulsed from the rune-etched iron head of Mjolnir. A blaze of red erupted opposite as Surtr drew his sword.

Both combatants shouted, their words unintelligible in the din. But the power and emotion of their voices drew the attention of those on both sides. The air itself crackled as the two powerful weapons drew close. Surtr swung for Thor's head, but the Aesir prince was prepared and ducked under it. His battle-hardened skills were more than a match for the novice Eldjotnar. However, compromised by rage and overconfidence, he swung wildly in a heavy, overhead arc. Surtr sidestepped it with ease, but Mjolnir's impact knocked the Eldjotnar off his feet. With the warhammer fully charged with all the power that he could imbue, Thor struck.

Surtr had enough presence of mind to hold on to the fiery sword and blocked, supporting the flat of the blade against his left hand. The contact caused the sword to flare brighter than it had ever done before, and the center of the Vigrid Plains erupted in a concussive blast of gold and red that swept through all of the combatants. None were left standing.

CHAPTER 40: ENEMY MINE, YOURS, OURS

From the broken rampart of the Bifrost Skjaldborg, Frigg regained her footing and looked over the battlements, her hands resting on the precision-cut stone. Even far above the battle and three hundred yards away from the epicenter of the explosion, the Asgardian defenders had been hit by the shock wave. Loose stone blocks began to fall from their positions along the edges where Garmr had attacked. Frigg concentrated, trying to call forth Mithlivald to hold the structure together. Try as she might, the flare of white light failed to manifest.

"Everyone, off!" Frigg shouted as she felt the vibrations continuing throughout the stone. "Sound the evacuation!" she shouted to Heimdall.

A series of sharp blasts from the warhorn jolted the Aesir soldiers to attention, and they hopped into action as they had been so thoroughly trained. The departure was quick and orderly, with Frigg and Heimdall ensuring everyone was safe before they brought up the rear amid crumbling masonry. Moments after they alighted from the stairs, the rest of the defensive wall came crashing down.

Frigg cursed and sheathed her Reginvald-infused weapons after they failed to cut through the debris. "Clear the rubble!" The entire wall had collapsed and a giant pile of shattered stones separated the defenders within Asgard from the battlefield.

"Clear the way!" Frigg ordered all within the courtyard. The army and all of the Einherjar were already fully deployed to the Vigrid Plains. But now the archers were no longer in a position to rain down arrows and support the defense.

Suddenly, an ethereal, almost spectral howl cut through the quiet, cold air. That howl was answered by another, and then another, and then dozens more.

"Hurry!" All able-bodied people increased their pace and set up brigade lines to remove the stones faster.

—

"No!" Hertha sat up as the howls were joined. Although disoriented, she easily recognized vargr calls and could even detect the rough vibrato signaling corrupted vargr. Those sounds were burned into her brain. Memories of her parents flashed through her mind. Looking up, Hertha saw that the cloud cover pulsed and grew thicker, darkening everything even as the lingering light and energy from the explosion dissipated.

"Hertha!" An Aesir soldier had his hands on her covering a blood-soaked patch of her torso. She could not be sure but she thought that they had been glowing white. Nothing about this scene made sense. An Aesir soldier had somehow crossed the front line and was calling her by name. Hertha squeezed her eyes shut to clear the disorientation. She rubbed her eyes and the figure came into greater focus. It was, indeed, an Aesir among the Allied forces.

"Who are you?" Hertha challenged as she pushed the stranger away and scrambled to her feet. Her voice was firm, with no lingering effects from the mortal wound. She reached for her sword, but her scabbard was empty. Several allied soldiers who had recovered from the blast seemed to just realize that there were enemies in their midst. They hurried to their feet and raised their weapons, taking up flanking, aggressive positions to defend their leader.

"It's just me—Loki," he answered and dropped his disguise in a flash of golden light. Hertha and the others emitted an audible gasp at the reveal.

"What are you…? How did you…? You're still alive?" Hertha stammered, unsure of which question she was asking and which she actually wanted answered first.

"Now's not the time for that," said a second Aesir soldier, approaching quickly, her arms outstretched as if she might try to give Hertha a hug.

Hertha grabbed a sword from a nearby soldier and pointed it at this newcomer, who stopped short with the blade tip inches from her throat.

"Wait, wait, wait." Loki stepped in; at his touch, the Aesir soldier's glamour vanished and Jorunn swept aside Hertha's sword and embraced her stunned sister in a crushing hug.

"Enough." Hertha regained her composure and pushed herself away from Jorunn's grasp. "Are we all dead? Is this Hel?" The Jotnar's mind raced with all the improbable things that had transpired in a handful of moments.

"No," Jorunn said. She placed her hands upon her sister's shoulders. Their weight and touch were reassuring and allowed Hertha the merest glimmer of hope that this reunion was real.

"We're all very much alive." Loki placed his own hand on her. "But we won't be if we just stand around here."

"Yes, now's not the time for reunions." Hertha pointed to the flattened field of soldiers on both sides. "Now is our chance to end the Aesir, once and for all."

"No!" Jorunn held her sister back by the shoulder and pointed towards the tree line. "Now is the time to put aside our differences and face the true nightmare upon us."

"Thor, the Aesir." Hertha spotted the downed figure of the Aesir prince. She could see him moving, still alive. "We have no better chance than now to finish this—"

The ear-splitting howl cut through the frosted air again. This time, it was clear and unobstructed as a flood of corrupted animals burst out of the northern woods. It was a blanket of undulating, inky figures blending into each other, racing into the massed armies.

Hertha rushed around to help up others who were still recovering. They were all disoriented and physically shaken; those at the center of the Vigrid Plains were the worst off. Brokkr, Sindri, and Eik were nearby and quick to recover and join Hertha, Loki, and Jorunn.

"In the north!" Eik called out as dark shapes began to emerge from the northern tree line.

Hertha's head snapped to see the stampeding horde. To her eyes, even the sky in that direction dimmed and the trees themselves looked to take on the same blight that was infecting the animals. The horizon disappeared into a black, shimmering haze. Even with no perceivable wind, the branches were rustling, inky tendrils having replaced the leaves.

CHAPTER 41: HEL COMES TO ASGARD

"Thor! Sire!" He could not be certain of how long the voice had been calling out. The ringing in his ears had finally died out enough for the sounds to cut through in intelligible words—although they were distant, like they were coming through a long tunnel.

As his vision cleared and came into focus, he recognized the valkyrie, Bodil, pulling him up into a sitting position. "I'm alright." Thor waved her off. But as he struggled to his feet, she pulled his arm over her shoulder. With that additional support, they both stood and he surveyed their decimated surroundings.

The Vigrid Plains looked like a poorly tilled field. The frozen ground was mixed with the snow and ice as the soldiers on both sides had dug in, trying to hold their ground or push their line into enemy territory. Shards of ice from issithar or frozen from the blood of Jotnar littered the ground. And just as it seemed the static charge and smell of charred air began to fade, the pressure shifted as a stormfront came out of nowhere. A wind picked up and the clouds themselves began to unleash the beginnings of a full blizzard. Hail and snow rolled in from the north, biting into the exposed flesh of all present.

"Where is he?" Thor faltered with his first few steps and had to lean upon the long haft of his warhammer. "Where's that cursed Eldjotnar?"

"There's no time for that, sire." Bodil tried to force his attention to the Vinwood. A wave of pure darkness was pouring out from the blackened, writhing trees, blotting out the ever-darkening sky.

"Shit," Thor muttered as he gave the marauding stampede a long, hard look. "We have to get back to the Bifrost Skjaldborg, where we can defend against—"

Bodil pointed to the pile of rubble that used to be the shield wall.

"Hel's taint." At first he did not quite process the possibility that everyone who had been on that wall could now be dead. Then, he exclaimed, "Mother!"

"We don't know what's happened," Bodil responded while still supporting him. "We can hear voices, but it's unclear how bad the damage is."

Thor took two steps back towards Asgard. Bodil held on to his arm and stopped him. "Sire, there's no time," she whispered. "There will be time to mourn later…"

"If we're still alive." With one last searching gaze across the slowly rising sea of bodies all around, he spat and hefted Mjolnir above his head. "Aesir, to me!" Thor's voice was strained and raspy, though it still thundered above the noise.

Frantic movement radiated out around the field as soldiers scrambled to their feet and helped their compatriots. Tensions flared at the front lines as troops on both sides eyed each other with extreme caution even as the coming onslaught drew ever closer.

"Attack!" Surtr roared. His unsteady gait was visible, though the ferocity of his ire burned bright in his eyes, trained on Thor.

Though the command was bellowed in Jotunmal, the meaning was clear to Thor and the Aesir. "Shields up! North and west!" His voice was sharp and the Aesir Army, drilled and trained as they were, closed ranks, ready for the impact to come.

But in that brief interlude between preparation and action, a figure emerged in the gap between the two armies, a pillar of ice erupting from the ground where he had struck it with the staff. Two smaller figures joined him.

"Wait!" Aric shouted, his gaze alternating between Surtr and Thor. Lif and Lifthrasir brandished their own weapons, each one facing opposite directions. "The real threat is there. That blight is going to destroy everything!" He pointed, the dark tide moments from impact. "Fight it with us!"

Surtr broke through the Allied lines and swung his sword at Aric, shouting, "The tyranny of the Aesir ends today!"

Freya's warning came just in time, and Aric brought the staff up to block. The impact reverberated through his thin frame, but the wood held against the flaming metal. Although surprised by the deflection, Surtr followed up with another strike, knocking Aric off his feet.

As he raised the sword again, the feral growls, snarls, and roars reached a crescendo and the animals hit the Aesir spears and shields on the north flank.

For all of their training and discipline, the line had no chance of holding against the deluge. Without Reginvald or Mithlivald, the beasts tore through the Aesir line and continued on through to the Allied Army.

As the clouds grew even more dense, the pale disc of the sun was blotted out, casting the field into darkness. A rolling wave of violence covered the ground. The occasional bursts of golden, white, or red light were the only points of illumination as Thor, Surtr, and Aric fought against the stampede.

Surtr's blade cut through swaths of beasts, raining entrails and rotted animal parts on everyone in proximity. With each strike of the gnarled piece of Yggdrasil, Aric dispelled the corruption from groups of beasts. Inky tendrils were flung away amid the burst of light and soldiers from both sides finished off the exposed animals. Mjolnir brought a bolt of lightning down from the sky when Thor attacked. The concussive impact threw the creatures back, several at a time. Fingers of electricity lingered and danced across each convulsing body.

"We have to work together!" Aric shouted as he tried to get the attention of Surtr and Thor. "We'll be overwhelmed if we keep fighting alone."

"You have to show them!" Freya called out to Aric. "They need to see your cooperation for themselves."

Aric nodded and worked his way towards Thor. Each step was fraught with peril as snapping jaws, tearing claws, and grasping tendrils struck at the Humans. Lif and Lifthrasir stayed close, finishing off animals cleansed of the blight. The ground was littered with corpses and viscera, further hampering their traversal.

When at last they reached Thor, his breathing was ragged and shallow. He turned on the Humans as they neared, almost striking them before checking his swing.

"I would tell you to flee to safety," Thor chuckled, before his expression soured, looking at the carnage surrounding them. "But there is no safe haven left, is there?"

"No," Aric replied. "But all is not lost."

Aric followed Freya's gesture as she reached out and placed a hand on Thor's shoulder. Upon contact, the staff burned bright and the surge in energy showed by the sudden glow in the Aesir's eyes. Thor took in a deep breath and stood taller. As another wave of blighted creatures rushed forward, he raised Mjolnir high overhead and brought it down with a thunderous explosion. A maelstrom of lightning erupted from the clouds above and struck in a spiraling vortex of electricity.

Both Aric and Thor collapsed to their knees. Lif ran to support Aric while Lifthrasir attended to Thor. The Aesir was quick to recover and regarded the Humans with a modicum of respect. From the corner of his eye, he caught torchlight coming from the east. Asgard was illuminated in firelight and a pathway had been cleared through the wreckage of the Skjaldborg. Thor assessed the state of the battle. The sound strategy would be to retreat east, across the Bifrost Bridge and defend from there as Odin had done long ago.

"Retrea—"

Before he could finish the command, an enormous shadow emerged from the chasm between the towering finger of rock that was Asgard and the rest of the continent. It shattered the Bifrost Bridge, and its long, lithe body slammed down across the western district of Asgard. Debris and bodies were crushed beneath its bulk while so many others were knocked off to plunge down to the thundering sea hundreds of feet below. As it thrashed and pulled more of itself up onto land, the site of the Bifrost Skjaldborg was consumed by the corruption pouring off the monster.

"Mother!" Thor cried out. He reached out his hand as if he might be able to reach across the hundreds of yards and somehow find Frigg and pull her to safety. The realization of what he was seeing slowly dawned on him, breaking through to the memories, long gone.

"Jormungandr," Thor whispered. The serpent had not been seen since the time before the Great Awakening. It had taken all of their united forces just to push the monster beneath Yggdrasil. Even with everyone working together, they had barely been able to trap it. Killing it had never been a possibility.

Covered in shadows, the already hulking serpent was even larger now. It rose up from the ruined Bifrost Bridge and towered a hundred feet above the Vigrid Plains. Yet despite its imposing height, the bulk of Jormungandr's body still lay submerged beneath the waters of the sea. Every figure froze in place as they eyed the awesome creature, not daring to move as the glowing eyes of this apex predator surveyed the Vigrid Plains.

A baleful howl broke the silence as the helhound, Garmr, returned. Once again, the gigantic hound was covered in a writhing mass of shadowy tendrils that seemed far more active and dense than before. All of the other infected animals surged with renewed fervor and redoubled their attack from the north and west.

As if they were coordinating, Jormungandr moved at the same time. The serpent struck with impossible speed for its size. Each snap of its jaws devoured three people whole. Its indiscriminate attacks scooped up people and beasts in equal measure.

The war was a distant memory as this became a fight for survival. Jotnar and Aesir stood side-by-side and closed ranks. Enemies mere moments ago now faced this existential threat together.

CHAPTER 42: TELLING FRIENDS FROM FOES

"Einherjar! Skjaldborg formation, north!" Brunhilda shouted, her gaze focused on the dark mass emerging from the tree line. The officer to her right brought a spiraled warhorn to her lips and trumpeted a series of notes. Aesir and Einherjar troops snapped into action with the speed and precision that weeks of grueling training had instilled in them. They redeployed with shields and spears locked together, facing outward, ignoring the Allied Army soldiers in their midst.

"Don't turn your back to me!" Hertha roared. Her own lines were a mass of confusion as they looked from the Aesir Army to the new threats. Those who had not encountered blighted creatures on the travels to Muspelheim feared these monstrosities more than the Aesir.

"*Stop!*" Jorunn grabbed Hertha's arm as she was about to charge into the distracted enemy ranks. *"Our true enemy is there."* She pointed as the giant dark shape of a hound emerged from the woods and let out another ear-piercing howl. *"Sister"*—Jorunn looked into Hertha's eyes—*"the Aesir might not have helped us, but it was the vargr who killed our parents and destroyed our home. We don't have to work together with the Aesir, but these creatures are the real danger."*

Hertha gave her a look of disgust and pulled free of her grasp. *"How could my own sister side with the Aesir? Do you even know that you're wearing the armor and uniform of the enemy?"*

"*Please.*" Jorunn reached out again. *"Mother would—"*

A blob of shadows in the approximate shape of a vargr bowled into Jorunn just then.

"*No!*" Hertha had a sudden flood of memories of the night their parents had died during an attack by slavering vargr. With a snarl curling her lips, she banished those images and leapt into action. She charged headlong, blade first, into the beast. Her momentum pushed the sword point deep into the corrupted animal and together they toppled off Jorunn, who quickly rolled over and scrambled to her feet.

Although they had rolled apart upon impact with the ground, inky strands stretched from the beast and clung to Hertha's weapon and armor. She swung the blade in wide arcs, attempting to sever her connection to the corruption. In that moment of distraction, the vargr attacked. It did not jump as much as the shadows burst forth like a dark fountain.

"*Hertha!*" Jorunn called out from several yards away.

Before the tide hit her, a wall of ice sprouted up from the trampled ground in front of the Jotnar. The shadows crashed with a trembling thud, but the ice held and Hertha looked around. From three yards to her right Loki stood, his hand out as if supporting the barrier from there.

As the shadows began to withdraw, Hertha noticed that the animal had not moved. The shadows had shot out and were now returning to its host. Then, with a sudden flash of steel, a Human Einherjar exploited the opportunity and beheaded the vargr before the blight could regroup. The body and corruption fell at the same time. And though the corpse was still, the inky blob thrashed as it sought out a new host. As it reached out towards Jorunn, the ice wall crashed down on top of it, burying it in place.

"Good job." Hertha nodded to Loki and the Human female.

"No time for that," she replied. "That's only one of thousands." Her hand shot out in an arc, and the Jotnar at last acknowledged the full scope of the tidal wave of shadows rushing rapidly towards them.

Hertha nodded and grabbed one of her soldiers who was backing away towards the south. "Stand your ground!" She shook the soldier until he snapped out of his fearful fugue. "Defense, left flank!" Her voice boomed and her troops jumped at the order. As those nearby fell into formation, the rest of the battalion followed suit. They were a far cry from the ordered and unbroken line of the Aesir, but they presented a formidable wall of their own.

―

If the blighted creatures were intimidated by the armies facing them, they did not show it. The flood of corrupted monsters crashed into the lines with a sickening crunch. Flesh tore, armor rent, and spears snapped. Inhuman growls and other terrible, animalistic sounds filled the air as the beasts tore through the armies. Without the Reginvald and Mithlivald energies reinforcing their weapons and armor, the defenders were at a significant disadvantage. Many of the animals simply vaulted over the front lines, catching those in the fourth and fifth ranks by surprise, sowing utter chaos among the less prepared Allied Army. And though many others rose to the challenge of these attacks, they were far less prepared to stand up to Garmr leaping into the fray.

While the threat imposed by the giant helhound sent most soldiers fleeing, the valkyries spread throughout the field of battle saw it as a worthy challenge, and they all congregated upon the terrible beast. Garmr stood over twelve feet tall at the shoulder, and its jaws could enclose a person's entire torso. The writhing tentacles of inky black gave it an even more threatening and sinister silhouette and still the valkyries encircled it, holding it at bay and preventing it from further decimating the armies. Even without their enchantments, the women warriors proved their mettle, working in unison, thrusting with their spears and weaving in and out, keeping the hound off balance and struggling to keep track of an individual target.

And yet their efforts did little to actually injure the great beast as the shadowy tentacles blocked or parried every strike. The stalemate broke when the blighted creature lunged forward with its snapping maw while the tentacles lashed out behind. Bodil pushed Brunhilda out of the way as she was snatched by the tendrils instead. Brunhilda crashed into the ground, losing her grip on her spear.

"Brunhilda!" Aric called out. He rushed forward, even as she recovered on her own. Garmr spun to face them and flung Bodil into the surging animal horde. The hound leapt forward, its gaping jaws closing in on Brunhilda.

She thrust forward on instinct, but her blade found nothing as a bright flash caused her to flinch. When her eyes adjusted, she saw that Aric had struck Garmr in its left shoulder with his staff.

"Now!" Aric shouted. His hit had cleared the blight away from the point of impact.

All of the valkyries who were in position reacted in a flash and attacked together. While it was not an opening for a lethal strike, the women hobbled Garmr's left foreleg before the blight recovered and the monster forced the valkyries back.

"Its head!" Brunhilda called out to Aric.

Even as the hound hobbled, the corruption appeared to flow and concentrate on the wounded area, allowing Garmr to pivot and move with most of its full range of motion and speed. The beast's keen eyes focused on Aric and the staff in his hands. It spun and whipped its tail at the surprised Human.

Caught unaware, Aric was knocked into the crowd and lost hold of the staff. Garmr kept it in sight and lunged for it, but its teeth closed on nothing but trampled ice and mud as the staff was yanked away by Lif. She dodged the gnashing teeth and looked for a way to get the staff back to Aric.

"Here!" Loki shouted to her.

With a moment's hesitation, she eyed the Jotnar but threw it just as Garmr struck again. She took a glancing blow and landed hard on the ground, the breath knocked from her lungs. Lifthrasir was at her side immediately, ready to defend her. His effort was appreciated though unneeded as the monster's attention had followed the staff.

"No!" Both Aric and Freya yelled as Loki caught the staff in his hand and squared up against the helhound. They both remembered what had happened the last time Loki had tried to use Ethlivald against a corrupted animal.

Loki remembered as well, and he struck the ground instead of a direct attack; pillars of ice erupted from the ground, impaling Garmr from multiple sides, lifting it off of the ground. "Here!" Loki yelled to Aric as he tossed it back to the Human.

Aric bobbled the catch but held on in the end. He rushed forward with Brunhilda close behind. Using his entire weight, he swung at the creature's head. In a shower of ice, Garmr broke free and snatched the staff in its mouth. Brunhilda struck at its jaws, but it was still protected by the blight, and with a flick of its head it knocked Aric and Brunhilda aside.

With a violent, full-bodied shake, the hound completely broke loose of the icy trap. Sparks of light and energy popped and burst as Garmr ground down on the staff in its teeth and the wood began to splinter. A spear struck the beast in the eye, and it dropped the staff as it recoiled. Hertha and Jorunn had joined the fight. Their triumphant entry was short-lived as the inky tendrils coiled around the spear and dislodged it, then covered the injury with a denser layer of writhing shadows.

In a flash, Loki dove beneath Garmr and grabbed the staff. Again he struck the ground, and an enormous frozen spike sprouted up directly below the hound. Half-blind and still reeling from the previous attack, Garmr was caught by surprise. The ice pierced its belly, lifting the creature twelve feet off the ground. And yet the blight still protected Garmr as it twisted and spun free of the ice shard. It landed deftly on its feet and snapped its jaws at Loki.

The Jotnar raised a sheath of ice around himself just in time. But Garmr's jaws flexed, and cracks radiated all along the ice. He threw the staff out to Aric a moment before the ice shattered and the teeth snapped shut.

With a flash of steel, Brunhilda leapt high and thrust her blade point down onto the hound's head. Although its enchantments were gone, the blow was powerful enough that Garmr flinched and pulled away, the ice-encased Loki still in its mouth. Brunhilda vaulted through the air as she was thrown off. When she landed, Aric was already on the offensive, swinging with the staff as Garmr bobbed and weaved, keeping its prize secure in its clenched teeth. The ichor thinned out over the injured eye, revealing the healed orb, just in time for the hound to flinch back again as Brunhilda and the others closed in.

"Here!" With the brief opening, Aric threw the staff to Brunhilda, who caught it on the run. A smile curled her lips as her sword flared with warm, golden light. From the sharp point all the way down to the golden swans on the pommel, the weapon shone with Reginvald energy. She charged the helhound, weapon ablaze, and cut into the beast's flesh, parting the blight and leaving a bright, glowing gash in its right flank. Garmr relinquished its prey and leapt back to where the blighted creatures pressed against the unified defenders, safe from the empowered spear.

"*Get up!*" Hertha reached down, pulling hard on Loki's arm and freeing him from the shattered ice debris that had nearly been his coffin. He winced in pain, his other arm clutched at his ribs.

"*Thanks,*" Loki eked out through gritted teeth.

Brunhilda pressed the attack, the golden blade flaring in the dim, gloomy light of the cloud-ridden sky. Amid the dark battlefield, that light served as a beacon to hearten the people as they fought. To the blighted animals, however, it also served as a point to focus their attack. They swarmed to Garmr's side and attacked with no regard for their individual safety. Like moths to a flame, they rushed forward, drawn to the power that Brunhilda channeled through her weapon.

The other defenders in close proximity were surprised as the runes on their own weapons and armor came back to life. Reginvald, Mithlivald, and even Ethlivald seemed available once again as she continued to tap into the Yggdrasil connection of the staff. Jotnar followed Loki's example and created defensive obstacles from ice, Eldjotnar lashed out at the beasts with flaming blades, and the Aesir and Vanir fought with renewed fervor, resplendent in the glow of their spelled regalia.

As the fighting continued to escalate around Brunhilda, all of that power flowing through her began to overwhelm her senses. Everything around her glowed in her vision and her skin prickled, the small hairs on her arms and neck standing on end, and there was a constant buzzing sound in her ears. Her perception of the battle was heightened, and all of the combatants appeared to move in slow motion. She bobbed and weaved, dodging and then cutting at the beasts in a spiraling dance of death. But the light continued to intensify and surge to the point of near blinding. Suddenly she was aware of a Jotnar hurtling towards her. It was Loki, and he was charging straight at her.

He was moving impossibly fast, and there seemed to be a ghost image of him, an illusory version that confused her. Brunhilda's mental alarms were blaring and she swung at him. But her weapon passed right through that image of him, and the real Loki tackled her to the ground and tore the staff from her hands.

Brunhilda's vision went dark all at once. Flashes of light burst here and there as the fighting continued and Yggdrasil's power continued to flow around her. Every part of her body felt leaden and stiff without the energy of the World Tree. But her muscle memory and combat instincts kicked in as she scrambled to her feet, sword at the ready. Brunhilda spun around, ready to fight Loki. Instead, she was just in time to see Garmr's jaws snap shut around him.

Brunhilda's mind reeled. Loki had saved her life. How had she not seen that huge, lumbering canine attack? She shook her head; this was no time to overthink. After that brief moment of hesitation, her battle-hardened instincts kicked in and she lunged at the beast. The runes on her sword flared gold, hotter and brighter than before.

Once again, Garmr retreated back behind the lines. But Brunhilda was driven and pressed her advantage. As she dove into the sea of blighted creatures, her blazing weapon cut them down like a farmer reaping a field of wheat. Following her path, Aesir, Jotnar, Humans, and the rest flooded behind her and pushed back against the inundating stampede.

Aric could only run after Brunhilda. He had picked up a weapon from a fallen soldier, but even with Freya's aid he could do little. With Jorunn, Lif, and Lifthrasir close by, he took it upon himself to protect them as he had been unable to do for Una and Dagmaer all those years ago.

However, these were no helpless babes fighting against hunger and want. They had learned and proven themselves to be capable warriors and survivors. Together they joined the second wave that pushed the corrupted animals back. The army had generated a burst of violence and energy, replacing the fear of the darkness with the catharsis of their renewed empowerment. But as the people attacked and waded into the miasma of the blight, the corruption reacted to the frenzy and infected the weapons and armor with each block and hit.

"Stay close!" Aric cautioned as the people rushed headlong, spreading the line thin. His head turned from side to side as he attempted to keep track of his friends. "Jorunn!"

Her normal, restrained demeanor had vanished, replaced by an intensity he had never seen before. The Jotnar's blade flew with wild abandon as she crashed into a pack of blighted vargr. Even in the dim light of the unnatural twilight, he could see the blight clinging, not only to her armor but also to Jorunn's exposed fur.

Aric grabbed Lif by the collar and pulled her along towards their friend. Lifthrasir followed close behind. But when they were just ten yards away, the glow of the Aesir weapons and armor faded and the monsters closed in again. They jumped on all of those who had fallen away from the staff, their enchantments now impotent.

"No!" Aric called out as he saw Jorunn consumed by a wave of inky shapes. He reached out but was stopped short. Now Lif was pulling on him, drawing him back as the army's charge collapsed against the horde.

Aric stopped struggling against Lif as they saw a dim golden figure streak across the sky just above their heads. Brunhilda crashed into a group of retreating Dokkalfar, knocking six of them to the ground. Aric and the others ran to her as the Dokkalfar scrambled to their feet and ran off on their own. The exhaustion on the valkyrie's face was clear. Her use of the Reginvald and staff had taken its toll on her. Her armor was battered and chunks of the metal had been torn off. Brunhilda's golden blood ran in rivulets, soaking her tunic. With Aric supporting her on her left and Lifthrasir on her right, they brought her to her feet. Before they could move her to safety, the dark, imposing shape of a giant dog landed in front of them with a seismic impact.

Brunhilda pushed the staff into Aric's hands. As he took hold of it, there was a brief flash of white at her abdomen where the most blood was spilling. Then she unsheathed her sword, which burst with a golden light before she pushed Aric back with the staff, into Lif and Lifthrasir.

"Sing of my deeds," she called over her shoulder. "Sing songs of all you have witnessed, Aric of Murtrborg!"

Brunhilda leapt at Garmr, her sword thrust straight forward into the gaping maw of the beast. The hound moved impossibly fast; only an inky afterimage where it had been remained. Its body had sidestepped in the blink of an eye and the valkyrie was hurtling in space toward nothing. With a snap, the golden light was doused, Brunhilda caught in the crushing jaws. With what Aric could only describe as disdain, the helhound spat out the mangled corpse of the valkyrie and her sword. As it lunged at the three Humans, Aric shielded Lif and Lifthrasir with his own body.

A wet thud boomed out as a dark, serpentine body flew out over the Vigrid Plains and crashed into the bounding beast at the apex of its jump. The two bodies skidded into the rubble of what remained of the Bifrost Skjaldborg before tumbling into the roaring waves far below.

Aric stood and turned to see a fading light on the battlefield from whence the serpent had come.

CHAPTER 43: THE WORLD SERPENT

Even as the ranks of former enemies formed impromptu alliances and worked together, a beacon of raging anger flashed at the center of the Vigrid Plains. Surtr and Thor resumed their duel, weapons flashing with power. With both weakened after their initial clash, their strikes carried very little actual power.

But in the ever-darkening twilight, those flashes drew the attention of Jormungandr. The two warriors disengaged just in time to dodge the monstrous serpent's strike.

Thor and Surtr regarded each other for a brief moment, the ire in their eyes cutting through the darkness. Their weapons flashed with energy, and their muscles tensed. Together they turned to face Jormungandr. Thor rooted his feet to the ground and wielded Mjolnir to block its attack, deflecting the monster towards Surtr. The Eldjotnar's blade cut into the monster's jaw but did little to arrest its momentum. It crashed into Surtr and knocked him back a dozen yards or more.

Now, with only one target, Jormungandr unleashed a barrage of strikes. The Aesir prince, though exhausted, called upon every ounce of strength and training to dodge and parry each attack. By now, Thor had begun to read the serpent's timing and tells. With the next snap of Jormungandr's maw, he was prepared and had imbued Mjolnir with a surge of power and swung it with all his might. Golden light exploded as the monster's head was flung back, crashing into Garmr in midair at the apex of the helhound's leap.

Thor, exhausted, collapsed to his knees. His breathing came fast and shallow as he struggled to hold himself up. He heard a hiss nearby and saw a pulsing, writhing shadow in the shape of a lindworm. His muscles were seized in a kind of palsy as he tried to recover. He only needed a moment to catch his breath. But the lindworm was not accommodating and charged forward. Before its jaws could close on the Aesir's throat, a bright flash of red came down and the beast's head flew past Thor, its gaping jaw limp and harmless.

The Aesir prince stared at Surtr with a mixture of respect and disdain, Thor's expression reflected in the Eldjotnar's face. The Aesir's eye flicked to the glowing blade in the Eldjotnar's hands.

"Your death will be at *my* hands," Surtr sneered. Another corrupted lindworm burst out of the dirt and snow at the Eldjotnar. Though he was knocked to the side, he stayed standing and, with a quick swing of his burning blade, cut its head off.

"After we kill these monsters," Thor said through heavy breaths.

Surtr stabbed the sword into the ground and had to pry his fingers from the hilt. Once the contact was broken, he breathed in deep, gulping breaths. The energy drain from wielding the sword was palpable. Surtr reached out his hand to help the Aesir up. Thor took a moment to consider the offer. Just as he moved to accept the help, Jormungandr leapt out once more from the sea and snapped its jaws around Surtr, swallowing him whole.

Thor staggered to his feet and recovered his fighting stance with urgency. There was a slight wobble in his knees, though he fought against it. As he forced his legs to remain steady, Thor saw the dark silhouette coil itself back for another attack. Once again he charged his warhammer with Reginvald energy and it flickered to life. He launched his attack, but the creature feinted and the strike missed the serpent's head. Thor was wheeling, off balance, his back exposed to this deadly foe.

Jormungandr did not hesitate at this opening. The riposte came with blinding speed, and its jaws closed around the Aesir. Thor used Mjolnir to stop the crushing jaws from closing completely. Undaunted, the serpent flicked its head back and tossed the Aesir up into the air and opened its mouth wide, waiting to swallow this morsel whole.

As Thor tumbled head over heels through the cold, dark sky, he briefly lost his bearings. In the darkness, he could not see the ground, and the wind blew snowflakes in all directions, not giving any indication of which way was up or down. Somehow he had kept hold of Mjolnir. Its reassuring weight gave him a sense of calm.

Despite only being aloft for mere seconds, he felt as if time had slowed, and he reflected on everything that had led up to this moment. Visions of Baldur, Freya, his father and mother came to mind… and then his thoughts turned to Jarnsaxa. An odd serenity filled his mind, and he sent out his thoughts and energies through Mjolnir.

The warhammer surged with the power and clouds above crackled with lightning. For one brief moment Mjolnir shone as bright as the sun, and the Vigrid Plains were lit as if it were midday. The gaping jaw of the waiting serpent was clear and visible below him. And as time appeared to resume its normal speed, Thor held Mjolnir out in front of him as he dove straight down.

CHAPTER 44: HAMMERFALL

Aric, Lif, and Lifthrasir had to shield their eyes from the sudden explosion of light. Even Freya turned her head and squinted at this artificial sun. The fighting ceased for a moment as every eye was drawn to the brilliant, dazzling light, so long absent from the cloud-shrouded realms during these three years of the fimbulvinter. Phantom images of the battlefield were seared into Aric's vision even through his shut eyelids. He thought that he could see shadowy afterimages of a person at the center of the nova.

The initial burst of the light dimmed as it coalesced into a bolt of lightning. From around the battlefield, all eyes followed that arc of energy as it raced downward. Fifty feet above the plains, everything plunged back into darkness as the massive jaws of the serpent snapped shut around it.

The quiet that followed stretched out. Nothing moved, and to Aric it felt as if time had stopped. But it was mere moments later when a deafening explosion of light and sound erupted from Jormungandr's throat. The serpent's body crashed onto the Vigrid Plains, crushing hundreds beneath its weighty bulk while thousands more were showered in gore. As Aric's vision returned, once again adjusted to the world blanketed in darkness, he caught movement all around him as the tidal wave of blighted creatures resurged and flooded the plains. The Aesir and Allied soldiers were slow to recover from the dazzling lights and put up little resistance against the renewed onslaught.

"There." Freya waved to direct Aric's attention. "Something's moving in the serpent's body."

Aric rushed up to the gaping wound in time to see Thor emerge from the bloody cavity in Jormungandr's body. He carried Mjolnir in one hand. Though its shaft had been broken in half, it glowed with a dim light. The pulsing, flickering arcs of Reginvald energy poured out from the shortened stub and crackled across the Aesir's body. Illuminated fissures shone out against the dark iron of the hammer's head.

"Thor," Aric called out perhaps a bit too loudly, his ears ringing from the explosion. "You did it, you killed…"

The Aesir had taken eight steps after leaving creature's bloody corpse. As Thor reacted to Aric's voice, Mjolnir slipped from his grasp, the iron shattering as it hit the ground. Energy evaporated from the cracks in glowing, ethereal ribbons. He took one more step and then fell, face first onto the ground. With the body prone, Aric saw something rising up out of his back. Running up to Thor, he realized that it was one of Jormungandr's fangs. It had pierced completely through the Aesir's body and must have broken off when Thor had been tossed into the air. As Aric came closer, he could see the ichor of the venom covering the tooth, seeping down into and out of the wound.

"Thor?" Aric's voice quavered. He had not seen any movement from Thor's body since it had fallen.

"He's dead," Freya stated, her voice flat and unemotional. "The Aesir dynasty has ended."

"I-I don't… what do we do now?" Aric stammered. He scanned the field nearby; even in the dim light, he recognized some of the fallen. Sigrid and Frode had been half-trampled. Their deaths were as anonymous now as their lives had been to the Aesir. Aric was almost certain that everyone he had known and met since Brunhilda had crossed his path not so long ago lay out there somewhere, dead with no one to remember them or their struggles.

"The blight is still coming." Aric's breath came in raspy and ragged. His voice cracked as he thought back to that fateful day. "There's no way to get to Yggdrasil now."

"There may yet be a way. It's fortunate that we have a piece of Yggdrasil with us." Freya placed her hand upon the gnarled staff.

"But we've had it this the whole time," Aric said, confusion in his voice. "Why now?"

Freya's eyes looked to the side. Aric followed her gaze to Thor's lifeless body.

"This has been about some kind of vendetta against the Aesir?" Aric was aghast. "It was never about saving the nine realms or finding justice for the other races?" He was pacing back and forth, his face buried in his hands. He stopped and raised his head and glared at Freya. "Then perhaps we do all deserve to die, to be wiped from existence, allow Yggdrasil to begin anew."

"At one point it was about that." Freya shook her head. "But I have learned much from you, Aric. I could have done none of this alone." Her hand stretched out and pointed to Surtr's blade, thrusting up from the ground just beyond Thor's body.

"What—how did we end up so near it?" asked a dumbfounded Aric.

"This was all fated, all prophesied," Freya replied. "I have seen much of this in the seidr rituals, trying to find a way to forestall or prevent Ragnarok."

"Ragnarok?"

"The end of days," Freya continued. "The end of our days at least."

She and Aric both looked to the unconscious forms of Lif and Lifthrasir lying on the ground nearby.

"Can you protect them?" Aric asked, looking at them with sad tenderness. His gaze turned to the encroaching blight. From all sides, the Aesir and Allied Army soldiers were falling to the monsters. Defeat was imminent.

"That is my intention," Freya replied. "But I need one more thing."

She stepped into Aric, their forms overlapping. One hand grasped the staff while the other went to the Brisingamen necklace that he wore.

"I have been incubating within you." Her voice quavered. "Loki had nearly killed me at Yggdrasil, and so I bound my essence to you, just as my father had bound himself to Yggdrasil. But unlike him, I am more powerful than my host. And now I must take my form back… back from you."

"What?!" Aric looked at Freya's hands as they closed on his.

"I think that I can use the runes and powers forged into this blade and the remaining connection to Yggdrasil in the staff to absorb and destroy the blight," Freya said. "But to do that, I need to be able to touch them myself. I cannot channel that through my bond with you. I need to be in control… I need to be the sole point of contact, with no distractions."

"I… I understand," Aric muttered. "I mean, I don't understand it at all. But I know what you're asking of me."

"Aric?"

A weak but familiar voice caught his ear. Aric searched the ground and saw Lif's head raised and her face looking at him. Blood and scratches marred the innocence that had reminded him of Una.

"What are you…" She trailed off and Aric saw her eyes shift, registering Freya's form.

"Don't worry, everything is going to be fine." Aric's voice was even and serene. He felt a sense of calm he had not known since leaving Murtrborg.

"No," Lif's voice quavered. Aric followed her gaze to his hands, still covered by Freya's. "You can't."

"I have to." He felt Freya's head nod in response. "This world is full… full of our hate and sorrow. It's full of all of our mistakes. It's up to you." Aric inclined his head towards her and then Lifthrasir. "Learn from us, build a better world."

"We need you," Lif implored.

Aric gave a little chuckle and shook his head. "You've never needed me. You are so strong and smart. The world you build will be so much better than this one." He closed his eyes. "My place is with my family."

"We're your family too," Lif said as a tear rolled down her cheek.

Aric did not reply. But tears began streaming from his closed eyes as he bowed his head. A barely restrained sob shook in his chest.

"Thank you, Aric," Freya said with a hint of regret in her voice. With her hand on the necklace, it shone with a warm, white light. Their body glowed as one. Lif shielded her eyes and cried out, though her words were drowned out, first by a loud thrumming, then by a thunderclap.

When the light had faded, all traces of Aric vanished and were replaced by Freya's features enshrouded in nothing save for the Brisingamen and the light of Mithlivald.

—

Now fully in control, the reborn Vanir took a brief moment to take in her form. Looking around, she saw that Lif lay unconscious, overwhelmed by the explosion. And even the blighted monsters had been stunned by the burst of light, though after a mere moment, they recovered and charged towards her. She had to act quickly. In a few short steps, she reached Surtr's blade and drew it up from the ground. Her right hand held the sword and her left, the staff. The horde of monsters closed in, faster and faster. As she brought her hands together, there was another eruption of light. A rainbow of colors streamed out in all directions, swirling in and among the dark, inky creatures.

It was a roiling vortex of energy, of light and shadow. The animals were drawn in, no longer moving of their own volition. Their dark energies were pulled in and joined the dancing light in all colors of the spectrum. The bright, white figure at the center of the maelstrom had a vaguely feminine form, though it appeared to be composed entirely of light, all solid matter having been burned off.

The specter raised the flaming sword and staff up on high and in one last conflagration, the light and shadows that churned and roiled across the Vigrid Plains collapsed into the central figure. It convulsed; its shape bulged and contracted as it struggled to contain all it had absorbed. In the darkness and calm of the now empty field, it was the only thing that moved.

With a scream, Freya exploded in a burst of light and a deafening roar. A beam of light pierced the sky, and the blanket of clouds gave way to the glittering sea of stars. Quiet and darkness returned to the Vigrid Plains. It was not the oppressive darkness of the fimbulvinter, but the cold and peaceful dark of a clear winter's night.

—

The clouds were gone and the cold light of the stars and moon shone bright overhead. Now they shared the vast dome of the heavens with a shimmering curtain of lights and shadows that swirled and danced across the celestial backdrop. Dark shapes moved among the whorls and vortices above, pushing and pulling in an eternal struggle that unfurled in a silent back-and-forth. On the ground, however, nothing moved, not even the wind. Corpses of all manner of person and beast lay strewn across the vast desolation of the Vigrid Plains.

In the distance to the east, the rock gave way beneath the limp coils of the world serpent. Its vast bulk appeared to move in slow motion as the body sloughed, slow at first and then faster as it plummeted down the sheer cliffs.

Caught in its collapse, the pillar of rock that held aloft the once bright city of Asgard fell into the sea far below. The din of rocks and buildings tumbling into the rolling waves broke the sepulchral silence.

Up on the Vigrid Plains—slowly, gradually—two figures stirred.

EPILOGUE

The sulfurous mists of the hot springs in the caldera shrouded the lush, verdant valley. Crops of barley and wheat grew wild and vast in unrestricted fields. Herds of livestock wandered and milled about with a bounty of food and no one to pen them in. A small shower of rocks cascaded along a portion of the southern wall that enclosed the bucolic caldera. In a flurry of activity, one of the larger rocks broke free of the vines that had sprouted into the cracks. An opening about two shoulders wide emerged as the rest of the stones came free and poured out into the interior.

"I told you I remembered where it was," Lifthrasir said as he stepped out onto the overgrown path. The youth now had a scruff of patchy hair adorning his jawline and upper lip.

"This was the third hillside that you wanted to try," Lif replied in a slightly annoyed tone. But even as she rolled her eyes, there was the hint of a smile on her lips as the familiar scents and sights engulfed her senses. "If I hadn't pulled you away, you would have wasted so much time and energy trying to dig into solid rock."

"Well, yeah, alright," he replied sheepishly. "You did live here longer than I did."

Lif smiled after taking in a deep breath.

"It looks like blocking off the path worked," Lifthrasir observed as he wrinkled his nose at the strong and pervasive odor of sulfur. "No vargr or lindworms would have sealed the passage behind them. The crops and livestock seem to have done well enough without our guidance."

As the two walked the path towards the moss-covered buildings at the valley's center, a motley group of people streamed in after them. Freya's sacrifice had saved more than just Lif and Lifthrasir. Whatever had happened in those final moments, Lif could not begin to comprehend, but dozens had been saved. Ljosalfar, Dokkalfar, and Humans had been among the survivors she had found upon waking to the decimation of the battle and the whimsical light display in the clear skies above. However, all of the Jotnar, Aesir, and Vanir bodies had vanished.

Many animal corpses had also littered the Vigrid Plains, though far fewer than Lif thought had fought on that fateful day. She recalled the final vision of that battle, Aric taking hold of Surtr's blade in one hand and his staff of Yggdrasil in the other before erupting in a flash of light. A single tear dropped from her eye before she blinked it away.

"Are you alright?" Lifthrasir asked, catching her movement from the corner of his eye.

"Yes," she said, her voice cracking. She straightened her posture and composed herself before she addressed the others. "Welcome to Hoddmimis Holt."

As they walked down into the valley, Lif began to sing quietly to herself:

Summer is ending
We have planted and played
Winter still slumbers
Look at all we have made

Oh, hark and be glad
Bright birds fly and fish splash
We reap the harvest
Wodensdaeg's come at last

Come friends and fam'ly
Come bounty of the year
Odin favors us
And brings to us great cheer

Celebrate as one
Bright birds fly and fish splash
Asgard smiles on all
Wodensdaeg's come at last

THE END

GLOSSARY

A

Aesir (singular and plural) – The second race of sentient beings birthed from Yggdrasil. They are a people characterized by a proclivity to order and structure. Their realm is Asgard; their capital city of the same name sits on an island off the east coast of the continent Ymir. It is connected to the mainland via Bifrost, the Rainbow Bridge. Their physical traits consist of various shades of blonde and red hair with fair skin complexion.

Aldrnari – Capital city of the realm of Muspelheim. Primary location for the forging and fabrication of tools, weapons, and armor for the nine realms.

Alfheim – Realm of the Ljosalfar, represented by emeralds. Dense forests form the basis for all of the lumber used in all of the realms. Their base resources are exchanged for the resources of the other realms.

Aric – Male. Human. Fisherman. Husband of Dagmaer, father of Una.

Asgard – Name of the realm and also the capital city for the Aesir, represented by quartz. On an island on the east coast, the city is connected to the continent via Bifrost, the Rainbow Bridge. The war room in the palace is adorned with trophies and relics from the hunts of the Great Awakening and the rites of passage of the pantheon. The table is eight feet in diameter, made from a single piece of oak with a detailed relief map of the nine realms carved into it. Capital of the nine realms, it currently provides no raw materials—despite its temperate climate and rich, arable lands—but is responsible for art and wealth.

Aska – Female. Eldjotnar. Freya in disguise. She is the organizer of the Eldjotnar resistance and teaches the Eldjotnar how to fight.

Asta – Female. Aesir Valkyrie. Comrade of Brunhilda.

aurochs (singular and plural) – A wooly, herd breed that provides resources and sustenance for many of the northern peoples. Their milk, wool, and meat supply food and clothes in the otherwise barren regions in Niflheim. They often serve as pack animals, capable of hauling heavy loads over long distances.

B

Baldur – Male. Aesir. Second son of Odin and Frigg. During the Jotnar Uprising was disguised at the Jotnar, Suttungr.

Barrel Stave Tavern – Tavern located near the docks in Knorrborg, a coastal town in the northwest of Midgard.

Bestla – Female. Jotnar. Leader during the Great Awakening, wife of Borr and mother of Odin.

Bifrost – The Rainbow Bridge. Several theories exist to explain the name. The single span bridge has only one immense arch underneath, recalling a rainbow. Also, the waterfalls that flow on each side of the bridge generate dense mists that refract brilliant rainbows throughout the day.

Bifrost Skjaldborg – The one-hundred-foot-tall wall that marks the western edge of Asgard. Erected after the Aesir-Vanir War, it is a semicircular bulwark that terminates on both ends at sheer cliffs, enclosing the merchant district of Asgard.

Birgjavale – Medium-sized city in Asgard territory proper.

Bjorn – Male. Vanir. Asgard City guard.

Bodil – Female. Aesir Valkyrie. Trainee under the tutelage of Brunhilda.

Boelthor – Male. Jotnar. First leader of Jotnar, spirit bound to Gungnir.

Boerborg – Human village in Midgard. Lifthrasir's former home.

Borghild – Female. Jotnar. Senior soldier in Jotnar Army.

Borr – Male. Aesir. Leader during the Great Awakening. Husband to Bestla, father of Odin.

Bragi – Male. Vanir. Husband of Ydun.

Brisingamen – A necklace imbued with Mithlivald power owned by Freya.

Brokkr – Male. Dokkalfar. Title for one of the two stewards of the Dokkalfar people in the realm of Svartalfheim. Named for one of the Dokkalfar brothers who helped to forge Mjolnir and Gungnir.

Bruborg – Large Human city bordering the former Vanaheim.

Brunhilda – Female. Aesir. Hot-headed valkyrie, red hair.

Buri – Male. Aesir. First leader, spirit bound to Mjolnir.

C

Calder Lake – A large lake in central northern Midgard near Jotunheim.

Calder River – Originating from Calder Lake, it flows northwest towards the Svelbjarg Mountains before emptying into the sea near the Human town of Murtrborg.

D

Dagmaer – Female. Human. Hunter. Wife of Aric, mother of Una.

Daudr Haf – The sea beyond the southernmost point of the continent of

Ymir.

Dokkalfar – The people who inhabit Svartalfheim. They are generally stout and stocky physically with pale skin since most of their lives are spent out of the sun in subterranean cities. With their primary industries being mining and smithing, they are often seen covered in grime and soot.

dragon – In the days before the Great Awakening, they were the dominant animal species. Solitary by nature, with broad wings and powerful claws, they dominated the land and the skies. The alliance of the Great Awakening eliminated them one by one until Nidhogg was the only one that remained. Their arsenal includes fiery breath, razor-sharp claws and teeth, and iron-hard scales that cover the entire body.

E

Eira – Female. Vanir. Chief healer of Asgard. Her title is Fostra Eira.

Eldjotnar (singular and plural) – The faction of the Jotnar population exiled to live in Muspelheim. Among the volcanic activity in the realm they developed into auburn- and brown-coated versions of the Jotnar of the north. Their Ethlivald similarly is more expressive of fire and heat.

Ethlivald – The spectrum of energy associated with Jotnar. Its effects enhance natural phenomena such as increasing plant growth or ambient weather conditions.

F

Fafnir – Female. Lindworm. This powerful lindworm brood mother was trapped as a result of the Great Awakening. After centuries beneath the World Tree, she absorbed much of the corruption that poisoned the tree as a result of the warring between the three prime races.

Fenrir – Male. Vargr. An extraordinary vargr produced as a result of artificial selective pressures of the Aesir rite of passage. Additionally empowered first by stray Mithlivald and Ethlivald energies and then by the energies stored beneath Yggdrasil, concentrated by the creatures trapped therein.

fjathrhamr – Cloak of falcon feathers. Crafted by the Vanir king, Njord. When worn, it turns its wearer into a larger-than-normal bird of prey aligned with the wearer's natural proclivities and skin and hair colors.

Folkvangr – The Vanir district of Asgard overseen by Freya and then Freyr after Freya's apparent death.

Freki – Female. Wolf that prowls Asgard as Frigg's companion. Always accompanied by Geri, male wolf.

Freya – Female. Vanir. Leader during the Aesir-Vanir War. Daughter of Njord, sister of Freyr.

Freyr – Male. Vanir. Son of Njord, brother of Freya.

Frigg – Female. Aesir. Queen and ruler of Asgard and the nine realms and the widow of Odin.

Frode – Male. Human. Gothi of Hoddmimis Holt.

G

Garmr – Male. Hound. A massive, feral dog of the Great Awakening also trapped by Njord.

Gastropnir (archaic) – Northern stronghold deep within Niflheim. Staging point for the final push of the Great Awakening.

Gastropnir (modern) – A small village nestled in the shadow of the ruins of the former stronghold.

Geri – Male. Wolf that prowls Asgard as Frigg's companion. Always accompanied by Freki, she-wolf.

Gjallarhorn – A massive trumpet fashioned from a giant dragon's horn. Wielded by Heimdall and only blown if enemies approach Asgard.

Gothi – Masculine. Title for leaders of Human cities and villages.

Great Awakening – The period of the world when the Aesir, Vanir, and Jotnar worked together with the other races to kill the giant monsters of old, or trap them beneath the roots of Yggdrasil if they could not be killed.

Groenborg – A town of Ljosalfar in Alfheim. As with most villages in Alfheim it is constructed up in the canopy of the trees in the forest with pathways made of vines and branches that were lashed together and have grown together over time. Ladders and counter-weighted lifts are the primary access points to the village.

Gungnir – Spear with a six-foot-long shaft and two-foot-long blade. Boelthor's spirit ties this weapon, covered with intricate knot patterns and runes, to the Ethlivald/chaotic end of the spectrum.

Gunnar – Female. Vanir. Leader of valkyries.

Gythja – Feminine. Title for leaders of Human cities and villages.

H

Halvard – Central commercial and military hub in the territory formerly known as Jotunheim. Situated on cliffs above Calder Lake. Site of the first major confrontation in the Jotnar Uprising.

Hege – Female. Human. Gythja of Murtrborg.

Heimdall – Male. Aesir. Herald of Asgard. Watchman and in charge of blowing the great trumpet Gjallarhorn to warn of approaching enemies.

Hel – Land of the dead, represented by onyx. A metaphysical realm that has no physical manifestation in the continent of Ymir.

helhound – Wild, canine animals that live in the wild forests and grasslands away from the population centers. Garmr is the pinnacle of this species from the days before the Great Awakening.

Hertha – Female. Jotnar. After Suttungr was revealed to be Baldur and subsequently defeated, Hertha took over leadership of the Jotnar.

Hilder – Female. Vanir. Valkyrie, serious and duty oriented. She is tall, broad, and muscular.

Hoddmimis Holt – Small hamlet hidden in a caldera nestled in the Svelbjarg Range. Traversing through it is the only other overland path through the Svelbjarg Mountains. The hot springs are a result of the volcanic activity of the underlying caldera. They are mineral rich and rejuvenating.

Hofborg – Medium-sized city in Vanaheim before unification with Asgard.

hrafnasueltir – Coward. Literally, raven starver.

hrodi (expletive, insult) – Literally, snot.

Huginn – Female. Raven. One of Odin's ravens. She watches and reports to Odin on the goings-on in the nine realms.

I

Isabrot – The town near Isabrot Pass that is the primary staging area for all Aesir Army action in Niflheim.

Isabrot Pass – Outpost guarding the only known overland path between Old Jotunheim/Asgard and Niflheim/New Jotunheim in the Svelbjarg Mountain Range.

Iss Ethlivald – Variant of Ethlivald that is an expression of the ice and cold of Nyr Jotunheim in Niflheim.

issithar – Jotnar soldiers specialized at using Ethlivald in combat.

Ivar – Male. Human. One of the members of the refugees with the Jotnar who arrive in Muspelheim.

J

Jarnsaxa – Female. Jotnar. Strong-willed sister of Loki.

Jormungandr – Female. Serpent. The first beast driven down beneath Yggdrasil. At the time of her imprisonment, she was a creature of average size and power. But having spent the most time nestled among Yggdrasil's roots, she has grown the most embittered and the most powerful of all the creatures imprisoned under the World Tree.

Jorunn – Female. Jotnar. Civilian, aurochs herder. Hertha's younger sister.

Jotnar (singular and plural) – The first race of sentient beings birthed from Yggdrasil.

Jotunheim – Jotnar, represented by emeralds. Jotnar are used as a permanent pool of indentured labor. Stone for building and aurochs are the primary resources of New Jotunheim. The original lands flourished with all manner of resources, primarily food and lumber.

K

Kari – Female. Aesir. Aesir soldier who has served as an Asgard City Guard before deploying to the Aesir Army around the nine realms.

Knute – Male. Jotnar. Civilian, bone-carver. An older-generation Jotnar who lived through the Aesir-Vanir War. Remembers the verdant Jotunheim and is an elder and leader of Gastropnir both in the past and the present.

L

Lif – Female. Human. Adoptive daughter of Aric and former resident of Hoddmimis Holt.

Lifthrasir – Male. Human. Traveled with Sigrid's band of human refugees before joining the Jotnar and Human band who fled to Muspelheim.

lindworm – Lizard-like creatures, they are wingless and have only two appendages. They slither/crawl on their bellies and are heavily armored on their dorsal side. Their broad, triangular heads make them ideal burrowers. Unlike dragons, lindworms do not breathe fire, but they do emit noxious gases and their saliva is quite poisonous.

Ljosalfar – The people of Alfheim. They live in villages built into the canopies of the trees of the vast forests in the south. They are the stewards of the trees and harvest the trees in a sustainable manner to provide high quality lumber for the nine realms. They are generally tall and lanky with darker complexions due to their time in their sun-dappled environments.

Loki – Male. Jotnar. Has a complicated relationship with the Aesir with specific ties to Baldur and his death. Brother to Jarnsaxa.

M

meinfretr (slang) – Stinky fart.

Midgard – Human realm, represented by pearls. Vast, open plains of farmlands and grazing pastures for animals. Humans work the land and produce the majority of food that is sent to the other realms.

Mithlivald – The spectrum of energy associated with the Vanir. It is a bridging energy that may be used to heal organic and inorganic material. It may also be utilized to amplify Reginvald or Ethlivald.

Mjolnir – A massive warhammer with a shaft four feet in length and a head with a blunted surface on one face and a spike on the other. The metal is embossed with a delicate filigree of knotwork. Imbued with Buri's life essence, the hammer leans to the ordered, Aesir/Reginvald spectrum.

Mothrgil Canyon – A canyon system to the northwest of Isabrot.

Muninn – Female. Raven. One of Odin's ravens. She watches and reports to Odin on the goings on in the nine realms.

Murtrborg – Small village along the coast in northwest Midgard, not far from the Svelbjarg Range.

Muspelheim – Eldjotnar realm, represented by garnet. Ingots of metal from Svartalfheim are brought to the forges here to be shaped into tools and weapons for the other realms.

N

Nidhogg – Indeterminate gender. Dragon. A powerful dragon from before the Great Awakening. The only monster to escape imprisonment beneath

Yggdrasil by Njord.

Niflheim – Realm of ice and cold, represented by sapphire. It is the buffer zone that surrounds and shelters Yggdrasil from encroachment.

Njord – Male. Vanir. First leader, father of Freya and Freyr. Spirit bound to Yggdrasil.

Nyr Jotunheim (New Jotunheim) – The new lands set aside for the Jotnar within Niflheim. Accessible only via Isabrot Pass. Though initially a desolate tundra, it has since become a thriving boreal forest region under the nurturing care of the Jotnar.

O

Odin – Male. Aesir (half Aesir, half Jotnar). Leader during the Aesir-Vanir War. Husband to Frigg, father of Thor and Baldur.

Odr – Male. Vanir. Husband of Freya. Leader of the Vanir during the Aesir-Vanir War alongside Freya. Freya's bargaining with Thor not only betrayed the Jotnar people, it undermined Odr's authority and standing. Though he was afforded a position within the unified Aesir-Vanir nation, he soon left, never to be heard from again. Freya often takes lengthy journeys supposedly to search for him.

oflati – Gaudy, ostentatious person.

Oydis – Female. Ljosalfar. One of the leaders of the bandits stealing from the caravans that travel through Alfheim. She is really Freya in disguise.

R

Reginvald – The spectrum of energy associated with the Aesir. Primarily a magic used to shape and bend the natural world into more ordered structures.

Rikrsmidja – The smithy within the Muspelheim city of Aldrnari where the furnace, anvil, and even the floors and walls of the chamber were scried with runes of Reginvald, Mithlivald, and Ethlivald allowing for the creating of the artifacts, Mjolnir and Gungnir.

Rite of Vinnask – Ritual hunt of vargr performed by Aesir hoping to prove themselves worthy of leadership positions within the Aesir government. Candidates must use weapons and armor that they have made on their own. Their success is measured by the size of the vargr carcass brought back and presented to Odin and the council of Asgard.

S

Sif – Female. Aesir. Commander of the Asgard City Guards and all domestic forces.

Sigrid – Female. Human. Leader of a band of Human refugees from the northern territories. Along with Frode, one of the Human leaders.

Sindri – Male. Dokkalfar. Title for one of the stewards of the Dokkalfar

people in Svartalfheim. Named for one of the first Dokkalfar who aided in the forging of Mjolnir and Gungnir.
Skjaldborg – A defensive wall, a bulwark
Skogul – Female. Half Aesir (father) half Vanir (mother). Valkyrie.
Skuld – Female. Human. Minstrel/actress with theater troupe.
Sleipnir – Male. Horse. One of the few friendly creatures of power that existed before the Great Awakening. Though forever wild, it created a bond with Borr that transferred to Odin after the ancient Aesir leader passed.
Svelbjarg ram – These elusive creatures climb the Svelbjarg range to heights that no other terrestrial creature could aspire to. Thus their hides are prized. They often defend territories by butting heads with rival males. The force of these impacts is so impressive that many are surprised that they can withstand such blows. As such, many Jotnar see their skulls as ideal for use as helmets, and their rarity makes such helmets one of the rare pieces of prestige among the Jotnar.
Suttungr – Male. Jotnar. Jotnar leader during uprising.
Svartalfheim – Realm of the Dokkalfar, represented by ruby. The mines provide metal ores and precious gems and minerals for artisans in Asgard, and the base materials for the military-industrial complex in Muspelheim.
Svelbjarg Mountains – Mountain range that forms the border between Jotunheim and Niflheim.
Sunnan Kaupstad – One of several hub cities in the nine realms. This is the city in the south along the border of Alfheim and Muspelheim.
swina bqllr (expletive) – Literally, pig penis/genitals.

T

Thor – Male. Aesir. First son of Odin and Frigg. Heir to Asgard.
Thrym – Male. Jotnar. Jotnar leader during Aesir-Vanir War.
Tyr – Male. Aesir. Accomplished military officer, still insists on leading field missions.

U

Una – Female. Human. Daughter of Aric and Dagmaer.
Utgard – Former capital city. Razed to the ground during the Aesir-Vanir War. Its ruins should exist somewhere south of the Svelbjarg Mountains.

V

Vanaheim – Realm of the Vanir, represented by amber. As with Old Jotunheim and Asgard, Vanaheim was a land well suited for the growth and production of all resources. Currently has merged with Asgard, though some lands are used as farms, worked by Human serfs.
Vali – Male. Vanir. Captain of the Aesir Army in Halvard.
vargr (singular and plural) – Though somewhat similar in appearance to wolves,

vargr are a separate species altogether. Their fur is much coarser, nearly like the back of a hedgehog. They are larger and more vicious, primarily solitary creatures. Other than for mating, it takes extraordinary circumstances for them to come together.

Veizlakr – Eastern farming community that produces much of the grain distributed throughout the realms.

Vigrid Plains – The vast grass plains that stretch out to the west of Asgard City. This was the site of the Siege of the Bifrost Skjaldborg led by Suttungr during the Jotnar Uprising.

Vinnask – Often used in reference to the ritual hunt of vargr. The act of overcoming, winning personal glory.

Y

Ydun – Female. Vanir. Wife of Bragi.

Yggdrasil – The World Tree. It is the source of the magical energies in the world: Reginvald, Mithlivald, and Ethlivald. It is said that all of the races sprang forth from beneath its roots. During the Great Awakening, many of the most fierce and dangerous monsters that could not be killed outright were driven back under the roots. The first Vanir King, Njord, bound his spirit to Yggdrasil so that he could keep the monsters trapped. Its trunk is over one hundred yards wide at the base, and the green, leafy canopy radiates out a mile in diameter.

Ymir – The name of the continent upon which all of the realms reside.

ACKNOWLEDGMENTS

This has been a crazy ten-year journey; from starting the outline for one novel to seeing it grow into a trilogy. And of course, that's not counting the early version that began as a graphic novel for my master's thesis ten years before that.

I want to thank everyone who has been a part of my life and journey along the way. Special thanks for the support and love from mom, dad, John, Dilek, Ela, and Zoey. Thank you to Kathleen and Jenny for bringing together the Absolute Dragons family of friends and for welcoming me into it.

Thank you for the continual hospitality of Marty, Gloria, Ember, and Marleau every Wednesday evening. It's always a great respite in the middle of the week to hang out with you all, James, Pam, Laura, Charles, Steph, Carl, Roland, Janice, and Kat.

I also want to give a special shout out to Hadley for commiserating with me on our individual writing journeys. I look forward to reading your novel soon. Thanks to my editor, Kristen. This final installment of the Hammerforged Saga is much more cohesive and consistent with part 2 because of her work and Kelly's proofreading work on both volumes.

And a final thanks to you, the reader. I hope that you enjoyed this story as much as I enjoyed writing it and that this provided a different and entertaining interpretation of Norse mythology.

ABOUT THE AUTHOR

Andy Wang lives in the San Francisco Bay Area where he works as a storyboard artist in the video game industry. Over the past sixteen years he has worked on creating and visualizing diverse and interesting game worlds.

As an undergraduate he studied Integrative Biology at UC Berkeley and then earned his Master of Fine Arts degree in illustration from the Academy of Art University in San Francisco. Andy's MFA coursework and thesis centered on sequential art and storytelling. His degree project was the first chapter for a proposed graphic novel exploring the characters, world, and themes of Norse mythology. That material laid the foundation for this book series.

FINALE

A biting breeze stirred the snow-covered tundra. It was a brisk winter evening beneath a clear canopy of sparkling stars; a thin, silvery crescent hung low, near the horizon. The shimmering, multicolored curtains of the aurora borealis swirled and danced above. A woman and child were bundled up tightly in anorak jackets, the fur-lined hoods pulled up over their heads. They were lying close to each other upon a pile of wool blankets spread out on the permafrost near a broad, low-domed tent.

"And that's where the northern lights came from," the woman said as they watched the spectacular celestial display.

"Is that really true?" asked the five-year-old girl, her voice a mixture of awe and skepticism.

"Of course it's true," she replied, her voice quiet but full of confidence. "At least that's what my grandmother told me."

"But Daddy said that it was light from the sun hitting gases high up in the atmosphere," the girl countered.

"Gases?" asked the mother. She blew out a long breath that clouded up in the chilly air. There was a lull in the wind and the fog lingered. Her hand swept through the mist, trying to make it dance like the aurora. "Your father says a lot of things." She tickled her daughter, who giggled even though her thick jacket surely insulated her from the mitten-encased fingers.

"I say a lot of things because I learned a lot of things." A man emerged from the tent. His glasses caught a hint of the green and purple aurora lights overhead.

"Both things can be true." She propped herself up and looked from him back up to the twinkling sky. "Freya and the blight continue to struggle against each other up there, part of those gases. Their eternal dance lit by the light of the sun." Leaning in close, she whispered, "You just need a little more imagination than your dad."

"Alright," he said with a laugh. Her whisper was quiet, but in the stillness of the wilderness, her words had been clear and audible. "Time for bed, you two."

They gathered up the blankets and all three walked over and entered the tent. Soon after, they extinguished the lantern, and the only light came from the glittering stars and the northern lights.

Made in the USA
Columbia, SC
25 November 2023